MANHATTAN NOIR 2

Manhattan Noir 2

The Classics

EDITED BY LAWRENCE BLOCK

AKASHIC BOOKS
NEW YORK

Published by Akashic Books | ©2008 Akashic Books
Series concept by Tim McLoughlin and Johnny Temple
Manhattan map by Sohrab Habibion

ISBN-13: 978-1-933354-57-6
Library of Congress Control Number: 2008925934
All rights reserved | First printing

Akashic Books | PO Box 1456 | New York, NY 10009
info@akashicbooks.com | www.akashicbooks.com

Grateful acknowledgment is made for permission to reprint the stories and poems in this anthology. "Johnny One-Eye" by Damon Runyon was originally published in *Collier's* (June 28, 1941). American Entertainment Rights Company, LLC is the copyright proprietor for the short story "Johnny One-Eye" by Damon Runyon, copyright © 1941 by P.F. Collier and Son, Inc., copyright renewal © 1968 by Damon Runyon, Jr. and Mary Runyon McCann. The copyright was assigned to American Entertainment Rights Company, LLC and it is the successor copyright proprietor pursuant to valid assignments from prior proper copyright proprietors; "My Aunt from Twelfth Street" by Jerome Weidman was originally published in the *New Yorker* (August 12, 1939), copyright © 1939 by Jerome Weidman, renewal © 1967 by Jerome Weidman, reprinted by permission of Brandt & Hochman Literary Agents, Inc.; "The Raven" by Edgar Allan Poe was originally published in *New York Evening Mirror* (January 29, 1845); "Mrs. Manstey's View" by Edith Wharton was originally published in *Scribner's Magazine* (July 1891); "A Poker Game" by Stephen Crane was originally published in *Last Words* by Stephen Crane (London: Digby, Long & Co., 1902); "The Furnished Room" by O. Henry was originally published in *The Four Million* (New York: Doubleday, 1906); the selected poems by Horace Gregory were originally published in *Chelsea Rooming House* by Horace Gregory (New York: Covici-Friede, 1930); "Spanish Blood" by Langston Hughes was originally published in *Metropolis* (December 29, 1934), licensed here from *Short Stories* by Langston Hughes, © 1996 by Ramona Bass and Arnold Rampersad, reprinted by permission of Hill and Wang, a division of Farrar, Straus and Giroux, LLC; "Sailor off the Bremen" by Irwin Shaw was originally published in the *New Yorker* (February 25, 1939), © 1939 by Irwin Shaw; "The Last Spin" by Evan Hunter was published in *Learning to Kill: Stories* by Ed McBain, copyright © 2006 by Hui Corp, reprinted by permission of Houghton Mifflin Harcourt Publishing Company. "The Last Spin" was originally published in *Manhunt* (September 1956); "The Luger Is a 9mm Handgun with a Parabellum Action" by Jerrold Mundis was originally published in *New Worlds* (March 1969), © 1969 by Jerrold Mundis; "New York Blues" by Cornell Woolrich was originally published in *Ellery Queen Mystery Magazine* (December 1970), © 1970 by Cornell Woolrich; "The Interceptor" by Barry N. Malzberg was originally published in *Mike Shayne Mystery Magazine* (August 1972), © 1972 by Barry N. Malzberg; "Crowded Lives" by Clark Howard was originally published in *Ellery Queen Mystery Magazine* (October 1989), © 1989 by Clark Howard; "Young Isaac" by Jerome Charyn was originally published in *The Armchair Detective* (Summer 1990), © 1990 by Jerome Charyn; "Love in the Lean Years," by Donald E. Westlake was originally published in *Playboy* (February 1992), © 1992 by Donald E. Westlake; "A Manhattan Romance" by Joyce Carol Oates was originally published in *American Short Fiction* (Winter 1997), © 1997 by Joyce Carol Oates; "In for a Penny" by Lawrence Block was originally published in *Ellery Queen Mystery Magazine* (December 1999), © 1999 by Lawrence Block; the selected poems by Geoffrey Bartholomew were originally published in *The McSorley Poems* by Geoffrey Bartholomew (New York: Charlton Street Press, 2001), © 2001 by Geoffrey Bartholomew.

"Johnny One-Eye" by Damon Runyon is reproduced by permission of American Entertainment Rights Company, LLC, the copyright proprietor.

Washington Heights
BRONX
Harlem
Upper West Side
NEW JERSEY
HUDSON RIVER
West 84th Street
Central Park
MANHATTAN
Central Park South
QUEENSBORO BRIDGE
QUEENS
Broadway
East 40s
East 37th Street
QUEENS MIDTOWN TUNNEL
Chelsea
Murray Hill
Eighth Avenue
Sixth Avenue
West Village
Greenwich Village
Alphabet City
EAST RIVER
East Village
Lower West Side
BROOKLYN
Lower East Side
WILLIAMSBURG BRIDGE
Wall Street
BROOKLYN BRIDGE
MANHATTAN BRIDGE

TABLE OF CONTENTS

PART III: DARKNESS VISIBLE

INTRODUCTION
It's Been Noir Around Here for Ages

M*anhattan Noir 2*. How did that happen?

Almost inevitably, it seems to me. Several years ago, Tim McLoughlin edited and Akashic Books published *Brooklyn Noir*. The book earned a warm reception from critics and readers, and spawned a series for the publisher that is rapidly taking over the world. Early on, I had the opportunity to turn the noir spotlight on my part of the world, the island of Manhattan. Because I had the good fortune to recruit some wonderful writers who sat down and wrote some wonderful stories, *Manhattan Noir* drew strong reviews and sold (and continues to sell) a gratifying number of copies.

Early on, Akashic expanded the franchise with *Brooklyn Noir 2: The Classics*, consisting of previously published stories. (I could hardly be unaware of the book, as Tim McLoughlin was gracious enough to reprint a story of mine, "By the Dawn's Early Light.") And this sequel, too, was very well received.

While I was editing *Manhattan Noir*, it struck me that Manhattan was a natural setting for noir material, not least because it had served that function ever since Peter Minuit's celebrated $24 land grab. I thought of all the writers who'd found a home in Manhattan, and of the dark stories they'd set here, and one day I e-mailed Johnny Temple at Akashic to propose the very book you now hold in your hand. Johnny, it turned out, had already noted in his calendar: *Q Block re:*

Manhattan Noir sequel. Great minds work alike, as you've no doubt been advised, and so do mine and Johnny's.

You would think compiling a reprint anthology would be a far simpler matter than putting together a book of original stories. I certainly thought so, or I might not have rushed to embrace the project. Curiously, it was the other way around.

For the first *Manhattan Noir*, all I had to do was persuade some of the best writers in the country to produce new dark stories set in Manhattan, and to do so for a fee that fell somewhere between honorarium and pittance. They turned in magnificent work, and I turned in the fruits of their labors, and that was pretty much it. Nice work if you can get it.

But this time around I had to find the stories, and that's not as easy as it sounds. I knew that I wanted to include O. Henry and Damon Runyon—but which O. Henry story? Which story of Runyon's? I did not want to resort to the anthologist's ploy of picking stories from other people's anthologies—this, of course, is one reason everybody knows "The Gift of the Magi" and "Little Miss Marker," while so many equally delightful stories remain unknown to the general reader. So what I had to do was read all of O. Henry's New York stories, and all of Damon Runyon's stories, and that was effortful and time-consuming but, I must admit, a very pleasurable way to get through the days. And then I had to narrow the field, until I'd selected a single story from each author.

I also had to filter everything for a Manhattan setting. For example, I knew I wanted to include a story by Jerome Weidman, author of works like *I Can Get It for You Wholesale* and *Fiorello!* And I even knew which one I wanted, a haunting story narrated by a young boy who has to find a way to inform his parents of the sudden death of a beloved cousin. I read that story forty or more years ago, and it stayed in my mind, and when I managed to track it down I discovered one aspect of it which had *not* stayed in my mind; to wit, the damn thing was set in Brooklyn.

No problem. Weidman wrote a good many stories, and I have now read them all, and I'm pleased to include herewith "My Aunt from Twelfth Street."

I've always had a problem with introductions to collections. If the material's good, what does it need with an anthologist's prefatory remarks? And if it's not good, who needs it?

Still, people who read anthologies seem to expect some concrete evidence of the editor's involvement in his material, even as those who publish them want to see proof that the an-thologist has expended sufficient effort to get words on paper. I won't say much about the stories, they don't require it, but I will say a word or two about the short story as a literary form, and its virtual disappearance in our time.

It should surprise no one with a feeling for noir that it all comes down to money.

Consider this: In 1902, William Sydney Porter, whom you and the rest of the world know as O. Henry, moved to New York after having served a prison sentence in Ohio. (He'd been convicted of embezzling $854.08 from a bank in Aus-tin, Texas.) Within a year he had been contracted to write a weekly short story for a newspaper, the *New York World*. For each story he was to receive $100.

This was at a time when a dollar a day was considered a satisfactory wage for a workingman, and when you could support a family quite acceptably on $20 a week. O. Henry published his first short story collection in 1904, and his tenth in 1910. He never wrote a novel. He never had to.

Consider Damon Runyon. Today's readers know him chiefly for *Guys and Dolls*, the brilliant musical based on his stories, but Runyon himself wrote short stories almost exclusively. "My measure of success is money," he wrote. "I have no interest in artistic triumphs that are financial losers. I would like to have an artistic success that also made money, of course, but if I had to make a choice between the two, I would take the dough."

Already a great success as a Broadway columnist, Runyon began publishing fiction in magazines in 1929, with the bulk of his work appearing in the '30s. Magazines like *Cosmopolitan*, *Collier's*, and the *Saturday Evening Post* paid him upwards of a dollar a word for his work.

Damon Runyon never wrote a novel. He never had to, either.

Throughout the 1930s and '40s, a majority of American writers made their living turning out short fiction for magazines. The upper crust wrote for the slicks, the lower echelon for the pulps, and in both tiers it was possible to make a decent living.

Then the world changed, and the publishing world with it. After the Second World War, inexpensive reprint fiction in the form of mass-market paperbacks killed off the pulp magazines almost overnight. Television finished the job and essentially took the slick magazines out of the fiction business. Few magazines published much in the way of short fiction, and those that did were able to pay only small sums for it.

And writers stopped producing short fiction.

Not entirely, to be sure. Samuel Johnson wasn't far off when he said that no one but a blockhead writes but for money, though the fact remains that virtually all writers are driven by more than the hope of financial reward. A poet, e.e. cummings once explained, is someone obsessed with the process of making things—and so is a writer of fiction. One may indeed make it in the hope of being well compensated for its manufacture, but one nevertheless makes it too for the sheer satisfaction of the task itself. Witness the many very fine stories being written today, rarely for more than an honorarium or a pittance, and often for magazines that pay the author in contributor's copies.

Still, money makes the mare run, or keeps her stalled in her traces. A surprising proportion of today's leading commercial writers have written no short fiction whatsoever, and few of them have written enough to be particularly good at it. They're not to be blamed, nor can one hold the publishing industry to account. If readers cared more about short fiction, more short fiction would be written.

And is the same thing even now happening to the novel? Are video games and hi-def cable and the World Wide Web doing to it what paperback novels and broadcast TV (Three networks! Small screens! Black-and-white pictures!) did to the short story?

But we don't really want to get into that, do we?

Before I could select a story for this volume, it had to meet two requirements. It had to be noir, and it had to be set in Manhattan.

The boundaries of noir, as we'll see, are hard to delineate. Those of Manhattan, on the other hand, are not. It's an island, and the waters that surround it make it pretty clear where it ends.

But two of my choices are rather less obvious in their Manhattan settings.

Evan Hunter knew Manhattan intimately, and set a large portion of his work here. His Ed McBain 87th Precinct novels are very clearly set in Manhattan, although for fictional purposes he tilts the borough ninety degrees and calls it *Isola*. (That's Italian for *island*, in case you were wondering.)

Hunter wrote a great deal of short fiction, all of it good and much of it superb. Many of the early stories were set in unspecified locales, and while he may well have had Manhattan in mind, there's no textual evidence to show it. The Matt Cordell stories, with their Bowery-bum private-eye hero, have specific Manhattan settings, but I opted instead for "The Last Spin," because I simply couldn't resist it; it's been a favorite story of mine ever since I read it fifty years ago.

But you have to read closely to determine that it takes place in Manhattan. The two characters, champions of warring teenage gangs, never get out of a featureless room. Still, the one called Dave makes it clear where they are. "My people come down from the Bronx," he says. When you come down from the Bronx, you inevitably land in Manhattan. Case closed.

If there's a line in "The Last Spin" that places the story firmly in Manhattan (and, I would guess, somewhere in the northern reaches thereof, East Harlem or Washington Heights, say), that's not a claim I can make for Edgar Allan Poe's entry. Now, you would think Poe would have set something in Manhattan, given that he spent so much time in residence here. He lived on West 3rd Street for a time, and there was a great outcry a few years ago when New York University, determined to turn all of Greenwich Village into dormitory space, set out to knock down the Poe House and build something in its place. And he also lived on West 84th Street, which the city fathers have subsequently named after him. (But don't give that street name to a cabby. These days it's hard enough to pick one who can find West 84th Street.)

I read my way through all of Poe's stories, or at least enough of each to determine where it took place, and while the man set stories in Charleston and Paris and in no end of murky landscapes, he doesn't seem to have set anything in Manhattan. He spent quite a few years here, and while they may not have been terribly happy years, well, how many of those did the man have, anyway?

And how could I leave this Manhattanite out of this volume?

So I stretched a point and selected "The Raven." He was living in Manhattan when he wrote it, and it takes place in the residence of the narrator, who is clearly a fictive equivalent of the author himself. How much of a stretch is it to presume that the book-lined chamber that serves as its setting (with its purple curtains and many a quaint and curious volume of forgotten lore) is situated like so many other book-lined chambers on Manhattan's Upper West Side? On, say, West 84th Street?

Works for me.

But wait, you say. (Yes, you. I can hear you.) Wait a minute. "The Raven." Uh, isn't it, well, a poem?

So?

Yes, "The Raven" is a poem—and a magnificent one at that. And Poe is not the only poet to be found herein. It's my great pleasure to present to you the work of two other poets, Horace Gregory and Geoffrey Bartholomew. Both are, to my mind, superb practitioners of their craft. Both are represented here by works set very specifically in Manhattan. And the works of both, like "The Raven," are indisputably noir.

I became acquainted with Horace Gregory's work almost as long ago as I read "The Last Spin," and it too made an enduring impression. Specifically, I was taken with a group of Gregory's early poems, originally published under the title *Chelsea Rooming House*, and consisting of poetic monologues by the various inhabitants of that building. There is a lingering darkness in the work that made my only problem that of deciding which of the poems to include, and the reader who samples these may well be moved to go on and read the rest of them.

Much more recently, Geoffrey Bartholomew published *The McSorley Poems*. McSorley's is an historic saloon in the East Village—*We were here before you were born*, proclaims the sign over its door, and the sign itself has been making that claim since, well, before you were born—and Bartholomew has been tending its bar for a quarter of a century. He's a longtime friend of mine, and when he offered me a prepublication look at *The McSorley Poems*, I found myself reminded of *Chelsea Rooming House*. The work of either of these poets, dark and rich and ironic and dripping in noir, would sweeten this book; together, they compliment one another; with "The Raven" for company, they make an even more vivid statement.

Yes, they're poems, all of them, and fine poems in the bargain. And who's to say that the notion of noir ought to confine us to prose? The term (which really only means *black* in French) first came into wide usage as a label for certain films of the 1940s and '50s. When it moved into prose fiction, it seemed early on to be inextricably associated with big cities, as if the term *urban noir* were redundant. The novels of Daniel Woodrell have since been categorized quite properly as *country noir*, and Akashic's great noir franchise, ranging as far afield as Havana and Dublin, makes it abundantly clear that noir knows no geographic limitations.

Nor does time serve as a boundary. If the term came about in the middle third of the past century, that doesn't mean that the noir sensibility had not been in evidence before then. Consider Stephen Crane; his first novel, *Maggie, A Girl of the Streets,* could hardly better epitomize the noir sensibility, and our selection, "A Poker Game," shows a dark soul indeed confounded by a rare example of innocent grace. Consider "Mrs. Manstey's View," the first published story of Edith Wharton, which appeared in *Scribner's Magazine* in 1891.

Noir seems to me to transcend form. Film and theater can fit comfortably in the shade of its dark canopy, and so surely can poetry. Some operas make the cut—Verdi's *Rigoletto,* it's worth noting, had its plot lifted in Damon Runyon's oft-anthologized "Sense of Humor." And who could look at Goya's black paintings and not perceive them as visual representations of noir? And what is Billie Holiday's recording of "Gloomy Sunday" if it isn't noir? Or the Beatles' Eleanor Rigby, who died in the church and was buried along with her name? I'd include them, and I'd pull in Beethoven's late quartets while I was at it.

Rather than exercise false modesty (which is the only sort of which I'm capable), I've included a story of my own, "In for a Penny." It was commissioned by the BBC, to be read aloud, and their request was quite specifically for a noir story. Such commissions rarely bring out the best in a writer, but in this case the resultant story was one with which I was well pleased, and I'm happy to offer it here.

Really, how could I resist? How could I pass up the opportunity to share a volume with Stephen Crane and O. Henry and Edgar Allan Poe and Damon Runyon and Irwin Shaw and Edith Wharton and, well, all of these literary superstars?

My mother would be so proud . . .

Lawrence Block
New York, NY
June 2008

PART I

THE OLD SCHOOL

MRS. MANSTEY'S VIEW

BY EDITH WHARTON

Greenwich Village

(Originally published in 1891)

T he view from Mrs. Manstey's window was not a strik-
ing one, but to her at least it was full of interest and
beauty. Mrs. Manstey occupied the back room on the
third floor of a New York boarding-house, in a street where
the ash-barrels lingered late on the sidewalk and the gaps in
the pavement would have staggered a Quintus Curtius. She
was the widow of a clerk in a large wholesale house, and his
death had left her alone, for her only daughter had married
in California, and could not afford the long journey to New
York to see her mother. Mrs. Manstey, perhaps, might have
joined her daughter in the West, but they had now been so
many years apart that they had ceased to feel any need of each
other's society, and their intercourse had long been limited to
the exchange of a few perfunctory letters, written with indifference by the daughter, and with difficulty by Mrs. Manstey,
whose right hand was growing stiff with gout. Even had she
felt a stronger desire for her daughter's companionship, Mrs.
Manstey's increasing infirmity, which caused her to dread the
three flights of stairs between her room and the street, would
have given her pause on the eve of undertaking so long a journey; and without perhaps formulating these reasons she had
long since accepted as a matter of course her solitary life in
New York.

She was, indeed, not quite lonely, for a few friends still toiled up now and then to her room; but their visits grew rare as the years went by. Mrs. Manstey had never been a sociable woman, and during her husband's lifetime his companionship had been all-sufficient to her. For many years she had cherished a desire to live in the country, to have a hen-house and a garden; but this longing had faded with age, leaving only in the breast of the uncommunicative old woman a vague tenderness for plants and animals. It was, perhaps, this tenderness which made her cling so fervently to her view from her window, a view in which the most optimistic eye would at first have failed to discover anything admirable.

Mrs. Manstey, from her coign of vantage (a slightly projecting bow-window where she nursed an ivy and a succession of unwholesome-looking bulbs), looked out first upon the yard of her own dwelling, of which, however, she could get but a restricted glimpse. Still, her gaze took in the topmost boughs of the ailanthus below her window, and she knew how early each year the clump of dicentra strung its bending stalk with hearts of pink.

But of greater interest were the yards beyond. Being for the most part attached to boarding-houses they were in a state of chronic untidiness and fluttering, on certain days of the week, with miscellaneous garments and frayed table-cloths. In spite of this Mrs. Manstey found much to admire in the long vista which she commanded. Some of the yards were, indeed, but stony wastes, with grass in the cracks of the pavement and no shade in spring save that afforded by the intermittent leafage of the clotheslines. These yards Mrs. Manstey disapproved of, but the others, the green ones, she loved. She had grown used to their disorder; the broken barrels, the empty bottles and paths unswept no longer annoyed her; hers was the happy faculty of dwelling on the pleasanter side of the prospect before her.

In the very next enclosure did not a magnolia open its hard white flowers against the watery blue of April? And was there not, a little way down the line, a fence foamed over every May by lilac waves of wistaria? Farther still, a horse-chestnut lifted its candelabra of buff and pink blossoms above broad fans of foliage; while in the opposite yard June was sweet with the breath of a neglected syringa, which persisted in growing in spite of the countless obstacles opposed to its welfare.

But if nature occupied the front rank in Mrs. Manstey's view, there was much of a more personal character to interest her in the aspect of the houses and their inmates. She deeply disapproved of the mustard-colored curtains which had lately been hung in the doctor's window opposite; but she glowed with pleasure when the house farther down had its old bricks washed with a coat of paint. The occupants of the houses did not often show themselves at the back windows, but the servants were always in sight. Noisy slatterns, Mrs. Manstey pronounced the greater number; she knew their ways and hated them. But to the quiet cook in the newly painted house, whose mistress bullied her, and who secretly fed the stray cats at nightfall, Mrs. Manstey's warmest sympathies were given. On one occasion her feelings were racked by the neglect of a housemaid, who for two days forgot to feed the parrot committed to her care. On the third day, Mrs. Manstey, in spite of her gouty hand, had just penned a letter, beginning: "Madam, it is now three days since your parrot has been fed," when the forgetful maid appeared at the window with a cup of seed in her hand.

But in Mrs. Manstey's more meditative moods it was the narrowing perspective of far-off yards which pleased her best.

She loved, at twilight, when the distant brown-stone spire seemed melting in the fluid yellow of the west, to lose herself in vague memories of a trip to Europe, made years ago, and now reduced in her mind's eye to a pale phantasmagoria of indistinct steeples and dreamy skies. Perhaps at heart Mrs. Manstey was an artist; at all events she was sensible of many changes of color unnoticed by the average eye, and dear to her as the green of early spring was the black lattice of branches against a cold sulphur sky at the close of a snowy day. She enjoyed, also, the sunny thaws of March, when patches of earth showed through the snow, like inkspots spreading on a sheet of white blotting-paper; and, better still, the haze of boughs, leafless but swollen, which replaced the clear-cut tracery of winter. She even watched with a certain interest the trail of smoke from a far-off factory chimney, and missed a detail in the landscape when the factory was closed and the smoke disappeared.

Mrs. Manstey, in the long hours which she spent at her window, was not idle. She read a little, and knitted numberless stockings; but the view surrounded and shaped her life as the sea does a lonely island. When her rare callers came it was difficult for her to detach herself from the contemplation of the opposite window-washing, or the scrutiny of certain green points in a neighboring flower-bed which might, or might not, turn into hyacinths, while she feigned an interest in her visitor's anecdotes about some unknown grandchild. Mrs. Manstey's real friends were the denizens of the yards, the hyacinths, the magnolia, the green parrot, the maid who fed the cats, the doctor who studied late behind his mustard-colored curtains; and the confidant of her tenderer musings was the church-spire floating in the sunset.

One April day, as she sat in her usual place, with knitting

cast aside and eyes fixed on the blue sky mottled with round clouds, a knock at the door announced the entrance of her landlady. Mrs. Manstey did not care for her landlady, but she submitted to her visits with ladylike resignation. To-day, however, it seemed harder than usual to turn from the blue sky and the blossoming magnolia to Mrs. Sampson's unsuggestive face, and Mrs. Manstey was conscious of a distinct effort as she did so.

"The magnolia is out earlier than usual this year, Mrs. Sampson," she remarked, yielding to a rare impulse, for she seldom alluded to the absorbing interest of her life. In the first place it was a topic not likely to appeal to her visitors and, besides, she lacked the power of expression and could not have given utterance to her feelings had she wished to.

"The what, Mrs. Manstey?" inquired the landlady, glancing about the room as if to find there the explanation of Mrs. Manstey's statement.

"The magnolia in the next yard—in Mrs. Black's yard," Mrs. Manstey repeated.

"Is it, indeed? I didn't know there was a magnolia there," said Mrs. Sampson, carelessly. Mrs. Manstey looked at her; she did not know that there was a magnolia in the next yard!

"By the way," Mrs. Sampson continued, "speaking of Mrs. Black reminds me that the work on the extension is to begin next week."

"The what?" it was Mrs. Manstey's turn to ask.

"The extension," said Mrs. Sampson, nodding her head in the direction of the ignored magnolia. "You knew, of course, that Mrs. Black was going to build an extension to her house? Yes, ma'am. I hear it is to run right back to the end of the yard. How she can afford to build an extension in these hard times I don't see; but she always was crazy about building. She used to keep a boarding-house in Seventeenth Street, and she nearly ruined herself then by sticking out bow-windows and what not; I should have thought that would have cured her of building, but I guess it's a disease, like drink. Anyhow, the work is to begin on Monday."

Mrs. Manstey had grown pale. She always spoke slowly, so the landlady did not heed the long pause which followed. At last Mrs. Manstey said: "Do you know how high the extension will be?"

"That's the most absurd part of it. The extension is to be built right up to the roof of the main building; now, did you ever?"

Mrs. Manstey paused again. "Won't it be a great annoyance to you, Mrs. Sampson?" she asked.

"I should say it would. But there's no help for it; if people have got a mind to build extensions there's no law to prevent 'em, that I'm aware of." Mrs. Manstey, knowing this, was silent. "There is no help for it," Mrs. Sampson repeated, "but if I *am* a church member, I wouldn't be so sorry if it ruined Eliza Black. Well, good-day, Mrs. Manstey; I'm glad to find you so comfortable."

So comfortable—so comfortable! Left to herself the old woman turned once more to the window. How lovely the view was that day! The blue sky with its round clouds shed a brightness over everything; the ailanthus had put on a tinge of yellow-green, the hyacinths were budding, the magnolia flowers looked more than ever like rosettes carved in alabaster. Soon the wistaria would bloom, then the horse-chestnut; but not for her. Between her eyes and them a barrier of brick and mortar would swiftly rise; presently even the spire would disappear, and all her radiant world be blotted out. Mrs. Manstey sent away untouched the dinner-tray brought to her that evening. She lingered in the window until the windy sunset died in bat-colored dusk; then, going to bed, she lay sleepless all night.

Early the next day she was up and at the window. It was raining, but even through the slanting gray gauze the scene had its charm—and then the rain was so good for the trees. She had noticed the day before that the ailanthus was growing dusty.

"Of course I might move," said Mrs. Manstey aloud, and turning from the window she looked about her room. She might move, of course; so might she be flayed alive; but she was not likely to survive either operation. The room, though far less important to her happiness than the view, was as much a part of her existence. She had lived in it seventeen years. She knew every stain on the wall-paper, every rent in the carpet; the light fell in a certain way on her engravings, her books had grown shabby on their shelves, her bulbs and ivy were used to their window and knew which way to lean to the sun. "We are all too old to move," she said.

That afternoon it cleared. Wet and radiant the blue reappeared through torn rags of cloud; the ailanthus sparkled; the earth in the flower-borders looked rich and warm. It was Thursday, and on Monday the building of the extension was to begin.

On Sunday afternoon a card was brought to Mrs. Black, as she was engaged in gathering up the fragments of the boarders' dinner in the basement. The card, black-edged, bore Mrs. Manstey's name.

"One of Mrs. Sampson's boarders; wants to move, I suppose. Well, I can give her a room next year in the extension. Dinah," said Mrs. Black, "tell the lady I'll be upstairs in a minute."

Mrs. Black found Mrs. Manstey standing in the long parlor garnished with statuettes and antimacassars; in that house she could not sit down.

Stooping hurriedly to open the register, which let out a cloud of dust, Mrs. Black advanced on her visitor.

"I'm happy to meet you, Mrs. Manstey; take a seat, please," the landlady remarked in her prosperous voice, the voice of a woman who can afford to build extensions. There was no help for it; Mrs. Manstey sat down.

"Is there anything I can do for you, ma'am?" Mrs. Black continued. "My house is full at present, but I am going to build an extension, and—"

"It is about the extension that I wish to speak," said Mrs. Manstey, suddenly. "I am a poor woman, Mrs. Black, and I have never been a happy one. I shall have to talk about myself first to—to make you understand."

Mrs. Black, astonished but imperturbable, bowed at this parenthesis.

"I never had what I wanted," Mrs. Manstey continued. "It was always one disappointment after another. For years I wanted to live in the country. I dreamed and dreamed about it; but we never could manage it. There was no sunny window in our house, and so all my plants died. My daughter married years ago and went away—besides, she never cared for the same things. Then my husband died and I was left alone. That was seventeen years ago. I went to live at Mrs. Sampson's, and I have been there ever since. I have grown a little infirm, as you see, and I don't get out often; only on fine days, if I am feeling very well. So you can understand my sitting a great deal in my window—the back window on the third floor—"

"Well, Mrs. Manstey," said Mrs. Black, liberally, "I could give you a back room, I dare say; one of the new rooms in the ex—"

"But I don't want to move; I can't move," said Mrs. Manstey, almost with a scream. "And I came to tell you that if you
build that extension I shall have no view from my window—
no view! Do you understand?"

Mrs. Black thought herself face to face with a lunatic, and
she had always heard that lunatics must be humored.

"Dear me, dear me," she remarked, pushing her chair back
a little way, "that is too bad, isn't it? Why, I never thought of
that. To be sure, the extension *will* interfere with your view,
Mrs. Manstey."

"You do understand?" Mrs. Manstey gasped.

"Of course I do. And I'm real sorry about it, too. But
there, don't you worry, Mrs. Manstey. I guess we can fix that
all right."

Mrs. Manstey rose from her seat, and Mrs. Black slipped
toward the door.

"What do you mean by fixing it? Do you mean that I can
induce you to change your mind about the extension? Oh,
Mrs. Black, listen to me. I have two thousand dollars in the
bank and I could manage, I know I could manage, to give you
a thousand if—" Mrs. Manstey paused; the tears were rolling
down her cheeks.

"There, there, Mrs. Manstey, don't you worry," repeated
Mrs. Black, soothingly. "I am sure we can settle it. I am sorry
that I can't stay and talk about it any longer, but this is such a
busy time of day, with supper to get—"

Her hand was on the door-knob, but with sudden vigor
Mrs. Manstey seized her wrist.

"You are not giving me a definite answer. Do you mean to
say that you accept my proposition?"

"Why, I'll think it over, Mrs. Manstey, certainly I will. I
wouldn't annoy you for the world—"

"But the work is to begin to-morrow, I am told," Mrs. Manstey persisted.

Mrs. Black hesitated. "It shan't begin, I promise you that; I'll send word to the builder this very night." Mrs. Manstey tightened her hold.

"You are not deceiving me, are you?" she said.

"No—no," stammered Mrs. Black. "How can you think such a thing of me, Mrs. Manstey?"

Slowly Mrs. Manstey's clutch relaxed, and she passed through the open door. "One thousand dollars," she repeated, pausing in the hall; then she let herself out of the house and hobbled down the steps, supporting herself on the cast-iron railing.

"My goodness," exclaimed Mrs. Black, shutting and bolting the hall-door, "I never knew the old woman was crazy! And she looks so quiet and ladylike, too."

Mrs. Manstey slept well that night, but early the next morning she was awakened by a sound of hammering. She got to her window with what haste she might and, looking out, saw that Mrs. Black's yard was full of workmen. Some were carrying loads of brick from the kitchen to the yard, others beginning to demolish the old-fashioned wooden balcony which adorned each story of Mrs. Black's house. Mrs. Manstey saw that she had been deceived. At first she thought of confiding her trouble to Mrs. Sampson, but a settled discouragement soon took possession of her and she went back to bed, not caring to see what was going on.

Toward afternoon, however, feeling that she must know the worst, she rose and dressed herself. It was a laborious task, for her hands were stiffer than usual, and the hooks and buttons seemed to evade her.

When she seated herself in the window, she saw that the

workmen had removed the upper part of the balcony, and that the bricks had multiplied since morning. One of the men, a coarse fellow with a bloated face, picked a magnolia blossom and, after smelling it, threw it to the ground; the next man, carrying a load of bricks, trod on the flower in passing.

"Look out, Jim," called one of the men to another who was smoking a pipe, "if you throw matches around near those barrels of paper you'll have the old tinder-box burning down before you know it." And Mrs. Manstey, leaning forward, perceived that there were several barrels of paper and rubbish under the wooden balcony.

At length the work ceased and twilight fell. The sunset was perfect and a roseate light, transfiguring the distant spire, lingered late in the west. When it grew dark Mrs. Manstey drew down the shades and proceeded, in her usual methodical manner, to light her lamp. She always filled and lit it with her own hands, keeping a kettle of kerosene on a zinc-covered shelf in a closet. As the lamp-light filled the room it assumed its usual peaceful aspect. The books and pictures and plants seemed, like their mistress, to settle themselves down for another quiet evening, and Mrs. Manstey, as was her wont, drew up her armchair to the table and began to knit.

That night she could not sleep. The weather had changed and a wild wind was abroad, blotting the stars with close-driven clouds. Mrs. Manstey rose once or twice and looked out of the window; but of the view nothing was discernible save a tardy light or two in the opposite windows. These lights at last went out, and Mrs. Manstey, who had watched for their extinction, began to dress herself. She was in evident haste, for she merely flung a thin dressing-gown over her night-dress and wrapped her head in a scarf; then she opened her closet and cautiously took out the kettle of kerosene. Having slipped a bundle of wooden matches into her pocket she proceeded, with increasing precautions, to unlock her door, and a few moments later she was feeling her way down the dark staircase, led by a glimmer of gas from the lower hall. At length she reached the bottom of the stairs and began the more difficult descent into the utter darkness of the basement. Here, however, she could move more freely, as there was less danger of being overheard; and without much delay she contrived to unlock the iron door leading into the yard. A gust of cold wind smote her as she stepped out and groped shiveringly under the clothes-lines.

That morning at three o'clock an alarm of fire brought the engines to Mrs. Black's door, and also brought Mrs. Sampson's startled boarders to their windows. The wooden balcony at the back of Mrs. Black's house was ablaze, and among those who watched the progress of the flames was Mrs. Manstey, leaning in her thin dressing-gown from the open window.

The fire, however, was soon put out, and the frightened occupants of the house, who had fled in scant attire, reassembled at dawn to find that little mischief had been done beyond the cracking of window panes and smoking of ceilings. In fact, the chief sufferer by the fire was Mrs. Manstey, who was found in the morning gasping with pneumonia, a not unnatural result, as everyone remarked, of her having hung out of an open window at her age in a dressing-gown. It was easy to see that she was very ill, but no one had guessed how grave the doctor's verdict would be, and the faces gathered that evening about Mrs. Sampson's table were awestruck and disturbed. Not that any of the boarders knew Mrs. Manstey well; she "kept to herself," as they said, and seemed to fancy herself too good for them; but then it is always disagreeable to have anyone dying in the house and, as one lady observed to another: "It might just as well have been you or me, my dear."

But it was only Mrs. Manstey; and she was dying, as she had lived, lonely if not alone. The doctor had sent a trained nurse, and Mrs. Sampson, with muffled step, came in from time to time; but both, to Mrs. Manstey, seemed remote and unsubstantial as the figures in a dream. All day she said nothing; but when she was asked for her daughter's address she shook her head. At times the nurse noticed that she seemed to be listening attentively for some sound which did not come; then again she dozed.

The next morning at daylight she was very low. The nurse called Mrs. Sampson and as the two bent over the old woman they saw her lips move.

"Lift me up—out of bed," she whispered.

They raised her in their arms, and with her stiff hand she pointed to the window.

"Oh, the window—she wants to sit in the window. She used to sit there all day," Mrs. Sampson explained. "It can do her no harm, I suppose?"

"Nothing matters now," said the nurse.

They carried Mrs. Manstey to the window and placed her in her chair. The dawn was abroad, a jubilant spring dawn; the spire had already caught a golden ray, though the magnolia and horse-chestnut still slumbered in shadow. In Mrs. Black's yard all was quiet. The charred timbers of the balcony lay where they had fallen. It was evident that since the fire the builders had not returned to their work. The magnolia had unfolded a few more sculptural flowers; the view was undisturbed.

It was hard for Mrs. Manstey to breathe; each moment it grew more difficult. She tried to make them open the window, but they would not understand. If she could have tasted the air, sweet with the penetrating ailanthus savor, it would have eased her; but the view at least was there—the spire was golden now, the heavens had warmed from pearl to blue, day was alight from east to west, even the magnolia had caught the sun.

Mrs. Manstey's head fell back and smiling she died.

That day the building of the extension was resumed.

A POKER GAME

BY STEPHEN CRANE

East 40s

(Originally published in 1902)

Usually a poker game is a picture of peace. There is no drama so low-voiced and serene and monotonous. If an amateur loser does not softly curse, there is no orchestral support. Here is one of the most exciting and absorbing occupations known to intelligent American manhood; here a year's reflection is compressed into a moment of thought; here the nerves may stand on end and scream to themselves, but a tranquility as from heaven is only interrupted by the click of chips. The higher the stakes, the more quiet the scene; this is a law that applies everywhere save on the stage.

And yet sometimes in a poker game things happen. Everybody remembers the celebrated corner on bay rum that was triumphantly consummated by Robert F. Cinch of Chicago assisted by the United States courts and whatever other federal power he needed. Robert F. Cinch enjoyed his victory four months. Then he died, and young Bobbie Cinch came to New York in order to more clearly demonstrate that there was a good deal of fun in twenty-two million dollars.

Old Henry Spuytendyvil owns all the real estate in New York save that previously appropriated by the hospitals and Central Park. He had been a friend of Bob's father. When Bob appeared in New York, Spuytendyvil entertained him correctly. It came to pass that they just naturally played poker.

One night they were having a small game in an uptown hotel. There were five of them, including two lawyers and a politician. The stakes depended on the ability of the individual fortune.

Bobbie Cinch had won rather heavily. He was as generous as sunshine, and when luck chases a generous man it chases him hard, even though he cannot bet with all the skill of his opponents.

Old Spuytendyvil had lost a considerable amount. One of the lawyers from time to time smiled quietly because he knew Spuytendyvil well, and he knew that anything with the name of loss attached to it sliced the old man's heart into sections.

At midnight, Archie Bracketts, the actor, came into the room. "How you holding 'em, Bob?" said he.

"Pretty well," said Bob.

"Having any luck, Mr. Spuytendyvil?"

"Blooming bad," grunted the old man.

Bracketts laughed and put his foot on the round of Spuytendyvil's chair. "There," said he. "I'll queer your luck for you." Spuytendyvil sat at the end of the table. "Bobbie," said the actor presently, as young Cinch won another pot, "I guess I better knock your luck." So he took his foot from the old man's chair and placed it on Bob's chair. The lad grinned good-naturedly and said he didn't care.

Bracketts was in a position to scan both of the hands. It was Bob's ante and old Spuytendyvil threw in a red chip. Everybody passed out up to Bobbie. He filled in the pot and drew a card.

Spuytendyvil drew a card. Bracketts, looking over his shoulder, saw him holding the ten, nine, eight, and seven of diamonds. Theatrically speaking, straight flushes are as frequent as berries on a juniper tree but as a matter of truth the reason that straight flushes are so admired is because they are not as common as berries on a juniper tree. Bracketts stared; drew a cigar slowly from his pocket, and, placing it between his teeth, forgot its existence.

Bobbie was the only other stayer. Bracketts flashed an eye for the lad's hand and saw the nine, eight, six, and five of hearts. Now there are but six hundred and forty-five emotions possible to the human mind, and Bracketts immediately had them all. Under the impression that he had finished his cigar, he took it from his mouth and tossed it toward the grate without turning his eyes to follow its flight.

There happened to be a complete silence around the green-clothed table. Spuytendyvil was studying his hand with a kind of contemptuous smile, but in his eyes there perhaps was to be seen a cold, stern light expressing something sinister and relentless.

Young Bob sat as he had sat. As the pause grew longer, he looked up once inquiringly at Spuytendyvil.

The old man reached for a white chip. "Well, mine are worth about that much," said he, tossing it into the pot. Thereupon he leaned back comfortably in his chair and renewed his stare at the five straight diamonds. Young Bob extended his hand leisurely toward his stack. It occurred to Bracketts that he was smoking, but he found no cigar in his mouth.

The lad fingered his chips and looked pensively at his hand. The silence of those moments oppressed Bracketts like the smoke from a conflagration.

Bobbie Cinch continued for some moments to coolly observe his cards. At last he breathed a little sigh and said, "Well, Mr. Spuytendyvil, I can't play a sure thing against you." He threw in a white chip. "I'll just call you. I've got a straight flush." He faced down his cards.

Old Spuytendyvil's roar of horror and rage could only be equaled in volume to a small explosion of gasolene. He dashed his cards upon the table. "There!" he shouted, glaring frightfully at Bobbie. "I've got a straight flush, too! And mine is Jack high!"

Bobbie was at first paralyzed with amazement, but in a moment he recovered and apparently observing something amusing in the situation he grinned.

Archie Bracketts, having burst his bond of silence, yelled for joy and relief. He smote Bobbie on the shoulder. "Bob, my boy," he cried exuberantly, "you're no gambler but you're a mighty good fellow, and if you hadn't been you would be losing a good many dollars this minute."

Old Spuytendyvil glowered at Bracketts. "Stop making such an infernal din, will you, Archie," he said morosely. His throat seemed filled with pounded glass. "Pass the whiskey."

THE FURNISHED ROOM

BY O. HENRY

Lower West Side

(Originally published in 1906)

Restless, shifting, fugacious as time itself is a certain vast bulk of the population of the red brick district of the lower West Side. Homeless, they have a hundred homes. They flit from furnished room to furnished room, transients forever—transients in abode, transients in heart and mind. They sing "Home, Sweet Home" in ragtime; they carry their *lares et penates* in a bandbox; their vine is entwined about a picture hat; a rubber plant is their fig tree.

Hence the houses of this district, having had a thousand dwellers, should have a thousand tales to tell, mostly dull ones, no doubt; but it would be strange if there could not be found a ghost or two in the wake of all these vagrant guests.

One evening after dark a young man prowled among these crumbling red mansions, ringing their bells. At the twelfth he rested his lean hand-baggage upon the step and wiped the dust from his hatband and forehead. The bell sounded faint and far away in some remote, hollow depths.

To the door of this, the twelfth house whose bell he had rung, came a housekeeper who made him think of an unwholesome, surfeited worm that had eaten its nut to a hollow shell and now sought to fill the vacancy with edible lodgers.

He asked if there was a room to let.

"Come in," said the housekeeper. Her voice came from

her throat; her throat seemed lined with fur. "I have the third-floor back, vacant since a week back. Should you wish to look at it?"

The young man followed her up the stairs. A faint light from no particular source mitigated the shadows of the halls. They trod noiselessly upon a stair carpet that its own loom would have forsworn. It seemed to have become vegetable; to have degenerated in that rank, sunless air to lush lichen or spreading moss that grew in patches to the staircase and was viscid under the foot like organic matter. At each turn of the stairs were vacant niches in the wall. Perhaps plants had once been set within them. If so they had died in that foul and tainted air. It may be that statues of the saints had stood there, but it was not difficult to conceive that imps and devils had dragged them forth in the darkness and down to the unholy depths of some furnished pit below.

"This is the room," said the housekeeper, from her furry throat. "It's a nice room. It ain't often vacant. I had some most elegant people in it last summer—no trouble at all, and paid in advance to the minute. The water's at the end of the hall. Sprowls and Mooney kept it three months. They done a vaudeville sketch. Miss B'retta Sprowls—you may have heard of her—oh, that was just the stage names—right there over the dresser is where the marriage certificate hung, framed. The gas is here, and you see there is plenty of closet room. It's a room everybody likes. It never stays idle long."

"Do you have many theatrical people rooming here?" asked the young man.

"They comes and goes. A good proportion of my lodgers is connected with the theatres. Yes, sir, this is the theatrical district. Actor people never stays long anywhere. I get my share. Yes, they comes and they goes."

He engaged the room, paying for a week in advance. He was tired, he said, and would take possession at once. He counted out the money. The room had been made ready, she said, even to towels and water. As the housekeeper moved away he put, for the thousandth time, the question that he carried at the end of his tongue.

"A young girl—Miss Vashner—Miss Eloise Vashner—do you remember such a one among your lodgers? She would be singing on the stage, most likely. A fair girl, of medium height and slender, with reddish, gold hair and a dark mole near her left eyebrow."

"No, I don't remember the name. Them stage people has names they change as often as their rooms. They comes and they goes. No, I don't call that one to mind."

No. Always no. Five months of ceaseless interrogation and the inevitable negative. So much time spent by day in questioning managers, agents, schools and choruses; by night among the audiences of theatres from all-star casts down to music halls so low that he dreaded to find what he most hoped for. He who had loved her best had tried to find her. He was sure that since her disappearance from home this great, water-girt city held her somewhere, but it was like a monstrous quicksand, shifting its particles constantly, with no foundation, its upper granules of to-day buried to-morrow in ooze and slime.

The furnished room received its latest guest with a first glow of pseudo-hospitality, a hectic, haggard, perfunctory welcome like the specious smile of a demirep. The sophistical comfort came in reflected gleams from the decayed furniture, the ragged brocade upholstery of a couch and two chairs, a foot-wide cheap pier glass between the two windows, from one or two gilt picture frames and a brass bedstead in a corner.

The guest reclined, inert, upon a chair, while the room, confused in speech as though it were an apartment in Babel, tried to discourse to him of its divers tenantry.

A polychromatic rug like some brilliant-flowered rectangular, tropical islet lay surrounded by a billowy sea of soiled matting. Upon the gay-papered wall were those pictures that pursue the homeless one from house to house—The Huguenot Lovers, The First Quarrel, The Wedding Breakfast, Psyche at the Fountain. The mantel's chastely severe outline was ingloriously veiled behind some pert drapery drawn rakishly askew like the sashes of the Amazonian ballet. Upon it was some desolate flotsam cast aside by the room's marooned when a lucky sail had borne them to a fresh port—a trifling vase or two, pictures of actresses, a medicine bottle, some stray cards out of a deck.

One by one, as the characters of a cryptograph become explicit, the little signs left by the furnished room's procession of guests developed a significance. The threadbare space in the rug in front of the dresser told that lovely women had marched in the throng. The tiny fingerprints on the wall spoke of little prisoners trying to feel their way to sun and air. A splattered stain, raying like the shadow of a bursting bomb, witnessed where a hurled glass or bottle had splintered with its contents against the wall. Across the pier glass had been scrawled with a diamond in staggering letters the name "Marie." It seemed that the succession of dwellers in the furnished room had turned in fury—perhaps tempted beyond forebearance by its garish coldness—and wreaked upon it their passions. The furniture was chipped and bruised; the couch, distorted by bursting springs, seemed a horrible monster that had been slain during the stress of some grotesque convulsion. Some more potent upheaval had cloven a great slice from the marble mantel. Each plank in the floor owned its particular cant and shriek as from a separate and individual agony. It seemed incredible that all this malice and injury had been wrought upon the room by those who had called it for a time their home; and yet it may have been the cheated home instinct surviving blindly, the resentful rage at false household gods that had kindled their wrath. A hut that is our own we can sweep and adorn and cherish.

The young tenant in the chair allowed these thoughts to file soft-shod, through his mind, while there drifted into the room furnished sounds and furnished scents. He heard in one room a tittering and incontinent, slack laughter; in others the monologue of a scold, the rattling of dice, a lullaby, and one crying dully; above him a banjo tinkled with spirit. Doors banged somewhere; the elevated trains roared intermittently; a cat yowled miserably upon a back fence. And he breathed the breath of the house—a dank savour rather than a smell—a cold, musty effluvium as from underground vaults mingled with the reeking exhalations of linoleum and mildewed and rotten woodwork.

Then suddenly, as he rested there, the room was filled with the strong, sweet odour of mignonette. It came as upon a single buffet of wind with such sureness and fragrance and emphasis that it almost seemed a living visitant. And the man cried aloud: "What, dear?" as if he had been called, and sprang up and faced about. The rich odour clung to him and wrapped him around. He reached out his arms for it, all his senses for the time confused and commingled. How could one be peremptorily called by an odour? Surely it must have been a sound. But, was it not the sound that had touched, that had caressed him?

"She has been in this room," he cried, and he sprang to

wrest from it a token, for he knew he would recognize the smallest thing that had belonged to her or that she had touched. This enveloping scent of mignonette, the odour that she had loved and made her own—whence came it?

The room had been but carelessly set in order. Scattered upon the flimsy dresser scarf were half a dozen hairpins—those discreet, indistinguishable friends of womankind, feminine of gender, infinite of mood and uncommunicative of tense. These he ignored, conscious of their triumphant lack of identity. Ransacking the drawers of the dresser he came upon a discarded, tiny, ragged handkerchief. He pressed it to his face. It was racy and insolent with heliotrope; he hurled it to the floor. In another drawer he found odd buttons, a theatre programme, a pawnbroker's card, two lost marshmallows, a book on the divination of dreams. In the last was a woman's black satin hair bow, which halted him, poised between ice and fire. But the black satin hair bow also is femininity's demure, impersonal common ornament and tells no tales.

And then he traversed the room like a hound on the scent, skimming the walls, considering the corners of the bulging matting on his hands and knees, rummaging mantel and tables, the curtains and hangings, the drunken cabinet in the corner, for a visible sign, unable to perceive that she was there beside, around, against, within, above him, clinging to him, wooing him, calling him so poignantly through the finer senses that even his grosser ones became cognizant of the call. Once again he answered loudly: "Yes, dear!" and turned, wild-eyed, to gaze on vacancy, for he could not yet discern form and colour and love and outstretched arms in the odour of mignonette. Oh, God! whence that odour, and since when have odours had a voice to call? Thus he groped. He burrowed in crevices and corners, and found corks and cigarettes. These he passed in passive contempt. But once he found in a fold of the matting a half-smoked cigar, and this he ground beneath his heel with a green and trenchant oath. He sifted the room from end to end. He found dreary and ignoble small records of many a peripatetic tenant; but of her whom he sought, and who may have lodged there, and whose spirit seemed to hover there, he found no trace.

And then he thought of the housekeeper.

He ran from the haunted room downstairs and to a door that showed a crack of light. She came out to his knock. He smothered his excitement as best he could.

"Will you tell me, madam," he besought her, "who occupied the room I have before I came?"

"Yes, sir. I can tell you again. 'Twas Sprowls and Mooney, as I said. Miss B'retta Sprowls it was in the theatres, but Missis Mooney she was. My house is well known for respectability. The marriage certificate hung, framed, on a nail over—"

"What kind of a lady was Miss Sprowls—in looks, I mean?"

"Why, black-haired, sir, short, and stout, with a comical face. They left a week ago Tuesday."

"And before they occupied it?"

"Why, there was a single gentleman connected with the draying business. He left owing me a week. Before him was Missis Crowder and her two children, that stayed four months; and back of them was old Mr. Doyle, whose sons paid for him. He kept the room six months. That goes back a year, sir, and further I do not remember."

He thanked her and crept back to his room. The room was dead. The essence that had vivified it was gone. The perfume of mignonette had departed. In its place was the old, stale odour of mouldy house furniture, of atmosphere in storage.

The ebbing of his hope drained his faith. He sat staring at the yellow, singing gaslight. Soon he walked to the bed and began to tear the sheets into strips. With the blade of his knife he drove them tightly into every crevice around windows and door. When all was snug and taut he turned out the light, turned the gas full on again, and laid himself gratefully upon the bed.

It was Mrs. McCool's night to go with the can for beer. So she fetched it and sat with Mrs. Purdy in one of those subterranean retreats where housekeepers foregather and the worm dieth seldom.

"I rented out my third-floor-back this evening," said Mrs. Purdy, across a fine circle of foam. "A young man took it. He went up to bed two hours ago."

"Now, did ye, Mrs. Purdy, ma'am?" said Mrs. McCool, with intense admiration. "You do be a wonder for rentin' rooms of that kind. And did ye tell him, then?" she concluded in a husky whisper laden with mystery.

"Rooms," said Mrs. Purdy, in her furriest tones, "are furnished for to rent. I did not tell him, Mrs. McCool."

"'Tis right ye are, ma'am; 'tis by renting rooms we kape alive. Ye have the rale sense for business, ma'am. There be many people will rayjict the rentin' of a room if they be tould a suicide has been after dyin' in the bed of it."

"As you say, we has our living to be making," remarked Mrs. Purdy.

"Yis, ma'am; 'tis true. 'Tis just one wake ago this day I helped ye lay out the third floor, back. A pretty slip of a colleen she was to be killin' herself wid the gas—a swate little face she had, Mrs. Purdy, ma'am."

"She'd a-been called handsome, as you say," said Mrs.

Purdy, assenting but critical, "but for that mole she had a-growin' by her left eyebrow. Do fill up your glass again, Mrs. McCool."

SPANISH BLOOD

BY LANGSTON HUGHES

Harlem

(Originally Published in 1934)

In that amazing city of Manhattan where people are forever building things anew, during prohibition times there lived a young Negro called Valerio Gutierrez whose mother was a Harlem laundress, but whose father was a Puerto Rican sailor. Valerio grew up in the streets. He was never much good at school, but he was swell at selling papers, pitching pennies, or shooting pool. In his teens he became one of the smoothest dancers in the Latin-American quarter north of Central Park. Long before the rhumba became popular, he knew how to do it in the real Cuban way that made all the girls afraid to dance with him. Besides, he was very good looking.

At seventeen, an elderly Chilean lady who owned a beauty parlor called La Flor began to buy his neckties. At eighteen, she kept him in pocket money and let him drive her car. At nineteen, younger and prettier women—a certain comely Spanish widow, also one Dr. Barrios' pale wife—began to see that he kept well dressed.

"You'll never amount to nothin'," Hattie, his brown-skinned mother, said. "Why don't you get a job and work? It's that foreign blood in you, that's what it is. Just like your father."

"*¿Qué va?*" Valerio replied, grinning.

"Don't you speak Spanish to me," his mama said. "You know I don't understand it."

"O.K., Mama," Valerio said. "*Yo voy a trabajar.*"

"You better *trabajar,*" his mama answered. "And I mean work, too! I'm tired o' comin' home every night from that Chinee laundry and findin' you gone to the dogs. I'm gonna move out o' this here Spanish neighborhood anyhow, way up into Harlem where some real *colored* people is, I mean American Negroes. There ain't nobody settin' a decent example for you down here 'mongst all these Cubans and Puerto Ricans and things. I don't care if your father was one of 'em, I never did like 'em real well."

"Aw, Ma, why didn't you ever learn Spanish and stop talking like a spook?"

"Don't you spook me, you young hound, you! I won't stand it. Just because you're straight-haired and yellow and got that foreign blood in you, don't you spook me. I'm your mother and I won't stand for it. You hear me?"

"Yes, m'am. But you know what I mean. I mean stop talking like most colored folks—just because you're not white you don't have to get back in a corner and stay there. Can't we live nowhere else but way up in Harlem, for instance? Down here in 106th Street, white and colored families live in the same house—Spanish-speaking families, some white and some black. What do you want to move further up in Harlem for, where everybody's all black? Lots of my friends down here are Spanish and Italian, and we get along swell."

"That's just what I'm talkin' about," said his mother. "That's just why I'm gonna move. I can't keep track of you, runnin' around with a fast foreign crowd, all mixed up with every what-cha-ma-call-it, lettin' all shades o' women give you money. Besides, no matter where you move, or what language you speak, you're still colored less'n your skin is white."

"Well, I won't be," said Valerio. "I'm American, Latin-American."

"Huh!" said his mama. "It's just by luck that you even got good hair."

"What's that got to do with being American?"

"A mighty lot," said his mama, "in America."

They moved. They moved up to 143rd Street, in the very middle of "American" Harlem. There Hattie Gutierrez was happier—for in her youth her name had been Jones, not Gutierrez, just plain colored Jones. She had come from Virginia, not Latin America. She had met the Puerto Rican seaman in Norfolk, had lived with him there and in New York for some ten or twelve years and borne him a son, meanwhile working hard to keep him and their house in style. Then one winter he just disappeared, probably missed his boat in some far-off port town, settled down with another woman, and went on dancing rhumbas and drinking rum without worry.

Valerio, whom Gutierrez left behind, was a handsome child, not quite as light as his father, but with olive-yellow skin and Spanish-black hair, more foreign than Negro. As he grew up, he became steadily taller and better looking. Most of his friends were Spanish-speaking, so he possessed their language as well as English. He was smart and amusing out of school. But he wouldn't work. That was what worried his mother, he just wouldn't work. The long hours and low wages most colored fellows received during depression times never appealed to him. He could live without struggling, so he did.

He liked to dance and play billiards. He hung out near the Cuban theater at 110th Street, around the pool halls and gambling places, in the taxi dance emporiums. He was all for getting the good things out of life. His mother's moving up to black 143rd Street didn't improve conditions any. Indeed, it just started the ball rolling faster, for here Valerio became what is known in Harlem as a big-timer, a young sport, a hep cat. In other words, a man-about-town.

His sleek-haired yellow star rose in a chocolate sky. He was seen at all the formal invitational affairs given by the exclusive clubs of Harlem's younger set, although he belonged to no clubs. He was seen at midnight shows stretching into the dawn. He was even asked to Florita Sutton's famous Thursday midnight-at-homes, where visiting dukes, English authors, colored tap dancers, and dinner-coated downtowners vied for elbow room in her small Sugar Hill apartment. Hattie, Valerio's mama, still kept her job ironing in the Chinese laundry—but nobody bothered about his mama.

Valerio was a nice enough boy, though, about sharing his income with her, about pawning a ring or something someone would give him to help her out on the rent or the insurance policies. And maybe, once or twice a week, Mama might see her son coming in as she went out in the morning or leaving as she came in at night, for Valerio often slept all day. And she would mutter, "The Lord knows, cause I don't, what will become of you, boy! You're just like your father!"

Then, strangely enough, one day Valerio got a job. A good job, too—at least, it paid him well. A friend of his ran an after-hours nightclub on upper St. Nicholas Avenue. Gangsters owned the place, but they let a Negro run it. They had a red-hot jazz band, a high-yellow revue, and bootleg liquor. When the Cuban music began to hit Harlem, they hired Valerio to introduce the rhumba. That was something he was really cut out to do, the rhumba. That wasn't work. Not at all, *hombre!* But it was a job, and his mama was glad.

Attired in a yellow silk shirt, white satin trousers, and a bright red sash, Valerio danced nightly to the throbbing drums and seed-filled rattles of the tropics—accompanied by the orchestra's usual instruments of joy. Valerio danced with a little brown Cuban girl in a red dress, Concha, whose hair was a mat of darkness and whose hips were nobody's business.

Their dance became the talk of the town—at least, of that part of the town composed of night-lifers—for Valerio danced the rhumba as his father had taught him to dance it in Norfolk when he was ten years old, innocently—unexpurgated, happy, funny, but beautiful, too—like a gay, sweet longing for something that might be had, sometime, maybe, someplace or other.

Anyhow, business boomed. Ringside tables filled with people who came expressly to see Valerio dance.

"He's marvelous," gasped ladies who ate at the Ritz any time they wanted to.

"That boy can dance," said portly gentlemen with offices full of lawyers to keep track of their income tax. "He can dance!" And they wished they could, too.

"Hot stuff," said young rumrunners, smoking reefers and drinking gin—for these were prohibition days.

"A natural-born eastman," cried a tan-skin lady with a diamond wristwatch. "He can have anything I got."

That was the trouble! Too many people felt that Valerio could have anything they had, so he lived on the fat of the land without making half an effort. He began to be invited to fashionable cocktail parties downtown. He often went out to dinner in the East Fifties with white folks. But his mama still kept her job in the Chinese laundry.

Perhaps it was a good thing she did in view of what finally happened, for to Valerio the world was nothing but a swagger world tingling with lights, music, drinks, money, and people who had everything—or thought they had. Each night, at the club, the orchestra beat out its astounding songs, shook its rattles, fingered its drums. Valerio put on his satin trousers with the fiery red sash to dance with the little Cuban girl who always had a look of pleased surprise on her face, as though amazed to find dancing so good. Somehow she and Valerio made their rhumba, for all their hip shaking, clean as a summer sun.

Offers began to come in from other nightclubs, and from small producers as well. "Wait for something big, kid," said the man who ran the cabaret. "Wait till the Winter Garden calls you."

Valerio waited. Meanwhile, a dark young rounder named Sonny, who wrote number bets for a living, had an idea for making money off of Valerio. They would open an apartment together where people could come after the nightclubs closed—come and drink and dance—and love a little if they wanted to. The money would be made from the sale of drinks—charging very high prices to keep the riffraff out. With Valerio as host, a lot of good spenders would surely call. They could get rich.

"O.K. by me," said Valerio.

"I'll run the place," said Sonny, "and all you gotta do is just be there and dance a little, maybe—you know—and make people feel at home."

"O.K.," said Valerio.

"And we'll split the profit two ways—me and you."

"O.K."

So they got a big Seventh Avenue apartment, furnished it with deep, soft sofas and lots of little tables and a huge icebox, and opened up. They paid off the police every week. They had good whisky. They sent out cards to a hundred downtown people who didn't care about money. They informed the best patrons of the cabaret where Valerio danced—the white folks who thrilled at becoming real Harlem initiates going home with Valerio.

From the opening night on, Valerio's flat filled with white

people from midnight till the sun came up. Mostly a sporty crowd, young blades accompanied by ladies of the chorus, race-track gentlemen, white cabaret entertainers out for amusement after their own places closed, musical-comedy stars in search of new dance steps—and perhaps three or four brownskin ladies-of-the-evening and a couple of chocolate gigolos, to add color.

There was a piano player. Valerio danced. There was impromptu entertaining by the guests. Often famous radio stars would get up and croon. Expensive nightclub names might rise to do a number—or several numbers if they were tight enough. And sometimes it would be hard to stop them when they really got going.

Occasionally guests would get very drunk and stay all night, sleeping well into the day. Sometimes one might sleep with Valerio.

Shortly, all Harlem began to talk about the big red road-ster Valerio drove up and down Seventh Avenue. It was all nickel-plated—and a little blond revue star known on two continents had given it to him, so folks said. Valerio was on his way to becoming a gigolo deluxe.

"That boy sure don't draw no color lines," Harlem commented. "No, Sir!"

"And why should he?" Harlem then asked itself rhetorically. "Colored folks ain't got no money—and money's what he's after, ain't it?"

But Harlem was wrong. Valerio seldom gave a thought to money—he was having too good a time. That's why it was well his mama kept her job in the Chinese laundry, for one day Sonny received a warning, "Close up that flat of yours, and close it damn quick!"

Gangsters!

"What the hell?" Sonny answered the racketeers. "We're payin' off, ain't we—you and the police, both? So what's wrong?"

"Close up, or we'll break you up," the warning came back. "We don't like the way you're running things, black boy. And tell Valerio to send that white chick's car back to her—and quick!"

"Aw, nuts!" said Sonny. "We're paying the police! You guys lay off."

But Sonny wasn't wise. He knew very well how little the police count when gangsters give orders, yet he kept right on. The profits had gone to his head. He didn't even tell Valerio they had been warned, for Sonny, who was trying to make enough money to start a number bank of his own, was afraid the boy might quit. Sonny should have known better.

One Sunday night about 3:30 A.M., the piano was going like mad. Fourteen couples packed the front room, dancing close and warm. There were at least a dozen folks whose names you'd know if you saw them in any paper, famous from Hollywood to Westport.

They were feeling good.

Sonny was busy at the door, and a brown bar-boy was collecting highball glasses, as Valerio came in from the club where he still worked. He went in the bedroom to change his dancing shoes, for it was snowing and his feet were cold.

O, rock me, pretty mama, till the cows come home . . .

sang a sleek-haired Harlemite at the piano.

Rock me, rock me, baby, from night to morn . . .

when, just then, a crash like the wreck of the Hesperus re-sounded through the hall and shook the whole house as five

Italian gentlemen in evening clothes who looked exactly like gangsters walked in. They had broken down the door.

Without a word they began to smash up the place with long axes each of them carried. Women began to scream, men to shout, and the piano vibrated, not from jazz-playing fingers, but from axes breaking its hidden heart.

"Lemme out," the piano player yelled. "Lemme out!" But there was panic at the door.

"I can't leave without my wrap," a woman cried. "Where is my wrap? Sonny, my ermine coat!"

"Don't move," one of the gangsters said to Sonny.

A big white fist flattened his brown nose.

"I ought to kill you," said a second gangster. "You was warned. Take this!"

Sonny spit out two teeth.

Crash went the axes on furniture and bar. Splintered glass flew, wood cracked. Guests fled, hatless and coatless. About that time the police arrived.

Strangely enough, the police, instead of helping protect the place from the gangsters, began themselves to break, not only the furniture, but also the *heads* of every Negro in sight. They started with Sonny. They laid the barman and the waiter low. They grabbed Valerio as he emerged from the bedroom. They beat his face to a pulp. They whacked the piano player twice across the buttocks. They had a grand time with their night sticks. Then they arrested all the colored fellows (and no whites) as the gangsters took their axes and left. That was the end of Valerio's apartment.

In jail Valerio learned that the woman who gave him the red roadster was being kept by a gangster who controlled prohibition's whole champagne racket and owned dozens of rum-running boats.

"No wonder!" said Sonny, through his bandages. "He got them guys to break up our place! He probably told the police to beat hell out of us, too!"

"Wonder how he knew she gave me that car?" asked Valerio innocently.

"White folks know everything," said Sonny.

"Aw, stop talking like a spook," said Valerio.

When he got out of jail, Valerio's face had a long night-stick scar across it that would never disappear. He still felt weak and sick and hungry. The gangsters had forbidden any of the nightclubs to employ him again, so he went back home to Mama.

"Umm-huh!" she told him. "Good thing I kept my job in that Chinee laundry. It's a good thing . . . Sit down and eat, son . . . What you gonna do now?"

"Start practicing dancing again. I got an offer to go to Brazil—a big club in Rio."

"Who's gonna pay your fare way down yonder to Brazil?"

"Concha," Valerio answered—the name of his Cuban rhumba partner whose hair was a mat of darkness. "Concha."

"A woman!" cried his mother. "I might a-knowed it! We're weak that way. My God, I don't know, boy! I don't know!"

"You don't know what?" asked Valerio, grinning.

"How women can help it," said his mama. "The Lord knows you're *just* like your father—and I took care o' him for ten years. I reckon it's that Spanish blood."

"¡*Qué va!*" said Valerio.

SAILOR OFF THE BREMEN

BY IRWIN SHAW

West Village

(Originally published in 1939)

They sat in the small white kitchen, Ernest and Charley and Preminger and Dr. Stryker, all bunched around the porcelain-topped table, so that the kitchen seemed to be overflowing with men. Sally stood at the stove turning griddle-cakes over thoughtfully, listening intently to what Preminger was saying.

"So," Preminger said, carefully working his knife and fork, "everything was excellent. The comrades arrived, dressed like ladies and gentlemen at the opera, in evening gowns and what do you call them?"

"Tuxedoes," Charley said. "Black ties."

"Tuxedoes," Preminger nodded, speaking with his precise educated German accent. "Very handsome people, mixing with all the other handsome people who came to say good-bye to their friends on the boat; everybody very gay, everybody with a little whisky on the breath; nobody would suspect they were Party members, they were so clean and upper class." He laughed lightly at his own joke. He looked like a young boy from a nice Middle Western college, with crew-cut hair and a straight nose and blue eyes and an easy laugh. His laugh was a little high and short, and he talked fast, as though he wanted to get a great many words out to beat a certain deadline, but otherwise, being a Communist in Germany and a deck officer on the *Bremen* hadn't made any obvious changes in him. "It is a wonderful thing," he said, "how many pretty girls there are in the Party in the United States. Wonderful!"

They all laughed, even Ernest, who put his hand up to cover the empty spaces in the front row of his teeth every time he smiled. His hand covered his mouth and the fingers cupped around the neat black patch over his eye, and he smiled secretly and swiftly behind that concealment, getting his merriment over with swiftly, so he could take his hand down and compose his face into its usual unmoved, distant expression, cultivated from the time he got out of the hospital. Sally watched him from the stove, knowing each step: the grudging smile, the hand, the consciousness and memory of deformity, the wrench to composure, the lie of peace when he took his hand down.

She shook her head, dumped three brown cakes onto a plate.

"Here," she said, putting them before Preminger. "Better than Childs restaurant."

"Wonderful," Preminger said, dousing them with syrup. "Each time I come to America I feast on these. There is nothing like it in the whole continent of Europe."

"All right," Charley said, leaning out across the kitchen table, practically covering it, because he was so big, "finish the story."

"So I gave the signal," Preminger said, waving his fork. "When everything was nice and ready, everybody having a good time, stewards running this way, that way, with champagne, a nice little signal and we had a very nice little demonstration. Nice signs, good loud yelling, the Nazi flag cut down, one, two, three, from the pole. The girls standing together singing like angels, everybody running there from all parts of the ship, everybody getting the idea very, very clear—a very nice little demonstration." He smeared butter methodically on the top cake. "So then, the rough business. Expected. Naturally. After all, we all know it is no cocktail party for Lady Astor." He pursed his lips and squinted at his plate, looking like a small boy making believe he's the head of a family. "A little pushing, expected, maybe a little crack over the head here and there, expected. Justice comes with a headache these days, we all know that. But my people, the Germans. You must always expect the worst from them. They organize like lightning. Method. How to treat a riot on a ship. Every steward, every oiler, every sailor, was there in a minute and a half. Two men would hold a comrade, the other would beat him. Nothing left to accident."

"The hell with it," Ernest said. "What's the sense in going through the whole thing again? It's all over."

"Shut up," Charley said.

"Two stewards got hold of Ernest," Preminger said softly. "And another one did the beating. Stewards are worse than sailors. All day long they take orders, they hate the world. Ernest was unlucky. All the others did their jobs, but they were human beings. The steward is a member of the Nazi party. He is an Austrian; he is not a normal man."

"Sally," Ernest said, "give Mr. Preminger some more milk."

"He kept hitting Ernest," Preminger tapped absently on the porcelain top with his fork, "and he kept laughing and laughing."

"You know who he is?" Charley asked. "You're sure know who he is?"

"I know who he is. He is twenty-five years old, very dark

and good-looking, and he sleeps with at least two ladies a voy-age." Preminger slopped his milk around in the bottom of his glass. "His name is Lueger. He spies on the crew for the Nazis. He has sent two men already to concentration camps. He is a very serious character. He knew what he was doing," Prem-inger said clearly, "when he kept hitting Ernest in the eye. I tried to get to him, but I was in the middle of a thousand people, screaming and running. If something happens to that Lueger that will be a very good thing."

"Have a cigar," Ernest said, pulling two out of his pocket.

"Something will happen to him," Charley said, taking a deep breath, and leaning back from the table. "Something will damn sure happen to him."

"You're a dumb kid," Ernest said, in the weary tone he used now in all serious discussions. "What do you prove if you beat up one stupid sailor?"

"I don't prove anything," Charley said. "I don't prove a goddamn thing. I am just going to have a good time with the boy that knocked my brother's eye out. That's all."

"It is not a personal thing," Ernest said, in the tired voice. "It is the movement of Fascism. You don't stop Fascism with a personal crusade against one German. If I thought it would do some good, I'd say, sure, go ahead . . ."

"My brother, the Communist," Charley said bitterly. "He goes out and he gets ruined and still he talks dialectics. The Red Saint with the long view. The long view gives me a pain in the ass. I am taking a very short view of Mr. Lueger. I am going to kick the living guts out of his belly. Preminger, what do you say?"

"Speaking as a Party member," Preminger said, "I approve of your brother's attitude, Charley."

"Nuts," Charley said.

"Speaking as a man, Charley," Preminger went on, "please put Lueger on his back for at least six months. Where is that cigar, Ernest?"

Dr. Stryker spoke up in his dry, polite, dentist's voice. "As you know," he said, "I am not the type for violence." Dr. Stryker weighed a hundred and thirty-three pounds and it was almost possible to see through his wrists, he was so frail. "But as Ernest's friends, I think there would be a definite satisfaction for all of us, including Ernest, if this Lueger was taken care of. You may count on me for anything within my powers." He was very scared, Dr. Stryker, and his voice was even drier than usual, but he spoke up after reasoning the whole thing out slowly and carefully, disregarding the fear, the worry, the possible great damage. "That is my opinion," he said.

"Sally," Ernest said, "talk to these damn fools."

"I think," Sally said slowly, looking steadily at her husband's face, always stiffly composed now, like a corpse's face, "I think they know what they're talking about."

Ernest shrugged. "Emotionalism. A large useless gesture. You're all tainted by Charley's philosophy. He's a football player. He has a football player's philosophy. Somebody knocks you down, you knock him down, everything is fine."

"I want a glass of milk, too," Charley said. "Please, Sally."

"Whom're you playing this week?" Ernest said.

"Georgetown."

"Won't that be enough violence for one week?" Ernest asked.

"Nope," Charley said. "I'll take care of Georgetown first, then Lueger."

"Anything I can do," Dr. Stryker said. "Remember, anything I can do. I am at your service."

"The coach'll be sore," Ernest said, "if you get banged up,

Charley."

"The hell with the coach. Please shut up, Ernest. I have got my stomachful of Communist tactics. No more. Get this in your head, Ernest." Charley stood up and banged the table. "I am disregarding the class struggle, I am disregarding the education of the proletariat, I am disregarding the fact that you are a good Communist. I am acting strictly in the capacity of your brother. If you'd had any brains you would have stayed away from that lousy boat. You're a painter, an artist, you make water colors, what the hell is it your business if lunatics're running Germany? But all right. You've got no brains. You go and get your eye beat out. O.K. Now I step in. Purely personal. None of your business. Shut your trap. I will fix everything to my own satisfaction. Please go and lie down in the bedroom. We have arrangements to make here."

Ernest stood up, hiding his mouth, which was twitching, and walked into the bedroom and closed the door and lay down on the bed, in the dark, with his eye open.

The next day, an hour before sailing time, Charley and Dr. Stryker and Sally went down to the *Bremen*, and boarded the ship on different gangplanks. They stood separately on the A Deck, up forward, waiting for Preminger. Preminger came, very boyish and crisp in his blue uniform, looked coldly past them, touched a steward on the arm, a dark, good-looking young steward, said something to him, and went aft. Charley and Dr. Stryker examined the steward closely, so that two weeks later, on a dark street, there would be no mistake, and left, leaving Sally there, smiling at Lueger.

"Yes," Sally said two weeks later, "it is very clear. I'll have dinner with him, and I'll go to a movie with him, and I'll get him to take at least two drinks, and I'll tell him I live on West Twelfth Street, near West Street. There is a whole block of apartment houses there, and I'll get him down to West Twelfth Street between a quarter to one and one in the morning, and you'll be waiting there, you and Stryker, under the Ninth Avenue L, and you'll say, 'Pardon me, can you direct me to Sheridan Square?' and I'll start running."

"That's right," Charley said, "that's fine." He blew reflectively on his huge hands, knotted and cleat-marked from last Saturday's game. "That is the whole story for Mr. Lueger. You'll go through with it now?" he asked. "You're sure you can manage it?"

"I'll go through with it," Sally said. "I had a long talk with him today when the boat came in. He is very . . . anxious. He likes small girls like me, he says, with black hair. I told him I lived alone, downtown. He looked at me very significantly. I know why he manages to sleep with two ladies a voyage, like Preminger says. I'll manage it."

"What is Ernest going to do tonight?" Dr. Stryker asked. In the two weeks of waiting his voice had become so dry he had to swallow desperately every five words. "Somebody ought to take care of Ernest tonight."

"He's going to Carnegie Hall tonight," Sally said. "They're playing Brahms and Debussy."

"That's a good way to spend an evening," Charley said. He opened his collar absently, and pulled down his tie. "The only place I can go with Ernest these days is the movies. It's dark, so I don't have to look at him."

"He'll pull through," Dr. Stryker said professionally. "I'm making him new teeth; he won't be so self-conscious, he'll adjust himself."

"He hardly paints any more," Sally said. "He just sits

around the house and looks at his old pictures."

"Mr. Lueger," Charley said. "Our pal, Mr. Lueger."

"He carries a picture of Hitler," Sally said. "In his watch. He showed me. He says he's lonely."

"How big is he?" Stryker asked nervously.

"He's a large, strong man," Sally said.

"I think you ought to have an instrument of some kind, Charley," Stryker said dryly. "Really, I do."

Charley laughed. He extended his two hands, palms up, the broken fingers curled a little, broad and muscular. "I want to do this with my own hands," he said. "I want to take care of Mr. Lueger with my bare fists. I want it to be a very personal affair."

"There is no telling what . . ." Stryker said.

"Don't worry, Stryker," Charley said. "Don't worry one bit."

At twelve that night Sally and Lueger walked down Eighth Avenue from the Fourteenth Street subway station. Lueger held Sally's arm as they walked, his fingers moving gently up and down, occasionally grasping tightly the loose cloth of her coat and the firm flesh of her arm just above the elbow.

"Oh," Sally said. "Don't. That hurts."

Lueger laughed. "It does not hurt much," he said. He pinched her playfully. "You don't mind if it hurt, nevertheless," he said. His English was very complicated, with a thick accent.

"I mind," Sally said. "Honest, I mind."

"I like you," he said, walking very close to her. "You are a good girl. You are made excellent. I am happy to accompany you home. You are sure you live alone?"

"I'm sure," Sally said. "Don't worry. I would like a drink."

"Aaah," Lueger said. "Waste time."

"I'll pay for it," Sally said. She had learned a lot about him in one evening. "My own money. Drinks for you and me."

"If you say so," Lueger said, steering her into a bar. "One drink, because we have something to do tonight." He pinched her hard and laughed, looking obliquely into her eyes with a kind of technical suggestiveness he used on the two ladies a voyage on the *Bremen*.

Under the Ninth Avenue L on Twelfth Street, Charley and Dr. Stryker leaned against an elevated post, in deep shadow.

"I . . . I . . ." Stryker said. Then he had to swallow to wet his throat so that the words would come out. "I wonder if they're coming," he said finally in a flat, high whisper.

"They'll come," Charley said, keeping his eyes on the little triangular park up Twelfth Street where it joins Eighth Avenue. "That Sally has guts. That Sally loves my dumb brother like he was the President of the United States. As if he was a combination of Lenin and Michelangelo. And he had to go and get his eye batted out."

"He's a very fine man," Stryker said. "Your brother Ernest. A man with true ideals. I am very sorry to see what has happened to his character since . . . Is that them?"

"No," Charley said. "It's two girls from the YWCA on the corner."

"He used to be a very merry man," Stryker said, swallowing rapidly. "Always laughing. Always sure of what he was saying. Before he was married we used to go out together all the time and all the time the girls, my girl and his girl, no matter who they were, would give all their attention to him. All the time. I didn't mind. I love your brother Ernest as if he was my young brother. I could cry when I see him sitting now, covering his eye and his teeth, not saying anything, just listening to what other people have to say."

"Yeah," Charley said. "Yeah. Why don't you keep quiet, Stryker?"

"Excuse me," Stryker said, talking fast and dry. "I don't like to bother you. But I must talk. Otherwise, if I just stand here keeping still, I will suddenly start running and I'll run right up to Forty-second Street. I can't keep quiet at the moment, excuse me."

"Go ahead and talk, Stryker," Charley said gently, patting him on the shoulder. "Shoot your mouth right off, all you want."

"I am only doing this because I think it will help Ernest," Stryker said, leaning hard against the post, in the shadow, to keep his knees straight. "I have a theory. My theory is that when Ernest finds out what happens to this Lueger, he will pick up. It will be a kind of springboard to him. It is my private notion of the psychology of the situation. We should have brought an instrument with us, though. A club, a knife, brass knuckles." Stryker put his hands in his pockets, holding them tight against the cloth to keep them from trembling. "It will be very bad if we mess this up. Won't it be very bad, Charley? Say, Charley . . ."

"Sssh," said Charley.

Stryker looked up the street. "That's them. That's Sally, that's her coat. That's the bastard. The lousy German bastard."

"Sssh, Stryker. Sssh."

"I feel very cold, Charley. Do you feel cold? It's a warm night but I . . ."

"For Christ's sake, shut up!"

"We'll fix him," Stryker whispered. "Yes, Charley, I'll shut up, sure, I'll shut up, depend on me, Charley . . ."

Sally and Lueger walked slowly down Twelfth Street.

Lueger had his arm around Sally's waist and their hips rubbed as they walked.

"That was a very fine film tonight," Lueger was saying. "I enjoy Deanna Durbin. Very young, fresh, sweet. Like you." He grinned at Sally in the dark and held tighter to her waist. "A small young maid. You are just the kind I like." He tried to kiss her. Sally turned her head away.

"Listen, Mr. Lueger," she said, not because she liked him, but because he was a human being and thoughtless and un-suspecting and because her heart was softer than she had thought. "Listen, I think you'd better leave me here."

"I do not understand English," Lueger said, enjoying this last coyness.

"Thank you very much for a pleasant evening," Sally said desperately, stopping in her tracks. "Thank you for tak-ing me home. You can't come up. I was lying to you. I don't live alone . . ."

Lueger laughed. "Little frightened girl. That's nice. I love you for it."

"My brother," Sally said. "I swear to God I live with my brother."

Lueger grabbed her and kissed her, hard, bruising her lips against her teeth, his hands pressing harshly into the flesh of her back. She sobbed into his mouth with the pain, helpless. He released her. He was laughing.

"Come," he said, holding her close. "I am anxious to meet your brother. Little liar."

"All right," she said, watching Charley and Stryker move out from the L shadow. "All right. Let's not wait. Let's walk fast. Very fast. Let's not waste time."

Lueger laughed happily. "That's it. That's the way a girl should talk."

They walked swiftly toward the elevated ramp, Lueger laughing, his hand on her hip in certainty and possession.

"Pardon me," Stryker said. "Could you direct me to Sheridan Square?"

"Well," said Sally, stopping, "it's . . ."

Charley swung and Sally started running as soon as she heard the wooden little noise a fist makes on a man's face. Charley held Lueger up with one hand and chopped the lolling head with the other. He carried Lueger back into the shadows against a high iron railing. He hung Lueger by his overcoat against one of the iron points, so he could use both hands on him. Stryker watched for a moment, then turned and looked toward Eighth Avenue.

Charley worked very methodically, getting his two hundred pounds behind short, accurate, smashing blows that made Lueger's head jump and loll and roll against the iron pikes. Charley hit him in the nose three times, squarely, using his fist the way a carpenter uses a hammer. Each time Charley heard the sound of bone breaking, cartilage tearing. When he got through with the nose, Charley went after the mouth, hooking along the side of the jaws with both hands, until teeth fell out and the jaw hung open, smashed, loose with the queer looseness of flesh that is no longer moored to solid bone. Charley started crying, the tears running down into his mouth, the sobs shaking him as he swung his fists. Even then Stryker didn't turn around. He just put his hands to his ears and looked steadfastly at Eighth Avenue.

When he started on Lueger's eye, Charley talked. "You bastard. Oh, you lousy goddamn bastard," came out with the sobs and the tears as he hit at the eye with his right hand, cutting it, smashing it, tearing it again and again, his hand coming away splattered with blood each time. "Oh, you dumb, mean, skirt-chasing sonofabitch, bastard." And he kept hitting with fury and deliberation at the shattered eye. . . .

A car came up Twelfth Street from the waterfront and slowed down at the corner. Stryker jumped on the running board. "Keep moving," he said, very tough, "if you know what's good for you."

He jumped off the running board and watched the car speed away.

Charley, still sobbing, pounded Lueger in the chest and belly. With each blow Lueger slammed against the iron fence with a noise like a carpet being beaten, until his coat ripped off the pike and he slid to the sidewalk.

Charley stood back, his fists swaying, the tears still coming, the sweat running down his face inside his collar, his clothes stained with blood.

"O.K.," he said, "O.K., you bastard."

He walked swiftly up under the L in the shadows, and Stryker hurried after him.

Much later, in the hospital, Preminger stood over the bed in which Lueger lay, unconscious, in splints and bandages.

"Yes," he said to the detective and the doctor. "That's our man. Lueger. A steward. The papers on him are correct."

"Who do you think done it?" the detective asked in a routine voice. "Did he have any enemies?"

"Not that I know of," Preminger said. "He was a very popular boy. Especially with the ladies."

The detective started out of the ward. "Well," he said, "he won't be a very popular boy when he gets out of here."

Preminger shook his head. "You must be very careful in a strange city," he said to the interne, and went back to the ship.

MY AUNT FROM TWELFTH STREET

BY JEROME WEIDMAN

Alphabet City

(Originally published in 1939)

When I was a child, the strangest thing to me about my Aunt Tessie from Twelfth Street was that she lived on Fifteenth Street. I liked her and she liked me, but I was not permitted to visit her very often because the rest of our family always considered her something of a renegade. She was a large woman, with a quick laugh, a generous purse, and a small tailor shop that her husband had left in her hands when he died, and she baked the largest and best sugar-covered cookies that I have ever eaten. But these virtues were impressive only to me. It was hard for my mother and father and our other relatives to forget that she did not live, by choice, among us.

We were Galicians and lived, quite properly, on East Fourth Street. Sixth Street was almost exclusively Hungarian, Fifth Street was full of Litvaks, Seventh and Eighth Streets were reserved for Russians, and so on. Nobody lived on Twelfth Street.

We all knew Aunt Tessie's explanation for not living with her own people—she said furnished rooms had been cheaper on Twelfth Street than in any other place in the city when she landed in America—but it was disregarded. The difference in rent between Twelfth and Fourth Streets was not enough to excuse such a lapse in nationalistic loyalty. Therefore, in our family she was always referred to, with an uncomplimentary twist of the lips, as Tessie from Twelfth Street.

Later, when she married the small tailor on Fifteenth Street and moved three blocks uptown to live in a tiny apartment behind the shop, she was still called that. Even after her husband died, Aunt Tessie showed no signs of capitulation. "You know Tessie," my father said with a shrug. "You say black, she says white. As long as she knows you want her to move to Fourth Street, where she belongs, she'll spend her life on Fifteenth Street, there, with the Italians and the Irish. That's Tessie from Twelfth Street for you."

It was hard to understand her loyalty to Fifteenth Street. From the few glimpses that I had had of her section of it, between Avenue A and First Avenue, the family accusation of stubbornness seemed justified. In fact, the street was so cold and dreary-looking, so shabby and lifeless, that I still don't know why I liked to go there. Fourth Street, where we lived, between Avenue D and Lewis, was no Coney Island, but at least it was cheerful and friendly, with plenty of movement and noise, if nothing else. But on Fifteenth Street the houses were dirty and old; no children played in the gutter; nobody yelled or laughed; no groups stood on the sidewalks and gossiped. Fifteenth Street was dead. But I liked it and never seemed to be able to visit it often enough.

Just after my tenth birthday, however, I was treated to what I considered a windfall. My mother, I was told, was about to "go away for a while." This puzzling phrase was delivered with a benevolent smile and later, in translation, proved to mean the addition of a baby sister to the household. The problem of getting rid of me for a few days became a choice between a Fourth Street neighbor and a Fifteenth Street aunt. Finally, and with reluctance, my parents decided on the latter.

Arrangements were made several weeks in advance, and one hot July evening my father delivered me at the small tailor shop with final instructions to be a good boy.

"Don't worry so much," Aunt Tessie told my father. "We're people here the same as you are on Fourth Street, not wild animals. I'll take care of him."

She started me off with a handful of her huge cookies and told me I could stand near the window of the shop and look out into the street while she prepared dinner.

"Can I go outside and sit on the stoop, Aunt Tess?" I asked.

"No," she said. "We'll be ready to eat soon. You can stand by the window and look out."

I was puzzled by her refusal. It was too hot to be indoors. But I couldn't disobey her, so I went to the front window and looked out into Fifteenth Street as I munched cookies. There wasn't much to see. The intense July heat had driven more people than usual out into the street, but they seemed curiously listless and disinterested. Occasionally an automobile drove through and once an ice wagon went by, but they did not stop. The only change that the heat seemed to have made in Fifteenth Street was that all the windows were open. I could tell by the way the curtains fluttered in and out whenever a faint breeze found its way into the block. On Fourth Street you could tell when a window was open because someone was almost always framed in it, leaning on a small pillow and usually yelling into the street or to a neighbor a floor or two above or below. But nobody leaned out of the windows on Fifteenth Street. The heat and the inactivity were depressing. I began to wonder why I had looked forward to this visit and by the time my aunt called me to dinner I was wishing I was back on Fourth Street.

After dinner I asked my aunt if I could go outside.

"No," she said.

"But it's so hot, Aunt Tess!" I protested.

"Well," she said hestitating; then, "All right. Wait till I finish the dishes and I'll go out with you."

When she was ready we carried two folding chairs out onto the stoop and I helped her set them up. She settled herself with her knitting in one of them and I took the other. The dinner hour was apparently over for most of the block, because a surprising number of people were sitting on the stoops of the houses, the men in shirt-sleeves and the women in house dresses, fanning themselves with folded newspapers. There was only one sign of activity on the block. A car was parked at the curb directly across the street from us. A handsome young man, with a tight, dark face and beautifully combed hair, was sitting in the front seat, leaning on the door and talking to three girls who stood on the sidewalk beside the car. The girls were quite pretty, or, rather, they seemed so without hats and in their light summer dresses. And the young man must have been very witty, because every few minutes they would all throw back their heads and laugh loudly at something he had said. Nobody on the block was paying any attention to them. I glanced quickly at my aunt once or twice. But she was engrossed in her knitting. She didn't seem to hear the loud laughter or see the bright little group on the other side of the street. I turned back to watch them.

Just as the sun was disappearing behind the L on First Avenue, another young man turned the corner and came down the block. He was carrying his hat and his hair was as thick and handsome and perfectly combed as that of the young man in the car. In fact, he looked almost exactly like the first young man, except that he seemed a little older and he wasn't smiling. He walked up to the car with an insolent swagger and put his foot on the running board and leaned his elbow on the door. The young man in the car smiled up at him and said something and everybody laughed. They talked for another minute or so and then the girls joined in a farewell burst of laughter and walked away, waving once or twice, leaving the two young men with the gleaming hair alone together.

They talked earnestly for a while in friendly fashion. Occasionally the first young man still seated in the car, would shake his head vigorously or smile. Finally he got out of the car and the two of them started to walk off together toward First Avenue. The first young man continued to shake his head as the other talked and a few times a snatch of his quick laughter came back to me on my aunt's stoop.

Then suddenly, as I watched them, an amazing thing happened. The second young man pulled something from his pocket, pointed it quickly at the first young man, and there was the single snapping crack of a gun. The first young man jerked himself erect, as though someone had taken him by surprise and poked him sharply in the small of the back, and then he crumpled quickly and fell into the gutter. The murderer ran the few steps to First Avenue, turned the corner, and disappeared.

"Aunt Tess!" I cried, jumping up.

In an instant the motionless block was full of a quivering, voiceless activity. Every stoop was bobbing with silent, swiftly moving people. Nobody yelled; nobody screamed; nobody ran toward the young man in the gutter. My aunt clutched my arm. "Come on," she said sharply. "But Aunt Tess!" "Come on," she repeated, and dragged me toward the door. Windows were being slammed shut all along the block. Both sidewalks were empty and in a moment every stoop was cleared. As my aunt pulled me through the door I had a last glimpse of Fifteenth Street. Except for the crumpled young man in the gutter, it was deserted and quiet.

My aunt hurried into the kitchen, dropped her knitting, and ran back into the store, where I was standing at the window.

"Get away from there," my aunt said.

She pushed me aside roughly and I watched her in amazement as she closed the windows and hauled down the long green shades.

"Aunt Tess, what—?"

"Keep quiet," she said.

She seized my arm again and dragged me into the kitchen, pushed me into a chair beside the kitchen table, and sat down at the other side, facing me. Then she picked up her knitting and began to work quickly. With all the windows shut, the heat was almost unbearable in the small room. The sweat gathered on my forehead and I could feel a thin trickle of it begin to work its way down my spine.

"Aunt Tess," I said, "what—?"

"Don't talk so much," she said.

Her voice was hard and frightened. She had never spoken like that to me before. She continued to knit determinedly, scowling at her nervously working fingers, without looking up and without wiping the sweat from her face.

"But Aunt Tess," I cried, "what happened? They—"

"Shut up," she said.

Not a sound came through to us from the street outside. The sweat was running into my eyes.

"It's hot in here!" I cried. "What—"

My aunt did not look at me. "Just shut up!" she said.

JOHNNY ONE-EYE

BY DAMON RUNYON

Broadway

(Originally published in 1941)

This cat I am going to tell you about is a very small cat, and in fact it is only a few weeks old, consequently it is really nothing but an infant cat. To tell the truth, it is just a kitten.

It is gray and white and very dirty and its fur is all frowzled up, so it is a very miserable-looking little kitten to be sure the day it crawls through a broken basement window into an old house in East Fifty-third Street over near Third Avenue in the city of New York and goes from room to room saying mer-ow, mer-ow in a low, weak voice until it comes to a room at the head of the stairs on the second story where a guy by the name of Rudolph is sitting on the floor thinking of not much.

One reason Rudolph is sitting on the floor is because there is nothing else to sit on as this is an empty house that is all boarded up for years and there is no furniture whatever in it, and another reason is that Rudolph has a .38 slug in his side and really does not feel like doing much of anything but sitting. He is wearing a derby hat and his overcoat as it is in the wintertime and very cold and he has an automatic Betsy on the floor beside him and naturally he is surprised quite some when the little kitten comes mer-owing into the room and he picks up the Betsy and points it at the door in case anyone he does not wish to see is with the kitten. But when he observes that it is all alone, Rudolph puts the Betsy down again and speaks to the kitten as follows:

"Hello, cat," he says.

Of course the kitten does not say anything in reply except mer-ow but it walks right up to Rudolph and climbs on his lap, although the chances are if it knows who Rudolph is, it will hightail it out of there quicker than anybody can say scat. There is enough daylight coming through the chinks in the boards over the windows for Rudolph to see that the kitten's right eye is in bad shape, and in fact it is bulged half out of its head in a most distressing manner and it is plain to be seen that the sight is gone from this eye. It is also plain to be seen that the injury happens recently and Rudolph gazes at the kitten a while and starts to laugh and says like this:

"Well, cat," he says, "you seem to be scuffed up almost as much as I am. We make a fine pair of invalids here together. What is your name, cat?"

Naturally the kitten does not state its name but only goes mer-ow and Rudolph says, "All right, I will call you Johnny. Yes," he says, "your tag is now Johnny One-Eye."

Then he puts the kitten in under his overcoat and pretty soon it gets warm and starts to purr and Rudolph says:

"Johnny," he says, "I will say one thing for you and that is you are plenty game to be able to sing when you are hurt as bad as you are. It is more than I can do."

But Johnny only goes mer-ow again and keeps on purring and by and by it falls sound asleep under Rudolph's coat, and Rudolph is wishing the pain in his side will let up long enough for him to do the same.

Well, I suppose you are saying to yourself, what is this Rudolph doing in an old empty house with a slug in his side, so I will explain that the district attorney is responsible for this situation. It seems that the D.A. appears before the grand jury and tells it that Rudolph is an extortion guy and a killer and I do not know what all else, though some of these statements are without doubt a great injustice to Rudolph as, up to the time the D.A. makes them, Rudolph does not kill anybody of any consequence in years.

It is true that at one period of his life he is considered a little wild but this is in the 1920's when everybody else is, too, and for seven or eight years he is all settled down and is engaged in business organization work, which is very respectable work, indeed. He organizes quite a number of businesses on a large scale and is doing very good for himself. He is living quietly in a big hotel all alone, as Rudolph is by no means a family guy, and he is highly spoken of by one and all when the D.A. starts poking his nose into his affairs, claiming that Rudolph has no right to be making money out of the businesses, even though Rudolph gives these businesses plenty of first-class protection.

In fact, the D.A. claims that Rudolph is nothing but a racket guy and a great knock to the community, and all this upsets Rudolph no little when it comes to his ears in a roundabout way. So he calls up his lawbooks and requests legal advice on the subject, and lawbooks says the best thing he can think of for Rudolph to do is to become as inconspicuous as possible right away but to please not mention to anyone that he gives this advice.

Lawbooks says he understands the D.A. is requesting indictments and is likely to get them and furthermore that he is rounding up certain parties that Rudolph is once associated with and trying to get them to remember incidents in Rudolph's early career that may not be entirely to his credit. Lawbooks says he hears that one of these parties is a guy by the name of Cute Freddy and that Freddy makes a deal with the D.A. to lay off of him if he tells everything he knows about Rudolph, so under the circumstances a long journey by Rudolph will be in the interest of everybody concerned.

So Rudolph decides to go on a journey but then he gets to thinking that maybe Freddy will remember a little matter that Rudolph long since dismisses from his mind and does not wish to have recalled again, which is the time he and Freddy do a job on a guy by the name of The Icelander in Troy years ago and he drops around to Freddy's house to remind him to be sure not to remember this.

But it seems that Freddy, who is an important guy in business organization work himself, though in a different part of the city than Rudolph, mistakes the purpose of Rudolph's visit and starts to out with his rooty-toot-toot, and in order to protect himself it is necessary for Rudolph to take his Betsy and give Freddy a little tattooing. In fact, Rudolph practically crochets his monogram on Freddy's chest and leaves him exceptionally deceased.

But as Rudolph is departing from the neighborhood, who bobs up but a young guy by the name of Buttsy Fagan, who works for Freddy as a chauffeur and one thing and another, and who is also said to be able to put a slug through a keyhole at forty paces without touching the sides, though I suppose it will have to be a pretty good-sized keyhole. Anyway, he takes a long-distance crack at Rudolph as Rudolph is rounding a corner but all Buttsy can see of Rudolph at the moment is a little piece of his left side and this is what Buttsy hits, although no one knows it at the time, except of course Rudolph, who just keeps on departing.

Now this incident causes quite a stir in police circles, and the D.A. is very indignant over losing a valuable witness, and when they are unable to locate Rudolph at once, a reward of five thousand dollars is offered for information leading to his capture alive or dead and some think they really mean dead. Indeed, it is publicly stated that it is not a good idea for anyone to take any chances with Rudolph as he is known to be armed and is such a character as will be sure to resent being captured, but they do not explain that this is only because Rudolph knows the D.A. wishes to place him in the old rocking chair at Sing Sing and that Rudolph is quite allergic to the idea.

Anyway, the cops go looking for Rudolph in Hot Springs and Miami and every other place except where he is, which is right in New York wandering around town with the slug in his side, knocking at the doors of old friends requesting assistance. But all the old friends do for him is to slam the doors in his face and forget they ever see him, as the D.A. is very tough on parties who assist guys he is looking for, claiming that this is something most illegal called harboring fugitives. Besides Rudolph is never any too popular at best with his old friends as he always plays pretty much of a lone duke and takes the big end of everything for his.

He cannot even consult a doctor about the slug in his side as he knows that nowadays the first thing a doctor will do about a guy with a gunshot wound is to report him to the cops, although Rudolph can remember when there is always a sure-footed doctor around who will consider it a privilege and a pleasure to treat him and keep his trap closed about it. But of course this is in the good old days and Rudolph can see they are gone forever. So he just does the best he can about the slug and goes on wandering here and there and around and about and the blats keep printing his picture and saying, Where is Rudolph?

Where he is some of the time is in Central Park trying to get some sleep, but of course even the blats will consider it foolish to go looking for Rudolph there in such cold weather, as he is known as a guy who enjoys his comfort at all times. In fact, it is comfort that Rudolph misses more than anything as the slug is commencing to cause him great pain and naturally the pain turns Rudolph's thoughts to the author of same and he remembers that he once hears somebody say that Buttsy lives over in East Fifty-third Street.

So one night Rudolph decides to look Buttsy up and cause him a little pain in return, and he is moseying through Fifty-third when he gets so weak he falls down on the sidewalk in front of the old house and rolls down a short flight of steps that lead from the street level to a little railed-in areaway and ground floor or basement door, and before he stops rolling he brings up against the door itself and it creaks open inward as he bumps it. After he lays there a while Rudolph can see that the house is empty and he crawls on inside.

Then, when he feels stronger, Rudolph makes his way upstairs because the basement is damp and mice keep trotting back and forth over him and eventually he winds up in the room where Johnny One-Eye finds him the following afternoon, and the reason Rudolph settles down in this room is because it commands the stairs. Naturally, this is important to a guy in Rudolph's situation, though after he is sitting there for about fourteen hours before Johnny comes along he can see that he is not going to be much disturbed by traffic. But he considers it a very fine place, indeed, to remain planted until he is able to resume his search for Buttsy.

Well, after a while Johnny One-Eye wakes up and comes from under the coat and looks at Rudolph out of his good eye and Rudolph waggles his fingers and Johnny plays with them, catching one finger in his front paws and biting it gently and this pleases Rudolph no little as he never before has any personal experience with a kitten. However, he remembers observing one when he is a boy down in Houston Street, so he takes a piece of paper out of his pocket and makes a little ball of it and rolls it along the floor and Johnny bounces after it very lively indeed. But Rudolph can see that the bad eye is getting worse and finally he says to Johnny like this:

"Johnny," he says, "I guess you must be suffering more than I am. I remember there are some pet shops over on Lexington Avenue not far from here and when it gets good and dark I am going to take you out and see if we can find a cat croaker to do something about your eye. Yes, Johnny," Rudolph says, "I will also get you something to eat. You must be starved."

Johnny One-Eye says mer-ow to this and keeps on playing with the paper ball but soon it comes on dark outside and inside, too, and, in fact, it is so dark inside that Rudolph cannot see his hand before him. Then he puts his Betsy in a side pocket of his overcoat and picks up Johnny and goes downstairs, feeling his way in the dark and easing along a step at a time until he gets to the basement door. Naturally, Rudolph does not wish to strike any matches because he is afraid someone outside may see the light and get nosey.

By moving very slowly, Rudolph finally gets to Lexington Avenue and while he is going along he remembers the time he walks from 125th Street in Harlem down to 110th with six slugs in him and never feels as bad as he does now. He gets to thinking that maybe he is not the guy he used to be, which of course is very true, as Rudolph is now forty-odd years of age and is fat around the middle and getting bald, and he also does some thinking about what a pleasure it will be to him to find this Buttsy and cause him the pain he is personally suffering.

There are not many people in the streets and those that are go hurrying along because it is so cold and none of them pay any attention to Rudolph or Johnny One-Eye either, even though Rudolph staggers a little now and then like a guy who is rummed up, although of course it is only weakness. The chances are he is also getting a little feverish and light-headed because finally he stops a cop who is going along swinging his arms to keep warm and asks him if he knows where there is a pet shop, and it is really most indiscreet of such a guy as Rudolph to be interviewing cops. But the cop just points up the street and goes on without looking twice at Rudolph and Rudolph laughs and pokes Johnny with a finger and says:

"No, Johnny One-Eye," he says, "the cop is not a dope for not recognizing Rudolph. Who can figure the hottest guy in forty-eight states to be going along a street with a little cat in his arms? Can you, Johnny?"

Johnny says mer-ow and pretty soon Rudolph comes to the pet shop the cop points out. Rudolph goes inside and says to the guy like this:

"Are you a cat croaker?" Rudolph says. "Do you know what to do about a little cat that has a hurt eye?"

"I am a kind of a vet," the guy says.

"Then take a glaum at Johnny One-Eye here and see what you can do for him," Rudolph says.

Then he hands Johnny over to the guy and the guy looks at Johnny a while and says:

"Mister," he says, "the best thing I can do for this cat is to put it out of its misery. You better let me give it something right now. It will just go to sleep and never know what happens."

Well, at this, Rudolph grabs Johnny One-Eye out of the guy's hands and puts him under his coat and drops a duke on the Betsy in his pocket as if he is afraid the guy will take Johnny away from him again and he says to the guy like this:

"No, no, no," Rudolph says. "I cannot bear to think of such a thing. What about some kind of an operation? I remember they take a bum lamp out of Joe the Goat at Bellevue one time and he is okay now."

"Nothing will do your cat any good," the guy says. "It is a goner. It will start having fits pretty soon and die sure. What is the idea of trying to save such a cat as this? It is no kind of a cat to begin with. It is just a cat. You can get a million like it for a nickel."

"No," Rudolph says, "this is not just a cat. This is Johnny One-Eye. He is my only friend in the world. He is the only living thing that ever comes pushing up against me warm and friendly and trusts me in my whole life. I feel sorry for him."

"I feel sorry for him, too," the guy says. "I always feel sorry for animals that get hurt and for people."

"I do not feel sorry for people," Rudolph says. "I only feel sorry for Johnny One-Eye. Give me some kind of stuff that Johnny will eat."

"Your cat wants milk," the guy says. "You can get some at the delicatessen store down at the corner. Mister," he says, "you look sick yourself. Can I do anything for you?"

But Rudolph only shakes his head and goes on out and down to the delicatessen joint where he buys a bottle of milk and this transaction reminds him that he is very short in the moo department. In fact, he can find only a five-dollar note in his pockets and he remembers that he has no way of getting any more when this runs out, which is a very sad predicament indeed for a guy who is accustomed to plenty of moo at all times.

Then Rudolph returns to the old house and sits down on

the floor again and gives Johnny One-Eye some of the milk in his derby hat as he neglects buying something for Johnny to drink out of. But Johnny offers no complaint. He laps up the milk and curls himself into a wad in Rudolph's lap and purrs.

Rudolph takes a swig of the milk himself but it makes him sick, for by this time Rudolph is really far from being in the pink of condition. He not only has the pain in his side but he has a heavy cold which he probably catches from lying on the basement floor or maybe sleeping in the park and he is wheezing no little. He commences to worry that he may get too ill to continue looking for Buttsy, as he can see that if it is not for Buttsy he will not be in this situation, suffering the way he is, but on a long journey to some place.

He takes to going off into long stretches of a kind of stupor and every time he comes out of one of these stupors the first thing he does is to look around for Johnny One-Eye and Johnny is always right there either playing with the paper ball or purring in Rudolph's lap. He is a great comfort to Rudolph but after a while Rudolph notices that Johnny seems to be running out of zip and he also notices that he is running out of zip himself especially when he discovers that he is no longer able to get to his feet.

It is along in the late afternoon of the day following the night Rudolph goes out of the house that he hears someone coming up the stairs and naturally he picks up his Betsy and gets ready for action when he also hears a very small voice calling kitty, kitty, kitty, and he realizes that the party that is coming can be nobody but a child. In fact, a minute later a little pretty of maybe six years of age comes into the room all out of breath and says to Rudolph like this:

"How do you do?" she says. "Have you seen my kitty?"

Then she spots Johnny One-Eye in Rudolph's lap and runs

over and sits down beside Rudolph and takes Johnny in her arms, and at first Rudolph is inclined to resent this and has a notion to give her a good boffing but he is too weak to exert himself in such a manner.

"Who are you?" Rudolph says to the little pretty, "and," he says, "where do you live and how do you get in this house?"

"Why," she says, "I am Elsie, and I live down the street and I am looking everywhere for my kitty for three days and the door is open downstairs and I know kitty likes to go in doors that are open so I came to find her and here she is."

"I guess I forgot to close it last night," Rudolph says. "I seem to be very forgetful lately."

"What is your name?" Elsie asks, "and why are you sitting on the floor in the cold and where are all your chairs? Do you have any little girls like me and do you love them dearly?"

"No," Rudolph says. "By no means and not at all."

"Well," Elsie says, "I think you are a nice man for taking care of my kitty. Do you love kitty?"

"Look," Rudolph says, "his name is not kitty. His name is Johnny One-Eye, because he has only one eye."

"I call her kitty," Elsie says. "But," she says, "Johnny One-Eye is a nice name too and if you like it best I will call her Johnny and I will leave her here with you to take care of always and I will come to see her every day. You see," she says, "if I take Johnny home Buttsy will only kick her again."

"Buttsy?" Rudolph says. "Do I hear you say Buttsy? Is his other name Fagan?"

"Why, yes," Elsie says. "Do you know him?"

"No," Rudolph says, "but I hear of him. What is he to you?"

"He is my new daddy," Elsie says. "My other one and my best one is dead and so my mamma makes Buttsy my new one.

My mamma says Buttsy is her mistake. He is very mean. He kicks Johnny and hurts her eye and makes her run away. He kicks my mamma too. Buttsy kicks everybody and everything when he is mad and he is always mad."

"He is a louse to kick a little cat," Rudolph says.

"Yes," Elsie says, "that is what Mr. O'Toole says he is for kicking my mamma but my mamma says it is not a nice word and I am never to say it out loud."

"Who is Mr. O'Toole?" Rudolph says.

"He is the policeman," Elsie says. "He lives across the street from us and he is very nice to me. He says Buttsy is the word you say just now, not only for kicking my mamma but for taking her money when she brings it home from work and spending it so she cannot buy me nice things to wear. But do you know what?" Elsie says. "My mamma says some day Buttsy is going far away and then she will buy me lots of things and send me to school and make me a lady."

Then Elsie begins skipping around the room with Johnny One-Eye in her arms and singing I am going to be a lady, I am going to be a lady, until Rudolph has to tell her to pipe down because he is afraid somebody may hear her. And all the time Rudolph is thinking of Buttsy and regretting that he is unable to get on his pins and go out of the house.

"Now I must go home," Elsie says, "because this is a night Buttsy comes in for his supper and I have to be in bed before he gets there so I will not bother him. Buttsy does not like little girls. Buttsy does not like little kittens. Buttsy does not like little anythings. My mamma is afraid of Buttsy and so am I. But," she says, "I will leave Johnny here with you and come back tomorrow to see her."

"Listen, Elsie," Rudolph says, "does Mr. O'Toole come home tonight to his house for his supper, too?"

"Oh, yes," Elsie says. "He comes home every night. Sometimes when there is a night Buttsy is not coming in for his supper my mamma lets me go over to Mr. O'Toole's and I play with his dog Charley but you must never tell Buttsy this because he does not like O'Toole either. But this is a night Buttsy is coming and that is why my mamma tells me to get in early."

Now Rudolph takes an old letter out of his inside pocket and a pencil out of another pocket and he scribbles a few lines on the envelope and stretches himself out on the floor and begins groaning oh, oh, oh, and then he says to Elsie like this:

"Look, Elsie," he says, "you are a smart little kid and you pay strict attention to what I am going to say to you. Do not go to bed tonight until Buttsy gets in. Then," Rudolph says, "you tell him you come in this old house looking for your cat and that you hear somebody groaning like I do just now in the room at the head of the stairs and that you find a guy who says his name is Rudolph lying on the floor so sick he cannot move. Tell him the front door of the basement is open. But," Rudolph says, "you must not tell him that Rudolph tells you to say these things. Do you understand?"

"Oh," Elsie says, "do you want him to come here? He will kick Johnny again if he does."

"He will come here, but he will not kick Johnny," Rudolph says. "He will come here, or I am the worst guesser in the world. Tell him what I look like, Elsie. Maybe he will ask you if you see a gun. Tell him you do not see one. You do not see a gun, do you, Elsie?"

"No," Elsie says, "only the one in your hand when I come in but you put it under your coat. Buttsy has a gun and Mr. O'Toole has a gun but Buttsy says I am never, never to tell anybody about this or he will kick me the way he does my mamma."

"Well," Rudolph says, "you must not remember seeing mine, either. It is a secret between you and me and Johnny One-Eye. Now," he says, "if Buttsy leaves the house to come and see me, as I am pretty sure he will, you run over to Mr. O'Toole's house and give him this note, but do not tell Buttsy or your mamma either about the note. If Buttsy does not leave, it is my hard luck but you give the note to Mr. O'Toole anyway. Now tell me what you are to do, Elsie," Rudolph says, "so I can see if you have got everything correct."

"I am to go on home and wait for Buttsy," she says, "and I am to tell him Rudolph is lying on the floor of this dirty old house with a fat stomach and a big nose making noises and that he is very sick and the basement door is open and there is no gun if he asks me, and when Buttsy comes to see you I am to take this note to Mr. O'Toole but Buttsy and my mamma are not to know I have the note and if Buttsy does not leave I am to give it to Mr. O'Toole anyway and you are to stay here and take care of Johnny my kitten."

"That is swell," Rudolph says. "Now you run along."

So Elsie leaves and Rudolph sits up again against the wall because his side feels easier this way and Johnny One-Eye is in his lap purring very low and the dark comes on until it is blacker inside the room than in the middle of a tunnel and Rudolph feels that he is going into another stupor and he has a tough time fighting it off.

Afterward some of the neighbors claim they remember hearing a shot inside the house and then two more in quick succession and then all is quiet until a little later when Officer O'Toole and half a dozen other cops and an ambulance with a doctor come busting into the street and swarm into the joint with their guns out and their flashlights going. The first thing they find is Buttsy at the foot of the stairs with two bullet wounds close together in his throat, and naturally he is real dead.

Rudolph is still sitting against the wall with what seems to be a small bundle of bloody fur in his lap but which turns out to be what is left of this little cat I am telling you about, although nobody pays any attention to it at first. They are more interested in getting the come-alongs on Rudolph's wrists, but before they move him he pulls his clothes aside and shows the doctor where the slug is in his side and the doctor takes one glaum and shakes his head and says:

"Gangrene," he says. "I think you have pneumonia, too, from the way you are blowing."

"I know," Rudolph says. "I know this morning. Not much chance, hey, croaker?"

"Not much," the doctor says.

"Well, cops," Rudolph says, "load me in. I do not suppose you want Johnny, seeing that he is dead."

"Johnny who?" one of the cops says.

"Johnny One-Eye," Rudolph says. "This little cat here in my lap. Buttsy shoots Johnny's only good eye out and takes most of his noodle with it. I never see a more wonderful shot. Well, Johnny is better off but I feel sorry about him as he is my best friend down to the last."

Then he begins to laugh and the cop asks him what tickles him so much and Rudolph says:

"Oh," he says, "I am thinking of the joke on Buttsy. I am positive he will come looking for me, all right, not only because of the little altercation between Cute Freddy and me but because the chances are Buttsy is greatly embarrassed by not tilting me over the first time, as of course he never knows he wings me. Furthermore," Rudolph says, "and this is the best reason of all, Buttsy will realize that if I am in his neighborhood it is by no means a good sign for him, even if he hears I am sick.

"Well," Rudolph says, "I figure that with any kind of a square rattle I will have a better chance of nailing him than he has of nailing me, but that even if he happens to nail me, O'Toole will get my note in time to arrive here and nab Buttsy on the spot with his gun on him. And," Rudolph says, "I know it will be a great pleasure to the D.A. to settle Buttsy for having a gun on him.

"But," Rudolph says, "as soon as I hear Buttsy coming on the sneaksby up the stairs, I can see I am taking all the worst of it because I am now wheezing like a busted valve and you can hear me a block away except when I hold my breath, which is very difficult indeed, considering the way I am already greatly tuckered out. No," Rudolph says, "it does not look any too good for me as Buttsy keeps coming up the stairs, as I can tell he is doing by a little faint creak in the boards now and then. I am in no shape to maneuver around the room and pretty soon he will be on the landing and then all he will have to do is to wait there until he hears me which he is bound to do unless I stop breathing altogether. Naturally," Rudolph says, "I do not care to risk a blast in the dark without knowing where he is, as something tells me Buttsy is not a guy you can miss in safety.

"Well," Rudolph says, "I notice several times before this that in the dark Johnny One-Eye's good glim shines like a big spark, so when I feel Buttsy is about to hit the landing, although of course I cannot see him, I flip Johnny's ball of paper across the room to the wall just opposite the door, and tough as he must be feeling Johnny chases after it when he hears it light. I figure Buttsy will hear Johnny playing with the paper and see his eye shining and think it is me and take a pop at it and that his gun flash will give me a crack at him.

"It all works out just like I dope it," Rudolph says, "but," he says, "I never give Buttsy credit for being such a marksman as to be able to hit a cat's eye in the dark. If I know this, maybe I will never stick Johnny out in front the way I do. It is a good thing I never give Buttsy a second shot. He is a lily. Yes," Rudolph says, "I can remember when I can use a guy like him."

"Buttsy is no account," the cop says. "He is a good riddance. He is the makings of a worse guy than you."

"Well," Rudolph says, "it is a good lesson to him for kicking a little cat."

Then they take Rudolph to a hospital and this is where I see him and piece out this story of Johnny One-Eye, and Officer O'Toole is at Rudolph's bedside keeping guard over him, and I remember that not long before Rudolph chalks out he looks at O'Toole and says to him like this:

"Copper," he says, "there is no chance of them outjuggling the kid on the reward moo, is there?"

"No," O'Toole says, "no chance. I keep the note you send me by Elsie saying she will tell me where you are. It is information leading to your capture just as the reward offer states. Rudolph," he says, "it is a nice thing you do for Elsie and her mother, although," he says, "it is not nearly as nice as icing Buttsy for them."

"By the way, copper," Rudolph says, "there is the remainders of a pound note in my pants pocket when I am brought here. I want you to do me a favor. Get it from the desk and buy Elsie another cat and name it Johnny, will you?"

"Sure," O'Toole says. "Anything else?"

"Yes," Rudolph says, "be sure it has two good eyes."

THE LAST SPIN

EVAN HUNTER

Washington Heights

(Originally published in 1956)

The boy sitting opposite him was his enemy.

The boy sitting opposite him was called Tigo, and he wore a green silk jacket with an orange stripe on each sleeve. The jacket told Dave that Tigo was his enemy. The jacket shrieked, "Enemy, enemy!"

"This is a good piece," Tigo said, indicating the gun on the table. "This runs you close to forty-five bucks, you try to buy it in a store. That's a lot of money."

The gun on the table was a Smith & Wesson .38 Police Special.

It rested exactly in the center of the table, its sawed-off, two-inch barrel abruptly terminating the otherwise lethal grace of the weapon. There was a checked walnut stock on the gun, and the gun was finished in a flat blue. Alongside the gun were three .38 Special cartridges.

Dave looked at the gun disinterestedly. He was nervous and apprehensive, but he kept tight control of his face. He could not show Tigo what he was feeling. Tigo was the enemy, and so he presented a mask to the enemy, cocking one eyebrow and saying, "I seen pieces before. There's nothing special about this one."

"Except what we got to do with it," Tigo said.

Tigo was studying him with large brown eyes. The eyes

were moist-looking. He was not a bad-looking kid, Tigo, with thick black hair and maybe a nose that was too long, but his mouth and chin were good. You could usually tell a cat by his mouth and his chin. Tigo would not turkey out of this particular rumble. Of that, Dave was sure.

"Why don't we start?" Dave asked. He wet his lips and looked across at Tigo.

"You understand," Tigo said, "I got no bad blood for you."

"I understand."

"This is what the club said. This is how the club said we should settle it. Without a big street diddlebop, you dig? But I want you to know I don't know you from a hole in the wall—except you wear a blue and gold jacket."

"And you wear a green and orange one," Dave said, "and that's enough for me."

"Sure, but what I was tryin to say . . ."

"We going to sit and talk all night, or we going to get this thing rolling?" Dave asked.

"What I'm tryin to say . . ." Tigo went on, "is that I just happened to be picked for this, you know? Like to settle this thing that's between the two clubs. I mean, you got to admit your boys shouldn't have come in our territory last night."

"I got to admit nothing," Dave said flatly.

"Well, anyway, they shot at the candy store. That wasn't right. There's supposed to be a truce on."

"Okay, okay," Dave said.

"So like . . . like this is the way we agreed to settle it. I mean, one of us and . . . and one of you. Fair and square. Without any street boppin', and without any law trouble."

"Let's get on with it," Dave said.

"I'm tryin to say, I never even seen you on the street before this. So this ain't nothin personal with me. Whichever way it turns out, like . . ."

"I never seen you neither," Dave said.

Tigo stared at him for a long time. "That's 'cause you're new around here. Where you from originally?"

"My people come down from the Bronx."

"You got a big family?"

"A sister and two brothers, that's all."

"Yeah, I only got a sister." Tigo shrugged. "Well." He sighed. "So." He sighed again. "Let's make it, huh?"

"I'm waitin," Dave said.

Tigo picked up the gun, and then he took one of the cartridges from the tabletop. He broke open the gun, slid the cartridge into the cylinder, and then snapped the gun shut and twirled the cylinder.

"Round and round she goes," he said, "and where she stops, nobody knows. There's six chambers in the cylinder and only one cartridge. That makes the odds five-to-one that the cartridge won't be in firing position when the cylinder stops whirling. You dig?"

"I dig."

"I'll go first," Tigo said.

Dave looked at him suspiciously.

"Why?"

"You want to go first?"

"I don't know."

"I'm giving you a break." Tigo grinned. "I may blow my head off first time out."

"Why you giving me a break?" Dave asked.

Tigo shrugged. "What the hell's the difference?" He gave the cylinder a fast twirl.

"The Russians invented this, huh?" Dave asked.

"Yeah."

"I always said they was crazy bastards."

"Yeah, I always . . ."

Tigo stopped talking. The cylinder was stopped now. He took a deep breath, put the barrel of the .38 to his temple, and then squeezed the trigger. The firing pin clicked on an empty chamber.

"Well, that was easy, wasn't it?" he asked. He shoved the gun across the table. "Your turn, Dave."

Dave reached for the gun. It was cold in the basement room, but he was sweating now. He pulled the gun toward him, then left it on the table while he dried his palms on his trousers. He picked up the gun then and stared at it.

"It's a nifty piece," Tigo said. "I like a good piece."

"Yeah, I do, too," Dave said. "You can tell a good piece just by the way it feels in your hand."

Tigo looked surprised. "I mentioned that to one of the guys yesterday, and he thought I was nuts."

"Lots of guys don't know about pieces," Dave said, shrugging.

"I was thinking," Tigo said, "when I get old enough, I'll join the Army, you know? I'd like to work around pieces."

"I thought of that, too. I'd join now, only my old lady won't give me permission. She's got to sign if I join now."

"Yeah, they're all the same," Tigo said, smiling. "Your old lady born here or the old country?"

"The old country," Dave said.

"Yeah, well you know they got these old-fashioned ideas."

"I better spin," Dave said.

"Yeah," Tigo agreed.

Dave slapped the cylinder with his left hand. The cylinder

whirled, whirled, and then stopped. Slowly, Dave put the gun to his head. He wanted to close his eyes, but he didn't dare. Tigo, the enemy, was watching him. He returned Tigo's stare, and then he squeezed the trigger. His heart skipped a beat, and then over the roar of his blood he heard the empty click. Hastily he put the gun down on the table.

"Makes you sweat, don't it?" Tigo said.

Dave nodded, saying nothing. He watched Tigo. Tigo was looking at the gun.

"Me now, huh?" Tigo said. He took a deep breath, then picked up the .38. He twirled the cylinder, waited for it to stop, and then put the gun to his head.

"Bang!" Tigo said, and then he squeezed the trigger. Again the firing pin clicked on an empty chamber. Tigo let out his breath and put the gun down.

"I thought I was dead that time," he said.

"I could hear the harps," Dave said.

"This is a good way to lose weight, you know that?" Tigo laughed nervously, and then his laugh became honest when he saw Dave was laughing with him.

"Ain't it the truth? You could lose ten pounds this way."

"My old lady's like a house," Dave said laughing. "She ought to try this kind of a diet." He laughed at his own humor, pleased when Tigo joined him.

"That's the trouble," Tigo said. "You see a nice deb in the street, you think it's crazy, you know? Then they get to be our people's age, and they turn to fat." He shook his head.

"You got a chick?" Dave asked.

"Yeah, I got one."

"What's her name?"

"Aw, you don't know her."

"Maybe I do," Dave said.

"Her name is Juana." Tigo watched him. "She's about five-two, got these brown eyes . . ."

"I think I know her," Dave said. He nodded. "Yeah, I think I know her."

"She's nice, ain't she?" Tigo asked. He leaned forward, as if Dave's answer was of great importance to him.

"Yeah, she's nice," Dave said.

"The guys rib me about her. You know, all they're after— well, you know—they don't understand something like Juana."

"I got a chick, too," Dave said.

"Yeah? Hey, maybe sometime we could . . ." Tigo cut himself short. He looked down at the gun, and his sudden enthusiasm seemed to ebb completely. "It's your turn," he said.

"Here goes nothing," Dave said. He twirled the cylinder, sucked in his breath, and then fired.

The empty click was loud in the stillness of the room.

"Man!" Dave said.

"We're pretty lucky, you know?" Tigo said.

"So far."

"We better lower the odds. The boys won't like it if we . . ." He stopped himself again, and then reached for one of the cartridges on the table. He broke open the gun again, and slipped the second cartridge into the cylinder. "Now we got two cartridges in here," he said. "Two cartridges, six chambers. That's four-to-two. Divide it, and you get two-to-one." He paused. "You game?"

"That's . . . that's what we're here for, ain't it?"

"Sure."

"Okay then."

"Gone," Tigo said, nodding his head. "You got courage, Dave."

"You're the one needs the courage," Dave said gently. "It's your spin."

Tigo lifted the gun. Idly, he began spinning the cylinder.

"You live on the next block, don't you?" Dave asked.

"Yeah." Tigo kept slapping the cylinder. It spun with a gently whirring sound.

"That's how come we never crossed paths, I guess. Also, I'm new on the scene."

"Yeah, well you know, you get hooked up with one club, that's the way it is."

"You like the guys in your club?" Dave asked, wondering why he was asking such a stupid question, listening to the whirring of the cylinder at the same time.

"They're okay." Tigo shrugged. "None of them really send me, but that's the club on my block, so what're you gonna do, huh?" His hand left the cylinder. It stopped spinning. He put the gun to his head.

"Wait!" Dave said.

Tigo looked puzzled. "What's the matter?"

"Nothin. I just wanted to say . . . I mean . . ." Dave frowned. "I don't dig too many of the guys in my club, either."

Tigo nodded. For a moment, their eyes locked. Then Tigo shrugged, and fired. The empty click filled the basement room.

"Phew," Tigo said.

"Man, you can say that again."

Tigo slid the gun across the table. Dave hesitated an instant. He did not want to pick up the gun. He felt sure that this time the firing pin would strike the percussion cap of one of the cartridges. He was sure that this time he would shoot himself.

"Sometimes I think I'm turkey," he said to Tigo, surprised that his thoughts had found voice.

"I feel that way sometimes, too," Tigo said.

"I never told that to nobody," Dave said. "The guys in my club would laugh at me, I ever told them that."

"Some things you got to keep to yourself. There ain't no-body you can trust in this world."

"There should be somebody you can trust," Dave said. "Hell, you can't tell nothing to your people. They don't understand."

Tigo laughed. "That's an old story. But that's the way things are. What're you gonna do?"

"Yeah. Still, sometimes I think I'm turkey."

"Sure, sure," Tigo said. "But it ain't only that, though. Like sometimes . . . well, don't you wonder what you're doing stomping some guy in the street? Like . . . you know what I mean? Like . . . who's the guy to you? What you got to beat him up for? 'Cause he messed with somebody else's girl?" Tigo shook his head. "It gets complicated sometimes."

"Yeah, but . . ." Dave frowned again. "You got to stick with the club. Don't you?"

"Sure, sure . . . no question."

Again, their eyes locked.

"Well, here goes," Dave said. He lifted the gun. "It's just . . ." He shook his head, and then twirled the cylinder. The cylinder spun, and then stopped. He studied the gun, wondering if one of the cartridges would roar from the barrel when he squeezed the trigger.

Then he fired.

Click.

"I didn't think you was going through with it," Tigo said.

"I didn't neither."

"You got heart, Dave," Tigo said. He looked at the gun. He picked it up and broke it open.

"What you doing?" Dave asked.

"Another cartridge," Tigo said. "Six chambers, three cartridges. That makes it even money. You game?"

"You?"

"The boys said . . ." Tigo stopped talking. "Yeah, I'm game," he added, his voice curiously low.

"It's your turn, you know."

"I know."

Dave watched as Tigo picked up the gun.

"You ever been rowboating on the lake?"

Tigo looked across the table at Dave, his eyes wide. "Once," he said. "I went with Juana."

"Is it . . . is it any kicks?"

"Yeah. Yeah, it's grand kicks. You mean you never been?"

"No," Dave said.

"Hey, you got to try it, man," Tigo said excitedly. "You'll like it. Hey, you try it."

"Yeah, I was thinking maybe this Sunday I'd . . ." He did not complete the sentence.

"My spin," Tigo said wearily. He twirled the cylinder. "Here goes a good man," he said, and he put the revolver to his head and squeezed the trigger.

Click.

Dave smiled nervously. "No rest for the weary," he said. "But, Jesus, you got heart, I don't know if I can go through with it."

"Sure, you can," Tigo assured him. "Listen, what's there to be afraid of?" He slid the gun across the table.

"We keep this up all night?" Dave asked.

"They said . . . you know . . ."

"Well, it ain't so bad. I mean, hell, we didn't have this operation, we wouldn'ta got a chance to talk, huh?" He grinned feebly.

"Yeah," Tigo said, his face splitting in a wide grin. "It ain't been so bad, huh?"

"No . . . it's been . . . well . . . you know, these guys in the club, who can talk to them?"

He picked up the gun.

"We could . . ." Tigo started.

"What?"

"We could say . . . well . . . like we kept shootin' an' nothin happened, so . . ." Tigo shrugged. "What the hell! We can't do this all night, can we?"

"I don't know."

"Let's make this the last spin. Listen, they don't like it, they can take a flying leap, you know?"

"I don't think they'll like it. We supposed to settle this for the clubs."

"Screw the clubs!" Tigo said vehemently. "Can't we pick our own . . ." The word was hard coming. When it came, he said it softly, and his eyes did not leave Dave's face. ". . . friends?"

"Sure we can," Dave said fervently. "Sure we can! Why not?"

"The last spin," Tigo said. "Come on, the last spin."

"Gone," Dave said. "Hey you know, I'm glad they got this idea. You know that? I'm actually glad!" He twirled the cylinder. "Look, you want to go on the lake this Sunday? I mean with your girl and mine? We could get two boats. Or even one if you want."

"Yeah, one boat," Tigo said. "Hey, your girl'll like Juana, I mean it. She's a swell chick."

The cylinder stopped. Dave put the gun to his head quickly.

"Here's to Sunday," he said. He grinned at Tigo, and Tigo grinned back, and then Dave fired.

The explosion rocked the small basement room, ripping away half of Dave's head, shattering his face. A small cry escaped Tigo's throat, and a look of incredulous shock knifed his eyes. Then he put his head on the table and began weeping.

NEW YORK BLUES

BY CORNELL WOOLRICH

East 37th Street

(Originally published in 1970)

I t's six o'clock; my drink is at the three-quarter mark—
three-quarters down, not three-quarters up—and the
night begins.

Across the way from me sits a little transistor radio, up
on end, simmering away like a teakettle on a stove. It's been
going steadily ever since I first came in here, two days, three
nights ago; it chisels away the stony silence, takes the edge off
the being alone. It came with the room, not with me.

Now there's a punctuation of three lush chords, and it
goes into a traffic report. "Good evening. The New York Mu-
nicipal Communications Service presents the 6:00 p.m. Traffic Advisory. Traffic through the Holland and Lincoln tunnels
and over the George Washington Bridge, heavy westbound,
light eastbound. Traffic on the crosscut between the George
Washington and Queens-Whitestone bridges, heavy in both
directions. Traffic through the Battery Tunnel, heavy out-
bound, very light inbound. Traffic on the West Side High-
way, bumper to bumper all the way. Radar units in operation
there. Traffic over the Long Island Expressway is beginning
to build, due to tonight's game at Shea Stadium. West 70th
Street between Amsterdam and West End avenues is closed
due to a water-main break. A power failure on the East Side
I.R.T. line between Grand Central and 125th Street is causing

delays of up to forty-five minutes. Otherwise all subways and buses, the Staten Island Ferry, the Jersey Central, the Delaware and Lackawanna, and the Pennsylvania railroads, and all other commuter services, are operating normally. At the three airports, planes are arriving and departing on time. The next regularly scheduled traffic advisory will be given one-half hour from now—"

The big weekend rush is on. The big city emptying itself out at once. Just a skeleton crew left to keep it going until Monday morning. Everybody getting out—everybody but me, everybody but those who are coming here for me tonight. We're going to have the whole damned town to ourselves.

I go over to the window and open up a crevice between two of the tightly flattened slats in one of the blinds, and a little parallelogram of a New York street scene, Murray Hill section, six-o'clock-evening hour, springs into view. Up in the sky the upper-echelon light tiers of the Pan Am Building are undulating and rippling in the humidity and carbon monoxide ("Air pollution index: normal, twelve percent; emergency level, fifty percent").

Down below, on the sidewalk, the glowing green blob of a street light, swollen to pumpkin size by foreshortened perspective, thrusts upward toward my window. And along the little slot that the parted slats make, lights keep passing along, like strung-up, shining, red and white beads. All going just one way, right to left, because 37th Street is westbound, and all going by twos, always by twos, headlights and tails, heads and tails, in a welter of slowed-down traffic and a paroxysm of vituperative horns. And directly under me I hear a taxi driver and would-be fares having an argument, the voices clearly audible, the participants unseen.

"But it's only to Fifty-ninth Street—"

"I don't ca-a-are, lady. Look, I already tolje. I'm not goin' up that way. Can'tje get it into your head?"

"Don't let's argue with him. Get inside. He can't put you out."

"No, but I can refuse to move. Lady, if your husband gets in here, he's gonna sit still in one place, 'cause I ain't budgin'."

New York. The world's most dramatic city. Like a permanent short circuit, sputtering and sparking up into the night sky all night long. No place like it for living. And probably no place like it for dying.

I take away the little tire jack my fingers have made, and the slats snap together again.

The first sign that the meal I phoned down for is approaching is the minor-key creak from a sharply swerved castor as the room-service waiter rounds a turn outside my door. I'm posted behind a high-backed wing chair, with my wrists crossed over the top of it and my hands dangling like loose claws, staring a little tensely at the door. Then there's the waiter's characteristically deferential knock. But I say "Who is it?" anyway, before I go over to open it.

He's an elderly man. He's been up here twice before, and by now I know the way he sounds.

"Room service," comes through in that high-pitched voice his old age has given him.

I release the double lock, then I turn the knob and open the door.

He wheels the little white-clothed dinner cart forward into the room, and as the hall perspective clears behind him I get a blurred glimpse of a figure in motion, just passing from view, then gone, too quickly to be brought into focus.

I stand there a moment, holding the door to a narrow slit, watching the hall. But it's empty now.

There's an innocuous explanation for everything. Everything is a coin that has two sides to it, and one side is innocuous but the other can be ominous. The hall makes a right-angle turn opposite my door, and to get to the elevators, those whose rooms are back of this turn have to pass the little setback that leads to my door.

On the other hand, if someone wanted to pinpoint me, to verify which room I was in, by sighting my face as I opened the door for the waiter, he would do just that: stand there an instant, then quickly step aside out of my line of vision. The optical snapshot I'd had was not of a figure in continuous motion going past my point of view, but of a figure that had first been static and then had flitted from sight.

And if it's that, now they know which room I'm in. Which room on which floor in which hotel.

"Did you notice anyone out there in the hall just now when you came along?" I ask. I try to sound casual, which only makes me not sound casual.

He answers with a question of his own. "*Was* there somebody out in the hall, sir?"

"That's what I asked you, did you see anyone?"

He explains that years of experience in trundling these food-laden carts across the halls have taught him never to look up, never to take his eyes off them, because an unexpected bump on the floor under the carpet might splash ice water out of the glass and wet the tablecloth or spill consommé into its saucer.

It sounds plausible enough. And whether it is or not, I know it's all I'm going to get.

I sign the check for the meal, add the tip, and tell him to put it on the bill. Then just as he turns to leave I remember something I want to do.

"Just a second; that reminds me." I shoot one of my cuffs forward and twist something out of it. Then the other one. And I hold out my hand to him with the two star-sapphire cuff links he admired so much last night. (Innocently, I'm sure, with no venal intent.)

He says I'm not serious, I must be joking. He says he can't take anything like that. He says all the things he's expected to say, and I override them. Then, when he can't come up with anything else, he comes up with, half-hopefully (hopeful for a yes answer): "You tired of them?"

"No," I say quite simply, "no—they're tired of me."

He thanks me over and thanks me under and thanks me over again, and then he's gone, and I'm glad he's gone.

Poor old man, wasting his life bringing people their meals up to their rooms for thirty-five, forty-odd years. He'll die in peace, though. Not in terror and in throes of resistance. I almost envy him.

I turn my head a little. The radio's caroling "Tonight," velvety smooth and young and filled with plaintive desire. Maria's song from *West Side Story*. I remember one beautiful night long ago at the Winter Garden, with a beautiful someone beside me. I tilt my nose and breathe in, and I can still smell her perfume, the ghost of her perfume from long ago. But where is she now, where did she go, and what did I *do* with her?

Our paths ran along so close together they were almost like one, the one they were eventually going to be. Then fear came along, fear entered into it somehow, and split them wide apart.

Fear bred anxiety to justify. Anxiety to justify bred anger. The phone calls that wouldn't be answered, the door rings that wouldn't be opened. Anger bred sudden calamity.

Now there aren't two paths anymore; there's only one,

only mine. Running downhill into the ground, running down-hill into its doom.

Tonight, tonight—there will be no morning star—Right, kid, there won't. Not for me, anyway.

There's a tap at the door, made with the tip of a key, not the tip of a finger. The voice doesn't wait, but comes right through before the signal has a chance to freeze me stiff. A woman's voice, soft-spoken, reassuring. "Night maid."

I wait a second to let a little of the white drain from my face before she sees me, and then I go over and let her in.

Her name is Ginny. She told me last night. I asked her, that's why she told me. I wanted to hear the sound of some-body's name, that's why I asked her. I was frightened and lonely, that's why I wanted to hear the sound of somebody's name.

On her face the beauty of two races blends, each con-tributing its individual hallmark. The golden-warm skin, the deep glowing eyes, the narrow-tipped nose, the economical underlip.

While she's turning back the bedcovers in a neat triangle over one corner, I remark, "I notice you go around the outside of the room to get to the bed, instead of cutting across the middle, which would be much shorter. Why do you?"

She answers plausibly, "People are often watching their television sets at this time, when I come in, and I don't want to block them off."

I point out, "But mine isn't on, Ginny."

I see how the pupils of her eyes try to flee, to get as far away from looking at me as possible, all the way over into their outside corners. And that gives it away. She's afraid of me. The rumors have already reached her. A hotel is like a beehive when it comes to gossip. *He never leaves his room, has all his meals sent up to him, and keeps his door locked all the time.*

"I want to give you something," I say to her. "For that little girl of yours you were telling me about."

I take a hundred-dollar bill out of the wallet on my hip. I fold the bill a few times so that the corner numerals disappear, then thrust it between two of her fingers.

She sees the "1" first as the bill slowly uncoils. Her face is politely appreciative.

She sees the first zero next—that makes it a ten. Her face is delighted, more than grateful.

She sees the last zero. Suddenly her face is fearful, stunned into stone; in her eyes I can see steel filings of mistrust glittering. Her wrist flexes to shove the bill back to me, but I ward it off with my hand upended.

I catch the swift side glance she darts at the fifth of rye on the side table.

"No, it didn't come out of that. It's just an impulse—came out of my heart, I suppose you could say. Either take it or don't take it, but don't spoil it."

"But why? What for?"

"Does there have to be a reason for everything? Sometimes there isn't."

"I'll buy her a new coat," she says huskily. "A new pink coat like little girls all seem to want. With a little baby muff of lamb's wool to go with it. And I'll say a prayer for you when I take her to church with me next Sunday."

It won't work, but—"Make it a good one."

The last part is all she hears.

Something occurs to me. "You won't have to do any explaining to her father, will you?"

"She has no father," she says quite simply. "She's never had. There's only me and her, sir."

Somehow I can tell by the quick chip-chop of her feet away from my door that it's not lost time she's trying to make up; it's the tears starting in her eyes that she wants to hide.

I slosh a little rye into a glass—a fresh glass, not the one before; they get rancid from your downbreaths that cling like a stale mist around the inner rim. But it's no help; I know that by now, and I've been dousing myself in it for three days. It just doesn't take hold. I think fear neutralizes alcohol, weakens its anesthetic power. It's good for small fears; your boss, your wife, your bills, your dentist; all right then to take a drink. But for big ones it doesn't do any good. Like water on blazing gasoline, it will only quicken and compound it. It takes sand, in the literal and the slang sense, to smother the bonfire that is fear. And if you're out of sand, then you must burn up.

I have it out now, paying it off between my fingers like a rosary of murder. Those same fingers that did it to her. For three days now I've taken it out at intervals, looked at it, then hidden it away again. Each time wondering if it really happened, hoping that it didn't, dreading that it did.

It's a woman's scarf; that much I know about it. And that's about all. But whose? Hers? And how did I come by it? How did it get into the side pocket of my jacket, dangling on the outside, when I came in here early Wednesday morning in some sort of traumatic daze, looking for room walls to hide inside of as if they were a folding screen. (I didn't even know I had it there; the bellboy who was checking me in spotted it on the way up in the elevator, grinned, and said something about a "heavy date.")

It's flimsy stuff, but it has a great tensile strength when pulled against its grain. The strength of the garotte. It's tinted in pastel colors that blend, graduate, into one another, all except one. It goes from a flamingo pink to a peach tone and then to a still paler flesh tint—and then suddenly an angry, jagged splash of blood color comes in, not even like the others. Not smooth, not artificed by some loom or by some dye vat. Like a star, like the scattered petals of a flower. Speaking of—I don't know how to say it—speaking of violence, of struggle, of life spilled out.

The blood isn't red anymore. It's rusty brown now. But it's still blood, all the same. Ten years from now, twenty, it'll still be blood; faded out, vanished, the pollen of, the dust of, blood. What was once warm and moving. And made blushes and rushed with anger and paled with fear. Like that night—

I can still see her eyes. They still come before me, wide and white and glistening with fright, out of the amnesiac darkness of our sudden, unpremeditated meeting.

They were like two pools of fear. She saw something that I couldn't see. And fear kindled in them. I feared and I mistrusted but I couldn't bear to see my fear reflected in her eyes. From her I wanted reassurance, consolation; only wanted to draw her close to me and hold her to me, to lean my head against her and rest and draw new belief in myself. Instead she met my fear with her fear. Eyes that should have been tender were glowing with unscreaming fear.

It wasn't an attack. We'd been together too many times before, made love together too many times before, for it to be that. It was just that fear had suddenly entered, and made us dangerous strangers.

She turned and tried to run. I caught the scarf from behind. Only in supplication, in pleading; trying to hold on to the only one who could save me. And the closer I tried to draw her to me, the less she was alive. Until finally I got her all the way back to me, where I wanted her to be, and she was dead.

I hadn't wanted that. It was only love, turned inside out. It was only loneliness, outgoing.

And now I'm alone, without any love.

And the radio, almost as if it were taking my pulse count, electrographing my heartbeats, echoes them back to me: *For, like caressing an empty glove, Is night without some love, The night was made for—*

The hotel room ashtrays are thick glass cubes, built to withstand cracking under heat of almost any degree. I touch my lighter to it, to the scarf compressed inside the cube. The flame points upward like a sawtoothed orange knife. There goes love. After a while it stops burning. It looks like a black cabbage, each leaf tipped by thin red lines that waver and creep back and forth like tiny red worms. Then one by one they go out.

I dump it into the bathroom bowl and flip the lever down. What a hell of a place for your love to wind up. Like something disemboweled.

I go back and pour out a little more. It's the seat belt against the imminent smash-up, the antidote for terror, the prescription against panic. Only it doesn't work. I sit there dejectedly, wrists looping down between my legs. I'm confused; I can't think it out. Something inside my mind keeps fogging over, like mist on a windshield. I use the back of my hand for a windshield wiper and draw it slowly across my forehead a couple times, and it clears up again for a little while.

"Remember," the little radio prattles. "Simple headache, take aspirin. Nervous tension, take—"

All I can say to myself is: there *is* no fix for the fix you're in now.

Suddenly the phone peals, sharp and shattering as the smashing of glass sealing up a vacuum. I never knew a sound could be so frightening, never knew a sound could be so dire. It's like a short circuit in my nervous system. Like springing a cork in my heart with a lopsided opener. Like a shot of sodium pentathol up my arm knocking out my will power.

All I keep thinking is: this is it. Here it is. It's not a hotel-service call, it can't be, not at this hour anymore. The waiter's been and gone, the night maid's been and gone. It can't be an outside call, because nobody on the outside knows I'm here in the hotel. Not even where I work, where I used to work, they don't know. This is it; it's got to be.

How will they put it? A polite summons. "Would you mind coming down for a minute, sir?" And then if I do, a sudden preventive twisting of my arm behind my back as I step out of the elevator, an unnoticeable flurry tactfully covered up behind the backs of the bellboys—then quickly out and away.

Why don't they come right up here to my door and get me? Is it because this is a high-class hotel on a high-class street? Maybe they don't want any commotion in the hall, for the sake of the other guests. Maybe this is the way they always do it.

Meanwhile it keeps ringing and ringing and ringing.

The damp zigzag path my spilled drink made, from where I was to where I am now, is slowly soaking into the carpet and darkening it. The empty glass, dropped on the carpet, has finished rocking on its side by now and lies still. And I've fallen motionless into the grotesque posture of a badly frightened kid. Almost prone along the floor, legs sprawled out in back of me in scissors formation, just the backs of my two hands grasping the edge of the low stand the phone sits on, and the rim of it cutting across the bridge of my nose so that just two big staring, straining eyes show up over the top.

And it rings on and on and on.

Then all at once an alternative occurs to me. Maybe it's a wrong-number call, meant for somebody else. Somebody in another room, or somebody in this room who was in it before I came. Hotel switchboards are overworked places: slip-ups like that can happen now and then.

I bet I haven't said a prayer since I finished my grammar-school final-exam paper in trigonometry (and flunked it; maybe that's why I haven't said a prayer since), and that was more a crossed-fingers thing held behind my back than a genuine prayer. I say one now. What a funny thing to pray for. I bet nobody ever prayed for a wrong number before, not since telephones first began. Or since prayers first began, either.

Please, make it a mistake and not for me. Make it a mistake.

Suddenly there's open space between the cradle and the receiver, and I've done it. I've picked it up. It's just as easy as pulling out one of your own teeth by the roots.

The prayer gets scratched. The call is for me, it's not a wrong number. For me, all right, every inch of the way. I can tell from the opening words. Only—it's not the one I feared; it's friendly, a friendly call no different from what other people get.

A voice from another world, almost. Yet I know it so well. Always like this, never a cloud on it; always jovial, always noisy. When a thing should be said softly, it says it loudly; when a thing should be said loudly, it says it louder still. He never identifies himself, never has to. Once you've heard his voice, you'll always know him.

That's Johnny for you—the pal of a hundred parties. The bar-kick of scores of binges. The captain of the second-string team in how many foursome one-night stands? Every man has had a Johnny in his life sometime or other.

He says he's been calling my apartment since Wednesday and no answer: what happened to me?

I play it by ear. "Water started to pour down through the ceiling, so I had to clear out till they get it repaired. . . . No, I'm not on a tear. . . . No, there's nobody with me, I'm by myself. . . . Do I? Sound sort of peculiar? No, I'm all right there's nothing the matter, not a thing."

I pass my free hand across the moist glisten on my forehead. It's tough enough to be in a jam, but it's tougher still to be in one and not be able to say you are.

"How did you know I was here? How did you track me to this place? . . . You went down the yellow pages, hotel by hotel, alphabetically. Since three o'clock yesterday afternoon? . . . Something to tell me?"

His new job had come through. He starts on Monday. With a direct line, and two, count 'em, two secretaries, not just one. And the old bunch is giving him a farewell party. A farewell party to end all farewell parties. Sardi's, on 44th. Then they'll move on later to some other place. But they'll wait here at Sardi's for me to catch up. Barb keeps asking, Why isn't your best-man-to-be here with us?

The noise of the party filters through into my ear. Ice clicking like dice in a fast-rolling game. Mixing sticks sounding like tiny tin flutes as they beat against glass. The laughter of girls, the laughter of men. Life is for the living, not the already dead.

"Sure, I'll be there. Sure."

If I say I won't be—and I won't, because I can't—he'll never quit pestering and calling me the rest of the night. So I say that I will, to get off the hook. But how can I go there, drag my trouble before his party, before his friends, before his girl? And if I go, it'll just happen there instead of here. Who wants a grandstand for his downfall? Who wants bleachers for his disgrace?

Johnny's gone now, and the night goes on.

Now the evening's at its noon, its meridian. The outgoing tide has simmered down, and there's a lull—like the calm in the eye of a hurricane—before the reverse tide starts to set in.

The last acts of the three-act plays are now on, and the after-theater eating places are beginning to fill up with early comers; Danny's and Lindy's—yes, and Horn & Hardart too. Everybody has got where they wanted to go—and that was out somewhere. Now everybody will want to get back where they came from—and that's home somewhere. Or as the coffee-grinder radio, always on the beam, put it at about this point: *New York, New York, it's a helluva town, The Bronx is up, the Battery's down, And the people ride around in a hole in the ground*—

Now the incoming tide rolls in; the hours abruptly switch back to single digits again, and it's a little like the time you put your watch back on entering a different time zone. Now the buses knock off and the subway expresses turn into locals and the locals space themselves far apart; and as Johnny Carson's face hits millions of screens all at one and the same time, the incoming tide reaches its crest and pounds against the shore. There's a sudden splurge, a slew of taxis arriving at the hotel entrance one by one as regularly as though they were on a conveyor belt, emptying out and then going away again.

Then this too dies down, and a deep still sets in. It's an around-the-clock town, but this is the stretch; from now until the garbage-grinding trucks come along and tear the dawn to shreds, it gets as quiet as it's ever going to get.

This is the deep of the night, the dregs, the sediment at

the bottom of the coffee cup. The blue hours; when guys' nerves get tauter and women's fears get greater. Now guys and girls make love, or kill each other or sometimes both. And as the windows on the *Late Show* title silhouette light up one by one, the real ones all around go dark. And from now on the silence is broken only by the occasional forlorn hoot of a bogged-down drunk or the gutted-cat squeal of a too sharply swerved axle coming around a turn. Or as Billy Daniels sang it in *Golden Boy*: *While the city sleeps, And the streets are clear, There's a life that's happening here—*

In the pin-drop silence a taxi comes up with an unaccompanied girl in it. I can tell it's a taxi, I can tell it's a girl, and I can tell she's unaccompanied; I can tell all three just by her introductory remark.

"Benny," she says, "will you come over and pay this for me?"

Benny is the hotel night-service man. I know his name; he brought drinks up to the room last night.

As the taxi drives away paid, Benny reminds her with aloof dignity, "You didn't give me my cut last week." Nothing personal, strictly business, you understand.

"I had a virus week before last," she explains. "And it took me all last week to pay off on my doctor bills. I'll square it with you tonight." Then she adds apprehensively, "I'm afraid he'll hurt me." Not her doctor, obviously.

"Na, he won't hurt you," Benny reassures.

"How would you know?" she asks, not unreasonably.

Benny culls from his store of call-girl-sponsorship experience. "These big guys never hurt you. They're meek as mice. It's the little shrimps got the sting."

She goes ahead in. A chore is a chore, she figures.

This of course is what is known in hotel-operational jar-

gon as a "personal call." In the earthier slang of the night bell-
men and deskmen it is simply a "fix" or a "fix-up." The taxi
fare, of course, will go down on the guest's bill, as "Misc." or
"Sundries." Which actually is what it is. From my second-floor
window I can figure it all out almost without any sound track
to go with it.

So much for the recreational side of night life in the upper-
bracket-income hotels of Manhattan. And in its root-origins
the very word itself is implicit with implication: re-create. Ana-
lyze it and you'll see it also means to reproduce. But clever,
ingenious Man has managed to sidetrack it into making life
more livable.

The wafer of ice riding the surface of my drink has melted
freakishly in its middle and not around its edges and now
looks like an onion ring. Off in the distance an ambulance
starts bansheeing with that new broken-blast siren they use,
scalp-crimping as the cries of pain of a partly dismembered
hog. Somebody dead in the night? Somebody sick and going
to be dead soon? Or maybe somebody going to be alive soon—
did she wait too long to start for the hospital?

All of a sudden, with the last sound there's been all night,
I can tell they're here. Don't ask me how, I only know they're
here. It's beginning at last. No way out, no way aside and no
way back.

Being silent is their business, and they know their
business well. They make less sound than the dinner cart
crunching along the carpeted hall, than Ginny's stifled sob
when I gave her that hundred-dollar bill, than the contes-
tants bickering over the taxi. Or that girl who was down
there just a little while ago on her errand of fighting loneliness for a fee.

How can I tell that they're here? By the absence of sound

more than by its presence. Or I should say by the absence of a complementary sound—the sound that belongs with another sound and yet fails to accompany it.

Like:

There's no sound of arrival, but suddenly two cars are in place down there along the hotel front. They must have come up on the glide, as noiselessly as a sailboat skimming over still water. No sound of tires, no sound of brakes. But there's one sound they couldn't quite obliterate—the cushioned thump of two doors closing after them in quick succession, staccato succession, as they spilled out and siphoned into the building. You can always tell a car door, no other door sounds quite like it.

There's only one other sound, a lesser one, a sort of follow-up: the scratch of a single sole against the abrasive sidewalk as they go hustling in. He either put it down off-balance or swiveled it too acutely in treading at the heels of those in front of him. Which is a good average, just one to sound off, considering that six or eight pairs of them must have been all going in at the same time and moving fast.

I've sprung to my feet from the very first, and I'm standing there now like an upright slab of ice carved in the outline of a man—burning-cold and slippery-wet and glassy with congealment. I've put out all the lights—they all work on one switch over by the door as you come in. They've probably already seen the lights though if they've marked the window from outside, and anyway, what difference does it make? Lighted up or dark, I'm still here inside the room. It's just some instinct as old as fear: you seek the dark when you hide, you seek the light when the need to hide is gone. All the animals have it too.

Now they're in, and it will take just a few minutes more

while they make their arrangements. That's all I have left, a few minutes more. Out of a time allotment that once stretched so far and limitlessly ahead of me. Who short-changed me, I feel like crying out in protest, but I know that nobody did; I short-changed myself.

"It," the heartless little radio jeers, "takes the worry out of being close."

Why is it taking them such a long time? What do they have to do, improvise as they go along? What for? They already knew what they had to do when they set out to come here.

I'm sitting down again now, momentarily; knees too rocky for standing long. Those are the only two positions I have left; no more walking, no more running, no more anything else now. Only stand up and wait or sit down and wait. I need a cigarette terribly bad. It may be a funny time to need one, but I do. I dip my head down between my outspread legs and bring the lighter up from below, so its shine won't glow through the blind-crevices. As I said, it doesn't make sense, because they know I'm here. But I don't want to do anything to quicken them. Even two minutes of grace is better than one. Even one minute is better than none.

Then suddenly my head comes up again, alerted. I drop the cigarette, still unlit. First I think the little radio has suddenly jumped in tone, started to come on louder and more resonant, as if it were spooked. Until it almost sounds like a car radio out in the open. Then I turn my head toward the window. It is a car radio. It's coming from outside into the room.

And even before I get up and go over to take a look, I think there's something familiar about it, I've heard it before, just like this, just the way it is now. This sounding-board effect, this walloping of the night like a drum, this ricochet of blast and din from side to side of the street, bouncing off the house fronts like a musical handball game.

Then it cuts off short, the after-silence swells up like a balloon ready to pop, and as I squint out, it's standing still down there, the little white car, and Johnny is already out of it and standing alongside.

He's come to take me to the party.

He's parked on the opposite side. He starts to cross over to the hotel. Someone posted in some doorway whistles to attract his attention. I hear it up at the window. Johnny stops, turns to look around, doesn't see anyone.

He's frozen in the position in which the whistle caught him. Head and shoulders turned inquiringly half around, hips and legs still pointed forward. Then a man, some anonymous man, glides up beside him from the street.

I told you he talks loud; on the phone, in a bar, on a street late at night. Every word he says I hear; not a word the other man says.

First, "Who is? What kind of trouble?"

Then, "You must mean somebody else."

Next, "Room 207. Yeah, that's right, 207."

That's my room number.

"How'd you know I was coming here?"

Finally, "You bugged the call I made to him before!"

Then the anonymous man goes back into the shadows, leaving Johnny in mid-street, taking it for granted he'll follow him as he was briefed to do, commanded to do.

But Johnny stands out there, alone and undecided, feet still one way, head and shoulders still the other. And I watch him from the window crevice. And the stakeout watches him from his invisible doorway.

Now a crisis arises. Not in my life, because that's nearly over; but in my illusions.

Will he go to his friend and try to stand by him, or will he let his friend go by?

He can't make it, sure I know that, he can never get in here past them; but he *can* make the try, there's just enough slack for him to do that. There's still half the width of the street ahead of him clear and untrammeled, for him to try to bolt across, before they spring after him and rough him up and fling him back. It's the token of the thing that would count, not the completion.

But it doesn't happen that way, I keep telling myself knowingly and sadly. Only in our fraternity pledges and masonic inductions, our cowboy movies and magazine stories, not in our real-life lives. For, the seventeenth-century humanist to the contrary, each man *is* an island complete unto himself, and as he sinks, the moving feet go on around him, from nowhere to nowhere and with no time to lose. The world is long past the Boy Scout stage of its development; now each man dies as he was meant to die, and as he was born, and as he lived: alone, all alone. Without any God, without any hope, without any record to show for his life.

My throat feels stiff, and I want to swallow but I can't. Watching and waiting to see what my friend will do.

He doesn't move, doesn't make up his mind, for half a minute, and that half a minute seems like an hour. He's doped by what he's been told, I guess. And I keep asking myself while the seconds are ticking off: What would *I* do? If there were me down there, and he were up here: What would *I* do? And I keep trying not to look the answer in the face, though it's staring at me the whole time.

You haven't any right to expect your friends to be larger

than yourself, larger than life. Just take them as they are, cut down to average size, and be glad you have them. To drink with, laugh with, borrow money from, lend money to, stay away from their special girls as you want them to stay away from yours, and above all, never break your word to, once it's been given.

And that is all the obligation you have, all you have the right to expect.

The half-minute is up, and Johnny turns, slowly and reluctantly, but he turns, and he goes back to the opposite side of the street. The side opposite to me.

And I knew all along that's what he would do, because I knew all along that's what I would have done too.

I think I hear a voice say slurredly somewhere in the shadows, "That's the smart thing to do," but I'm not sure. Maybe I don't, maybe it's me I hear.

He gets back in the car, shoulders sagging, and keys it on. And as he glides from sight the music seems to start up almost by itself; it's such second nature for him to have it on by now. It fades around the corner building, and then a wisp of it comes back just once more, carried by some cross-current of the wind: *Fools rush in, Where wise men never dare to go*—and then it dies away for good.

I bang my crushed-up fist against the center of my forehead, bring it away, then bang it again. Slow but hard. It hurts to lose a long-term friend, almost like losing an arm. But I never lost an arm, so I really wouldn't know.

Now I can swallow, but it doesn't feel good anymore.

I hear a marginal noise outside in the hall, and I swing around in instant alert. It's easy enough to decipher it. A woman is being taken from her room nearby—in case the going gets too rough around here in my immediate vicinity, I suppose.

I hear them tap, and then she comes out and accompanies them to safety. I hear the slap-slap of her bedroom slippers, like the soft little hands of children applauding in a kindergarten, as she goes hurrying by with someone. Several someones. You can't hear them, only her, but I know they're with her. I even hear the soft *sch sch* of her silk wrapper or kimono as it rustles past. A noticeable whiff of sachet drifts in through the door seam. She must have taken a bath and powdered herself liberally just moments ago.

Probably a nice sort of woman, unused to violence or emergencies of this sort, unsure of what to bring along or how to comport herself.

"I left my handbag in there," I hear her remark plaintively as she goes by. "Do you think it'll be all right to leave it there?"

Somebody's wife, come to meet him in the city and waiting for him to join her. Long ago I used to like that kind of woman. Objectively, of course, not close-up.

After she's gone, another brief lull sets in. This one is probably the last. But what good is a lull? It's only a breathing spell in which to get more frightened. Because anticipatory fear is always twice as strong as present fear. Anticipatory fear has both fears in it at once—the anticipatory one and the one that comes simultaneously with the dread happening itself. Present fear only has the one, because by that time anticipation is over.

I switch on the light for a moment, to see my way to a drink. The one I had is gone—just what used to be ice is sloshing colorlessly in the bottom of the glass. Then when I put the recharged glass down again, empty, it seems to pull me after it, as if it weighed so much I couldn't let go of it from an upright position. Don't ask me why this is, I don't know. Probably simple loss of equilibrium for a second, due to the massive infusion of alcohol.

Then with no more warning, no more waiting, with no more of anything, it begins. It gets under way at last.

There is a mild-mannered knuckle rapping at the door. They use my name. A voice, mild-mannered also, says in a conciliatory way, "Come out, please. We want to talk to you." "Punctilious," I guess, would be a better word for it. The etiquette of the forcible entry, of the break-in. They're so considerate, so deferential, so attentive to all the niceties. Hold your head steady, please, we don't want to nick your chin while we're cutting your throat.

I don't answer.

I don't think they expected me to. If I had answered, it would have astonished them, thrown them off their timing for a moment.

The mild-voiced man leaves the door and somebody else takes his place. I can sense the shifting over more by intuition than by actual hearing.

A wooden toolbox or carryall of some sort settles down noisily on the floor outside the door. I can tell it's wooden, not by its floor impact but by the "settling" sound that accompanies it, as if a considerable number of loose and rolling objects in it are chinking against its insides. Nails and bolts and awls and screwdrivers and the like. That tells me that it's a kit commonly used by carpenters and locksmiths and their kind.

They're going to take the lock off bodily from the outside.

A cold surge goes through me that I can't describe. It isn't blood. It's too numbing and heavy and cold for that. And it breaks through the skin surface, which blood doesn't ordinarily do without a wound, and emerges into innumerable sting pin pricks all over me. An ice-sweat.

I can see him (not literally, but just as surely as if I could), down on one knee, and scared, probably as scared as I am myself, pressing as far back to the side out of the direct line of the door as he can, while the others, bunched together farther back, stand ready to cover him, to pile on me and bring me down if I should suddenly break out and rush him.

And the radio tells me sarcastically to "Light up, you've got a good thing going."

I start backing away, with a sleepwalker's fixity, staring at the door as I retreat, or staring at where I last saw it, for I can't see it in the dark. What good would it do to stay close to it, for I can't hold it back, I can't stop it from opening. And as I go back step after step, my tongue keeps tracking the outside outline of my lips, as if I wondered what they were and what they were there for.

A very small sound begins. I don't know how to put it. Like someone twisting a small metal cap to open a small medicine bottle, but continuously, without ever getting it off. He's started already. He's started coming in.

It's terrible to hear that little thing move. As if it were animate, had a life of its own. Terrible to hear it move and to know that a hostile agency, a hostile presence, just a few feet away from me, is what is making it move. Such a little thing, there is almost nothing smaller, only the size of a pinhead perhaps, and yet to create such terror and to be capable of bringing about such a shattering end-result: entry, capture, final loss of reason, and the darkness that is worse than death. All from a little thing like that, turning slowly, secretively, but avidly, in the lockplate on the door, on the door into my room.

I have to get out of here. Out. I have to push these walls apart, these foursquare tightly seamed walls, and make space wide enough to run in, and keep running through it, running and running through it, running and running through it, and never stopping. Until I drop. And then still running on and on, inside my head. Like a watch with its case smashed open and lying on the ground, but with the works still going inside it. Or like a cockroach when you knock it over on its back so that it can't ambulate anymore, but its legs still go spiraling around in the air.

The window. They're at the door, but the window—that way out is still open. I remember when I checked in here the small hours of Wednesday, I didn't ask to be given a room on the second floor, they just happened to give me one. Then when I saw it later that day in the light, I realized the drop to the ground from one of the little semicircular stone ledges outside the windows wouldn't be dangerous, especially if you held a pillow in front of you, and remembered to keep your chin tilted upward as you went over. Just a sprawling shake-up fall maybe, that's all.

I pull at the blind cords with both hands, and it spasms upward with a sound like a lot of little twigs being stepped on and broken. I push up the window sash and assume a sitting position on the sill, then swing my legs across and I'm out in the clear, out in the open night.

The little stone apron has this spiked iron rail guard around it, with no space left on the outer side of it to plant your feet before you go over. You have to straddle it, which makes for tricky going. Still, necessity can make you dexterous, terror can make you agile. I won't go back inside for the pillow, there isn't time. I'll take the leap neat.

The two cars that brought them here are below, and for a moment, only for a moment, they look empty, dark and still and empty, standing bumper to bumper against the curb. Someone gives a warning whistle—a lip whistle, I mean, not a metal one. I don't know who, I don't know where, somewhere around. Then an angry, ugly, smoldering, car-bound orange moon starts up, lightens to yellow, then brightens to the dazzling white of a laundry-detergent commercial. The operator guiding it slants it too high at first, and it lands over my head. Like a halo. *Some* halo and *some time* for a halo. Then he brings it down and it hits me as if someone had belted me full across the face with a talcum-powder puff. You can't see through it, you can't see around it.

Shoe leather comes padding from around the corner—maybe the guy that warded off Johnny—and stops directly under me. I sense somehow he's afraid, just as I am. That won't keep him from doing what he has to do, because he's got the backing on his side. But he doesn't like this. I shield my eyes from the light on one side, and I can see his anxious face peering up at me. All guys are scared of each other, didn't you know that? I'm not the only one. We're all born afraid.

I can't shake the light off. It's like ghostly flypaper. It's like slapstick-thrown yoghurt. It clings to me whichever way I turn.

I hear his voice talking to me from below. Very near and clear. As if we were off together by ourselves somewhere, just chatting, the two of us.

"Go back into your room. We don't want you to get hurt." And then a second time: "Go back in. You'll only get hurt if you stand out here like this."

I'm thinking, detached, as in a dream: I didn't know they were this considerate. Are they always this considerate? When I was a kid back in the forties, I used to go to those tough-guy movies a lot. Humphrey Bogart, Jimmy Cagney. And when they had a guy penned in, they used to be tough about it, snarling: "Come on out of there, yuh rat, we've got yuh covered!" I wonder what has changed them? Maybe it's just that time has moved on. This is the sixties now.

What's the good of jumping now? Where is there to run to now? And the light teases my eyes. I see all sorts of interlocked and colored soap bubbles that aren't there.

It's more awkward getting back inside than it was getting out. And with the light on me, and them watching me, there's a self-consciousness that was missing in my uninhibited outward surge. I have to straighten out one leg first and dip it into the room toes forward, the way you test the water in a pool before you jump in. Then the other leg, and then I'm in. The roundness of the light beam is broken into long thin tatters as the blind rolls down over it, but it still stays on out there.

There are only two points of light in the whole room—I mean, in addition to the indirect reflection through the blind. Which gives off a sort of phosphorescent haziness—two points so small that if you didn't know they were there and looked for them, you wouldn't see them. And small as both are, one is even smaller than the other. One is the tiny light in the radio, which, because the lens shielding the dial is convex, glows like a miniature orange scimitar. I go over to it to turn it off. It can't keep the darkness away anymore; the darkness is here.

"Here's to the losers," the radio is saying. "Here's to them all—"

The other point of light is over by the door. It's in the door itself. I go over there close to it, peering with my head bowed, as if I were mourning inconsolably. And I am. One of the four tiny screwheads set into the corners of the oblong plate that holds the lock is gone, is out now, and if you squint at an acute angle you can see a speck of orange light shining through it from the hall. Then, while I'm standing there, something falls soundlessly, glances off the top of my shoe with no more weight than a grain of gravel, and there's a second speck of orange light at the opposite upper corner of the plate. Two more to go now. Two and a half minutes of deft work left, maybe not even that much.

What careful planning, what painstaking attention to detail, goes into extinguishing a man's life! Far more than the hit-or-miss, haphazard circumstances of igniting it.

I can't get out the window, I can't go out the door. But there *is* a way out, a third way. I can escape inward. If I can't get away from them on the outside, I can get away from them on the inside.

You're not supposed to have those things. But when you have money you can get anything, in New York. They were on a prescription, but that was where the money came in—getting the prescription. I remember now. Some doctor gave it to me—sold it to me—long ago. I don't remember why or when. Maybe when fear first came between the two of us and I couldn't reach her anymore.

I came across it in my wallet on Wednesday, after I first came in here, and I sent it out to have it filled, knowing that this night would come. I remember the bellboy bringing it to the door afterward in a small bright-green paper wrapping that some pharmacists use. But where is it now?

I start a treasure hunt of terror, around the inside of the room in the dark. First into the clothes closet, wheeling and twirling among the couple of things I have hanging in there like a hopped-up discothèque dancer, dipping in and out of pockets, patting some of them between my hands to see if they're flat or hold a bulk. As if I were calling a little pet dog to me by clapping my hands to it. A little dog who is hiding away from me in there, a little dog called death.

Not in there. Then the drawers of the dresser, spading

them in and out, fast as a card shuffle. A telephone directory, a complimentary shaving kit (if you're a man), a complimentary manicure kit (if you're a girl).

They must be down to the last screwhead by now.

Then around and into the bathroom, while the remorseless dismantling at the door keeps on. It's all white in there, white as my face must be. It's dark, but you can still see that it's white against the dark. Twilight-colored tiles. I don't put on the light to help me find them, because there isn't enough time left; the lights in here are fluorescent and take a few moments to come on, and by that time they'll be in here.

There's a catch phrase that you all must have heard at one time or another. You walk into a room or go over toward a group. Someone turns and says with huge emphasis: "*There* he is." As though you were the most important one of all. (And you're not.) As though you were the one they were just talking about. (And they weren't.) As though you were the only one that mattered. (And you're not.) It's a nice little tribute, and it don't cost anyone a cent.

And so I say this to them now, as I find them on the top glass slab of the shallow medicine cabinet: *There* you are. Glad to see you—you're important in my scheme of things.

As I bend for some running water, the shower curtain twines around me in descending spiral folds—don't ask me how, it must have been ballooning out. I sidestep like a drunken Roman staggering around his toga, pulling half the curtain down behind me while the pins holding it to the rod about tinkle like little finger cymbals, dragging part of it with me over one shoulder, while I bend over the basin to drink.

No time to rummage for a tumbler. It's not there anyway—I'd been using it for the rye. So I use the hollow of one hand for a scoop, pumping it up and down to my open mouth and alternating with one of the nuggets from the little plastic container I'm holding uncapped in my other hand. I've been called a fast drinker at times. Johnny used to say—never mind that now.

I only miss one—that falls down in the gap between me and the basin to the floor. That's a damned good average. There were twelve of them in there, and I remember the label read: *Not more than three to be taken during any twenty-four-hour period.* In other words, I've just killed myself three times, with a down payment on a fourth time for good measure.

I grab the sides of the basin suddenly and bend over it, on the point of getting them all out of me again in rebellious upheaval. I don't want to, but they do. I fold both arms around my middle, hugging myself, squeezing myself, to hold them down. They stay put. They've caught on, taken hold. Only a pump can get them out now. And after a certain point of no return (I don't know how long that is), once they start being assimilated into the bloodstream, not even a pump can get them out.

Only a little brine taste shows up in my mouth, and gagging a little, still holding my middle, I go back into the other room. Then I sit down to wait. To see which of them gets to me first.

It goes fast now, like a drumbeat quickening to a climax. An upended foot kicks at the door, and it suddenly spanks inward with a firecracker sound. The light comes fizzing through the empty oblong like gushing carbonation, too sudden against the dark to ray clearly at first.

They rush in like the splash of a wave that suddenly has splattered itself all around the room. Then the lights are on, and they're on all four sides of me, and they're holding me hard and fast, quicker than one eyelid can touch the other in a blink.

My arms go behind me into the cuffless convolutions of a strait jacket. Then as though unconvinced that this is enough precaution, someone standing back there has looped the curve of his arm around my throat and the back of the chair, and holds it there in tight restraint. Not choking-tight as in a mugging, but ready to pin me back if I should try to heave out of the chair.

Although the room is blazing-bright, several of them are holding flashlights, all lit and centered inward on my face from the perimeter around me, like the spokes of a blinding wheel. Probably to disable me still further by their dazzle. One beam, more skeptical than the others, travels slowly up and down my length, seeking out any bulges that might possibly spell a concealed offensive weapon. My only weapon is already used, and it was a defensive one.

I roll my eyes toward the ceiling to try and get away from the lights, and one by one they blink and go out.

There they stand. The assignment is over, completed. To me it's my life, to them just another incident. I don't know how many there are. The man in the coffin doesn't count the number who have come to the funeral. But as I look at them, as my eyes go from face to face, on each one I read the key to what the man is thinking.

One face, soft with compunction: Poor guy, I might have been him, he might have been me.

One, hard with contempt: Just another of those creeps something went wrong with along the way.

Another, flexing with hate: I wish he'd shown some fight; I'd like an excuse to—

Still another, rueful with impatience: I'd like to get this over so I could call her unexpectedly and catch her in a lie; I bet she never stayed home tonight like she told me she would.

And yet another, blank with indifference, its thoughts a thousand miles away: And what's a guy like Yastrzemski got, plenty of others guy haven't got too? It's just the breaks, that's all—

And I say to my own thoughts dejectedly: Why weren't you that clear, that all-seeing, the other night, that terrible other night. It might have done you more good then.

There they stand. And there I am, seemingly in their hands but slowly slipping away from them.

They don't say anything. I'm not aware of any of them saying anything. They're waiting for someone to give them further orders. Or maybe waiting for something to come and take me away.

One of them hasn't got a uniform on or plainsclothes either like the rest. He has on the white coat that is my nightmare and my horror. And in the crotch of one arm he is upending two long poles intertwined with canvas.

The long-drawn-out death within life. The burial-alive of the mind, covering it over with fresh graveyard earth each time it tries to struggle through to the light. In this kind of death you never finish dying.

In back of them, over by the door, I see the top of someone's head appear, then come forward, slowly, fearfully forward. Different from their short-clipped, starkly outlined heads, soft and rippling in contour, and gentle. And as she comes forward into fullface view, I see who she is.

She comes up close to me, stops, and looks at me.

"Then it wasn't—you?" I whisper.

She shakes her head slightly with a mournful trace of smile. "It wasn't me," she whispers back, without taking them into it, just between the two of us, as in the days before. "I didn't go there to meet you. I didn't like the way you sounded."

But someone was there, I came across someone there. Someone whose face became hers in my waking dream. The scarf, the blood on the scarf. It's not my blood, it's not my scarf. It must belong to someone else. Someone they haven't even found yet, don't even know about yet.

The preventive has come too late.

She moves a step closer and bends toward me.

"Careful—watch it," a voice warns her.

"He won't hurt me," she answers understandingly without taking her eyes from mine. "We used to be in love."

Used to? Then that's why I'm dying. Because I still am. And you aren't anymore.

She bends and kisses me, on the forehead, between the eyes. Like a sort of last rite.

And in that last moment, as I'm straining upward to find her lips, as the light is leaving my eyes, the whole night passes before my mind, the way they say your past life does when you're drowning: the waiter, the night maid, the taxi argument, the call girl, Johnny—it all meshes into start-to-finish continuity. Just like in a story. An organized, step-by-step, timetabled story.

This story.

Afterword to "New York Blues": "New York Blues" (Ellery Queen Mystery Magazine, *December 1970) is the last, best, and bleakest of the original stories EQMM founding editor Frederic Dannay bought from Woolrich during their long association. Within its minimalist storyline we find virtually every motif, belief, device that had pervaded Woolrich's fiction for generations: flashes of word magic, touches of evocative song lyrics, love and loneliness, madness and death, paranoia, partial amnesia, total despair. If this was the last story Woolrich completed, he couldn't have ended his career more fittingly.*

PART II

The Poets

THE RAVEN

EDGAR ALLAN POE

West 84th Street

(Originally published in 1845)

Once upon a midnight dreary, while I pondered, weak
    and weary,
Over many a quaint and curious volume of forgotten lore—
While I nodded, nearly napping, suddenly there came a
    tapping,
As of some one gently rapping, rapping at my chamber
    door—
"'Tis some visiter," I muttered, "tapping at my chamber
    door—
        Only this and nothing more."

Ah, distinctly I remember it was in the bleak December;
And each separate dying ember wrought its ghost upon the
    floor.
Eagerly I wished the morrow;—vainly I had sought to
    borrow
From my books surcease of sorrow—sorrow for the lost
    Lenore—
For the rare and radiant maiden whom the angels name
    Lenore—
        Nameless *here* for evermore.

And the silken, sad, uncertain rustling of each purple curtain

Thrilled me—filled me with fantastic terrors never felt
   before;
So that now, to still the beating of my heart, I stood
   repeating,
"'Tis some visiter entreating entrance at my chamber
   door—
Some late visiter entreating entrance at my chamber
   door;—
           This it is and nothing more."

Presently my soul grew stronger; hesitating then no longer,
"Sir," said I, "or Madam, truly your forgiveness I implore;
But the fact is I was napping, and so gently you came
   rapping,
And so faintly you came tapping, tapping at my chamber
   door,
That I scarce was sure I heard you"—here I opened wide
   the door;—
           Darkness there and nothing more.

Deep into that darkness peering, long I stood there
   wondering, fearing,
Doubting, dreaming dreams no mortal ever dared to dream
   before;
But the silence was unbroken, and the stillness gave no
   token,
And the only word there spoken was the whispered word,
   "Lenore?"
This I whispered, and an echo murmured back the word,
   "Lenore!"
           Merely this and nothing more.

Back into the chamber turning, all my soul within me
    burning,
Soon again I heard a tapping somewhat louder than before.
"Surely," said I, "surely that is something at my window
    lattice;
Let me see, then, what thereat is, and this mystery
    explore—
Let my heart be still a moment and this mystery explore;—
       'Tis the wind and nothing more!"

Open here I flung the shutter, when, with many a flirt and
    flutter,
In there stepped a stately Raven of the saintly days of yore;
Not the least obeisance made he; not a minute stopped or
    stayed he;
But, with mien of lord or lady, perched above my chamber
    door—
Perched upon a bust of Pallas just above my chamber door—
       Perched, and sat, and nothing more.

Then this ebony bird beguiling my sad fancy into smiling,
By the grave and stern decorum of the countenance it wore,
"Though thy crest be shorn and shaven, thou," I said, "art
    sure no craven,
Ghastly grim and ancient Raven wandering from the Nightly
    shore—
Tell me what thy lordly name is on the Night's Plutonian
    shore!"
       Quoth the Raven "Nevermore."

Much I marvelled this ungainly fowl to hear discourse so
    plainly,

Though its answer little meaning—little relevancy bore;
For we cannot help agreeing that no living human being
Ever yet was blessed with seeing bird above his chamber
    door—
Bird or beast upon the sculptured bust above his chamber
    door,
        With such name as "Nevermore."

But the Raven, sitting lonely on the placid bust, spoke only
That one word, as if his soul in that one word he did
    outpour.
Nothing further then he uttered—not a feather then he
    fluttered—
Till I scarcely more than muttered "Other friends have flown
    before—
On the morrow He will leave me, as my Hopes have flown
    before."
        Then the bird said "Nevermore."

Startled at the stillness broken by reply so aptly spoken,
"Doubtless," said I, "what it utters is its only stock and store
Caught from some unhappy master whom unmerciful Disaster
Followed fast and followed faster till his songs one burden
    bore—
Till the dirges of his Hope that melancholy burden bore
        Of 'Never—nevermore.'"

But the Raven still beguiling my sad fancy into smiling,
Straight I wheeled a cushioned seat in front of bird, and
    bust and door;
Then, upon the velvet sinking, I betook myself to linking
Fancy unto fancy, thinking what this ominous bird of yore—

What this grim, ungainly, ghastly, gaunt and ominous bird
   of yore
       Meant in croaking "Nevermore."

This I sat engaged in guessing, but no syllable expressing
To the fowl whose fiery eyes now burned into my bosom's
   core;
This and more I sat divining, with my head at ease reclining
On the cushion's velvet lining that the lamp-light gloated o'er,
But whose velvet-violet lining with the lamp-light gloating
   o'er,
       She shall press, ah, nevermore!

Then, methought, the air grew denser, perfumed from an
   unseen censer
Swung by seraphim whose foot-falls tinkled on the tufted
   floor.
"Wretch," I cried, "thy God hath lent thee—by these
   angels he hath sent thee
Respite—respite and nepenthe, from thy memories of
   Lenore;
Quaff, oh quaff this kind nepenthe and forget this lost
   Lenore!"
       Quoth the Raven "Nevermore."

"Prophet!" said I, "thing of evil!—prophet still, if bird or
   devil!—
Whether Tempter sent, or whether tempest tossed thee here
   ashore,
Desolate yet all undaunted, on this desert land enchanted—
On this home by Horror haunted—tell me truly, I
   implore—

Is there—*is* there balm in Gilead?—tell me—tell me, I
    implore!"
        Quoth the Raven "Nevermore."

"Prophet!" said I, "thing of evil!—prophet still, if bird or
    devil!
By that Heaven that bends above us—by that God we both
    adore—
Tell this soul with sorrow laden if, within the distant
    Aidenn,
It shall clasp a sainted maiden whom the angels name
    Lenore—
Clasp a rare and radiant maiden whom the angels name
    Lenore."
        Quoth the Raven "Nevermore."

"Be that word our sign in parting, bird or fiend!" I shrieked,
    upstarting—
"Get thee back into the tempest and the Night's Plutonian
    shore!
Leave no black plume as a token of that lie thy soul hath
    spoken!
Leave my loneliness unbroken!—quit the bust above my
    door!
Take thy beak from out my heart, and take thy form from
    off my door!"
        Quoth the Raven "Nevermore."

And the Raven, never flitting, still is sitting, *still* is sitting
On the pallid bust of Pallas just above my chamber door;
And his eyes have all the seeming of a demon's that is
    dreaming,

And the lamp-light o'er him streaming throws his shadow
    on the floor;
And my soul from out that shadow that lies floating on the
    floor
        Shall be lifted—nevermore!

SELECTIONS FROM
CHELSEA ROOMING HOUSE

BY HORACE GREGORY

Chelsea

(Originally published in 1930)

LONGFACE MAHONEY DISCUSSES HEAVEN

If someone said, Escape,
let's get away from here,
you'd see snow mountains thrown
against the sky,
cold, and you'd draw your breath and feel
air like cold water going through your veins,
but you'd be free, up so high,
or you'd see a row of girls dancing on a beach
with tropic trees and a warm moon
and warm air floating under your clothes
and through your hair.
Then you'd think of heaven
where there's peace, away from here
and you'd go some place unreal
where everybody goes after something happens,
set up in the air, safe, a room in a hotel.
A brass bed, military hair brushes,
a couple of coats, trousers, maybe a dress
on a chair or draped on the floor.
This room is not on earth, feel the air,
warm like heaven and far away.

This is a place
where marriage nights are kept
and sometimes here you say, Hello
to a neat girl with you
and sometimes she laughs
because she thinks it's funny to be sitting here
for no reason at all, except perhaps,
she likes you daddy.
Maybe this isn't heaven but near
to something like it,
more like love coming up in elevators
and nothing to think about, except, O God,
you love her now and it makes no difference
if it isn't spring. All seasons are warm
in the warm air
and the brass bed is always there.

If you've done something
and the cops get you afterwards, you
can't remember the place again,
away from cops and streets—
it's all unreal—
the warm air, a dream
that couldn't save you now.
No one would care
to hear about it,
it would be heaven
far away, dark and no music,
not even a girl there.

TIME AND ISIDORE LEFKOWITZ

It is not good to feel old
for time is heavy,
time is heavy
on a man's brain,
thrusting him down,
gasping into the earth,
out of the way of the sun
and the rain.

Look at Isidore Lefkowitz,
biting his nails, telling how
he seduces Beautiful French Canadian
Five and Ten Cent Store Girls,
beautiful, by God, and how they cry
and moan, wrapping their arms
and legs around him
when he leaves them
saying:
Good bye,
good bye.

He feels old when he tells
these stories over and over,
(how the Beautiful Five and Ten Cent Store
Girls go crazy when he puts on
his clothes and is gone),
these old lies
that maybe nobody at all believes.
He feels old thinking how
once he gave five

dollars to a girl
who made him feel like other men
and wonders if she is still alive.
If he were a millionaire,
if he could spend five dollars now,
he could show them how
he was strong and handsome then,
better than other men.

But it is not good to feel old,
time is too heavy,
it gets a man
tired, tired
when he thinks how time wears
him down
and girls, milk-fed, white,
vanish with glorious smiling millionaires
in silver limousines.

BRIDGEWATER JONES: IMPROMPTU IN A SPEAKEASY

When you've been through what I've been through
over in France where war was hell
and everything turned to blood and mud
and you get covered with blood and rain
and rain and mud
then you come back home again,
come back home and make good in business.
You don't know how and you don't know why;
it's enough to make God stand still and wonder.

It's something that makes you sit down and think
and you want to say something that's clear and deep,
something that someone can understand:
that's why I got to be confidential
and see things clear and say what I mean,
something that's almost like a sermon,
O world without end,
amen.

When you can't see things then you get like Nelly
and somebody has to put you out
and somebody has to put you away
but you can always see through Nelly.
She unrolled like a map on the office floor,
you could see her in the dark—
a blind pink cat
in the back seat of the Judge's car.
But she'd get cold in the Globe Hotel,
singing songs like the Songs of Solomon,
making the Good Book sound immoral
then she'd say she was Mother Mary
and the strength of sin is the law.
World without end
amen.

Gentlemen, I had to fire Nelly,
she didn't see when a man's in business,
she didn't know when a man's a Christian
you can't go singing the Songs of Solomon,
shouting Holy, holy, holy,
making Mother of Christ a whore,
cold as rain,

dead blood and rain like the goddam war,
cold as Nelly telling you hell you killed her baby,
then she couldn't take a letter
but would sit down and cry
like rain.

It got so bad I couldn't sleep
with her hair and eyes and breasts and belly
and arms around me
like rain, rain,
rain without end
amen.

I tell you gentlemen almighty God,
I didn't kill her dead baby,
it was the rain
falling on men and girls and cities.
Ask the Judge (he's got a girl)
about a baby:
a baby wants life and sun, not rain by God that's death
         when you float a baby down the sewer into the
                              East River with its lips
making foam at the stern of ships
head on for Liverpool in rain.

You can't see what happens in rain
(only God knows, world without end)
maybe war, maybe a dead baby.
There's no good when rain falls on a man;
I had to make it clear,
that's what I wanted to explain.

SELECTIONS FROM
THE MCSORLEY POEMS

BY GEOFFREY BARTHOLOMEW

East Village

(Originally published in 2001)

MISYCK, THE NIGHT WATCHMAN

I sit alone here at night, listening
        doors and windows twisted
        by McSorley's heavy sag
        everything out of whack
        creak and groan of ghosts
        they speak, you know
        but Woodrow Wilson there
        I can't understand him
        he garbles his words

My brother Jerzy's dead thirty years tonight
        we grew up here on 7th Street
        St. George's, God and girls
        stickball, cars and beer
        then we started the skag
        Jerzy shot up first
        I was belting my arm
        when he sat back
        his eyes went real wide

like flooring the Buick
feeling that crazy rush

Bill McSorley up there by the icebox
        resembles Teddy Roosevelt
        a smaller moustache
        timid eyes, sour mouth
        really did love his old man
        vowed to keep the bar *as is*
        kill time in this real place
        now just a face on the wall
        the bar a mute witness
        to Bill's doomed love

My favorite relic is the playbill from the 1880s
        a windmill and two dutchgirls
        on a forlorn spit of land
        the ocean a white-capped menace
        What Are The Wild Waves Saying?
        some March nights it blows
        so hard against the windows
        I'd swear it's Jerzy's voice

Larry, homeless black wraith, taps the window
        I make him a liverwurst on rye
        some nights he has d.t.s
        tonight he's souful
        I fucked up, he says
        shoeless, he begins again
        his scabrous circle
        East Village Odysseus

The ripe nude in the painting back there
      I don't like her much
      she knows she's got it
      that mouth of plump disdain
      the parrot probably trained
      to do weird shit, yeah
      they liked that stuff back then

And on every wall this guy Peter Cooper
      rich and famous in 1860
      John McSorley's buddy
      they say he brought Lincoln here
      after some Great Hall speech
      that's real strange, me here
      where Lincoln once drank

At night I oil the old bar
      there's a sag in the middle
      the mahogany a wornout horse
      I know it's stupid, but I think
      Jerzy's going to appear one night
      we're all gonna sit here and talk
      him and Cooper and McSorley,
      Lincoln, Woodrow Wilson,
      maybe the fat nude, too

MAD DEEGAN

On the bustling sidewalk
as the last gray light slides
     between concrete walls
I move brokenly, madness
a hunched raven on my shoulder
behind Dean & DeLuca's glass
the elegant consume
     and defecate elsewhere
invisible yet ubiquitous
I shit on dark corners
urinate with the feral
apologia to Lowry
     but I am his pariah dog
     still alive in the ravine
howling, quietly howling

Educated with the elite
Stuyvesant then Yale
in the Seminary I became
     a brother of inculcation
so I taught God's children
the nun Betty and I
     fell in love's despair
we quit our vows to marry
     we ate acid
quickly madness won us over
with fists we fought
our words weapons of delight

Betty took a train to

somewhere, leaving then
this tunnel in my brain
a small black smudge
with their pills the shrinks
    would me heal a hole

At McSorley's I swept up
for simple cash and food
washed pots and pans despite
the burgeoning smear
    which one night
blotted the running bullshit
    leaving the mind a nub
    where the raven pecks
I am searching the streets
catching the last sliding light
    on my hunched form
the pariah dog is here
    is here somewhere

THE LIFE OF JIMMY FATS

Call me Jimmy
I'm not fat, I'm obese
nowhere to hide, pal
but I learned something
people love you
    if you're real fat
I mean, really huge
you save them

So I got my first job
      in Coccia's on 7th Street
      Italian sit-down deli
Jewish actors from Second Avenue
Ukey Moms from the block
laborers, clerks from Wannamaker's
number-runners an' schoolkids
      you know the years
      how they quietly roar by
I was the best short-order guy
      ate like a champ
then Artie sold the building

Two doors up was the saloon
busy lunch an' lazy afternoons
nights packed with young guys
J.J. the owner knew me from when
I was a kid, burned my arm on
his '48 Buick, Irish guys laughing
that fat kid in the photo, that's
me, walking by the bar in 1950

Stampalia the chef had just died
      announcing lunch
      he'd sound an old bugle
      this time his aorta blew
I got the job
old guys in the bar whispered
but I was big, fast, an' funny
no bugles, just Jimmy Fats
I won 'em over with laughs
I loved that place

In the doo-wop band
    I sang lead, us guys
     from Aviation High
we cut some songs, never made it
Joey overdosed on skag
Lou got married with kids
Willy stepped on a mine in Nam
me, I kept cooking an' eating

McSorley's in the '70s
    me & an' Frank the Slob
    we humped it all
Ray the waiter, then George
    he was the best
    took care of everyone
workers, cops, students, firemen
we played nags an' numbers
    then George quit
    oldtimers died off
Frank's fuckin' bitch drone began
waiters coming an' going
    the only sane ones
Minnie the cat an' me

Shit, I was up to 630 by '79
when I fell in love
Lace was beautiful and big
so we starved an' screwed to 260
after the baby, she got mental
nights she cried a lot
it sounded like me far off
but I can't remember when

One black night I woke up
      Lace was gone
note said she went to L.A.
      that was it
I don't think it was love
just some kind of lonely thing
      fat people get

Still, I was McSorley's chef
I was 500 an' floating
      little Tanya screaming
      Daddy! Daddy! Daddy!
raising a kid alone ain't easy
the fucking dog Blacky
      big Lab, shedding
hated the heat he always did
I was on the throne when he
ripped her head halfway off
      broke her neck
the funeral was like Ma's
at Lancia's on Second Avenue
next to the old 21 Place
the guys from the bar
murmured condolences
      shook their heads
if Lacey hadn't run away
if I hadn't been on the shitter
if, if, a million *ifs*

Back at work
Frank's *fuckin' bitch*
      became a foul mantra

nothing to say nor do
that's when I began
        to eat
really eat

I couldn't get out of bed
fucking buzz in my ear
        a numb hissing
        finally I got up
then the buzz was a hornet
the floor rose up, stung me
sideways the last thing I saw
some pizza crust and the doll
Tanya's dusty Barbie

That was the end of Jimmy Fats
they buried me out in Queens
        between Tanya an' Ma
the stone says 1939-1990
but how's anybody to know
        you know
what *really* happened?

PART III

Darkness Visible

THE LUGER IS A 9MM AUTOMATIC HANDGUN WITH A PARABELLUM ACTION

BY JERROLD MUNDIS

Central Park

(Originally published in 1969)

Two years ago I was walking in Central Park around the shallow bowl of water beneath the dollhouse Norman castle that is the weather station. I had approached from the north. I was not thinking.

Ahab said, "You are despondent." He mushed his conso-nants. His *s* was lisped. A five-foot branch was wedged rather far back in his mouth. The bark was rough. A string of blood and saliva dipped and swayed from his jaw.

I considered a little. "Disconsolate."

He gagged, dropped the branch and insisted on despon-dence. His consonants were clear and his lisp was gone. I shrugged. We went on in silence. Padding alongside, he cocked his head up at intervals to look at me. Then he stopped and began snuffing the air. He pinpointed the direction and trot-ted off with a light springy step. His vibrancy sometimes fires me with jealousy. It was an oak, which he read with his nose. Then he made a tight circle, deciding, balanced on three legs and urinated.

He returned and said, "Disconsolation suggests an edge of emotional keenness, whereas despondence—"

"I'd rather not talk about it."

"You err. Whereas, as I was saying, despondence is essentially ennui, a moribund state lightly salted with bitterness."

"You cut me up, moving the way you do."

"Do I?" The corners of his long mouth pulled back in his equivalent of a smile, which is not grotesque, but which, neither, is the legitimate article. You must project certain responses to understand that it is a smile. "That's improvement," he said.

"I don't see it."

"Sure you do."

"I don't like this conversation."

He sat down and scratched his ear. He asked me if I would like to throw a stick for him to chase. He was attempting rapprochement, but he was also going for himself. Like everyone. Though why this should matter, I don't know. Quivering, poised, eager, focused, he was naked and ugly in his exposure. Ordinarily I wouldn't have minded. That is what he is, that is what he is about. But he had made me angry. And the walk had not helped. I was still weary, incredibly. Often the walks were successful. Watching him run and cavort and do all his healthy animal things, my shuffle would lengthen to a stride and I would begin to feel vigorous and defined, primed with purpose. "No, I don't want to throw a stick for you."

"I sigh," he said. "Langorously."

"Shutup."

Climbing the walk to the weather station we came upon seven fat pigeons pecking bread crumbs in a semicircle around a thin young girl in a skirt that, it being short and she being seated, was well up her skinny thighs. She wore no stockings. Her knees were bony, like flattened golf balls. Ahab's ears clicked forward and his shoulders bunched. He went into his stifflegged walk. Fifteen feet from the fat pigeons. His mouth opened, drops of spittle appeared. Ten feet from the fat pigeons. He breathed with explosive little pants. Five feet from the fat pigeons. He now looked a sloppily worked marionette. Four feet from the fat pigeons. . . .

I caught him an instant before he lunged, an instant so close to the act that they shredded into one another. "Ahab, *heel!*"

He jerked, half wheeled, went up on his hind legs and scored the pavement with his claws when he struck, but there was no forward progress.

In place, eyes wild on the seven fat pigeons thrashing the air in panicked escape, he performed a zealot's dance, a dance of possession. He was a *plastique* detonated within a steel room, all that power, all that energy—contained.

The skinny girl was on her feet. She was not pretty. Her skin was the color of sour milk. She was jabbing her finger at me and shrieking. It had to do with Ahab and the birds.

Ahab said, "Kill, kill," and turned to her with ferocious urgency.

I grabbed his collar and slammed him back. It is a pinch-collar, misnomered by many as a spike-collar. When the short sliding length of chain is pulled, the linked circle tightens. This causes blunt prongs to meet, pinching the neck. It is an effective, and with Ahab, a necessary collar. There is no question, however, that he would disregard the pain of pinched flesh if he thought that killing were really appropriate.

"Overprotective," I said to the skinny not pretty girl who was the color of sour milk and had knees like flattened golf balls and who was shrieking and jabbing her finger at me. Shrieking, she did not hear me. "Fuck you," I said. Jabbing her finger, she did not hear me. I don't know if I said anything. If I did say overprotective and fuck you, then neither one of us heard anything and they were passionless sounds without significance, like fog, and they disappeared under the bright summer sun.

"Heel," I said to Ahab.

He said nothing more. I believe he was thinking, with a growing sense of injustice or some such, of the seven fat pigeons and the way in which I had stopped him an instant before he lunged, an instant so close to the act that they shredded into one another. But I might very well be wrong.

We went home.

Ahab remained silent—that is, he did not say anything, in words, for more than a year. Most surely he carried on dialogues in the style assumed natural.

We were again at the park late one pleasant fall night, some fifteen months after our initial conversation. We had just entered and were walking down the ramp and I had not yet unsnapped the leash from his collar.

"Freedom *now*, freedom *now*," he chanted.

He had recently spent several afternoons playing with a bitch in the yard of a garden apartment down the street. Apartment and bitch were owned by a militant blueblack oboe player and his wife, both of whom wore their hair natural.

"Freedom in a minute, there's a squad car passing."

"Baby, I'm not gonna wait no longer. You don't like it, that's your lookout."

"What are you going to do if I keep the leash on?"

"Like the man says, violence is as American as cherry pie. Take it from there."

"Shit on America, you're violent by nature, that's all."

"True. What are you by nature?"

"You mean am I violent or not?"

"Don't jive me, baby. You dig the question."

"You know, if I do keep you on the leash, you won't touch me. Matter of fact, if I clobbered the hell out of you, you wouldn't touch me. That's your nature too."

"True, very true. You have the knowledge, man, but unfortunately not the wisdom."

I unsnapped his leash. "Thanks," he said, raced in wide circles, then went foraging into the darkness. He came back, fell in step with me and said, "Been thinkin' on your nature?"

"No."

"Well, wouldn't help anyhow. You ain't got none."

"Seems the only reason you say anything is to needle me."

"You people, man, you operate at three and three while the rest of it's at fifty and fifty."

"Rest of what?"

"Everything."

"You know that for a fact?"

"No."

"Well . . . listen, how come you talk? I thought about that a while back."

"I'm an atavism."

"Oh. Sorry."

"Why?"

"I don't know. It seems the thing to say."

He swung in front of me and sat. He cocked his head to one side. "Hey, man. Hey."

"Yeah?"

"I love you."

"I know. I love you."

"Does it help, loving?"

"It helps. Sometimes, but it's not nearly enough."

He nodded.

We resumed walking. I said, "The thing is, there's no significance. Nothing makes any difference. Nothing is more valuable than anything else. Which means there isn't any such thing as value."

"Uh-huh."

"How do you endure it?"

"I don't."

"I don't understand you."

"You won't survive then."

"Is that really important?"

"No, it isn't."

Without Ahab I would have gone mad, if there is such a state. That is, in a negative sense. Which I don't believe. I was sinking. Interminably. From nowhere, to nowhere. I am still sinking, all of us are, interminably. But now there is a vital difference—I have the key, the *raison d'être*; better, the *mode d'être*. It is the answer, the only answer. Thank you, Ahab.

Sometimes I called him Ahab Flying Death Defier. I would throw one of his rubber toys and he would leap high, with grace, and close his powerful jaws about it in midflight, then land erect with light resilience. Now and then I would say, "It's a dynamite stick! Catch it, boy, or we're done for!" And he would snatch it from the air. I laughed. He wriggled pleasurably and came to get his ears scratched, his chest rubbed. We loved each other. For whatever that was worth.

I functioned well. The vicissitudes of my life went smoothly and successfully. Everything was, however, uniformly neutral. Everything still is, on that higher level. Or that lower level. Deterioration is not always symbolically manifest, nor even literally manifest. But that is what our dialogues had been about. Because deterioration is dominant, although deterioration is perhaps not the proper word: it implies values. And there is the crux of it all.

"Self-determination and a positive outlook," Ahab said. "We must pull ourselves up by the bootstraps, so to speak."

It was winter in the park. The sky was corrupt. The snow on the ground had been three days rotting. It was soot and sickly ice crystals. We had just come through a city election.

"It requires will, strong will. Immediate investment. A sacrifice on all our parts, which, I point out, will not be easy. But I tell you that a sacrifice made easily and without effort is no sacrifice at all and is therefore without consequence. Invest now and in a little time you will reap benefits one hundred, nay even one thousand–fold."

"Where is this taking us?" I asked him.

"To our logical, our inescapable conclusion, my fellow countryman."

Three boys in leather were approaching.

"Why didn't you tell me earlier there was one?"

"You weren't desperate enough. Now is the time. The iron is hot."

"Is it cusp?"

"It is cusp."

"I suspected that, dimly. But it doesn't make any difference."

"True enough. That is why you must recognize its importance." The boys in leather came scuffling closer. Ahab's walk stiffened. "Discover your nature!"

"You said I didn't have any."

"You don't."

"Nothing does!"

"Nothing is!"

"Then how can—"

"Hey, Jack, you got any butts?"

"No, sorry."

"Pull that mother back, or he's dead!"

"He's dead anyway. Come on, your wallet, Jack."

They held thin steel in their hands, fine implements from the looks of them. I never knew much of cutlery. But they made good, solid metallic clacks when they sprang open. Discriminating buyers, I am told, look for that sound. I marked the absence of Ahab's customary barks; this time there was only a low rumbling in his throat. He moved. The nearest one, the tallest, screamed. Ahab had opened his wrist. I could see a tendon. The knife fell. All three of them ran. Ahab loped after them, furrowed a calf, but broke off and returned when I called him.

"Thank you," I said.

"My pleasure."

"How do you feel?"

"Full. Brimming." He raced ahead, spun, raced back, spun . . . "Overflowing," he said.

"Functioning as you're meant to gives you such joy?"

"Functioning, yes. As I'm meant to, that's a non sequitur."

"Everything has an intended function."

"Bullshit."

"The function is to die."

"Puppycock."

"Mountains erode. Organisms wither, drop and decay. Physically, we are eating ourselves. Spiritually, we are disintegrating. Psychologically, we are being gnawed from within. Everything is collapsing."

Ahab chewed angrily at some irritation on his flank. "So?"

"So *a priori* there is no question of ultimate survival,

and temporary survival can be obtained only through self-neutralization."

"Temporary survival *is* total survival, triumph even, since in the grave nothing, including defeat, can be experienced. And survival is dependent on frameworks and structures."

"None exist."

"Right, so discover them."

"Create them?"

"What can be created already exists; discover them. React. In a completely voluntary, and systematically arbitrary way. Reacting, you will act, which will cause reactions in the form of new actions. But it must be codified, all of it. And you must function within the system as if it were built upon categorical absolutes. Never question, never waver. You will have to do it, your species will have to do it. Perversely, you've forced yourselves to see the meaninglessness of your lives and values. So now you have no lives and values. You must rebuild."

"Why, why should we? What's the point?"

Ahab shrugged.

"It's stupid," I said.

"Someone suggested it wasn't?"

I thought a few moments. "If, I mean just if someone wanted to do that, how would he go about it?"

"Plunge into it. Dramatically. Unequivocally. Your commitment has to be total."

"And it works?"

"It works."

"What about you?"

"I told you. I'm an atavism. Old primal race memories come to a head in me sometimes."

"Then it's not perfect."

"Put it this way. Out of uncountable organisms over millions of years there have been only a few minor deviations. That's not bad. Or not good, depending on your point of view."

"I don't have one."

"That's what we've been talking about."

I sat up all that night looking out and down through my window at a street light and at the few people who passed hurriedly beneath it. In the morning I washed my face. I took Ahab to the park again. He made no mention of yesterday's conversation. He made no mention of anything. He frolicked, rolled and burrowed in the rotten snow, delighted with this unexpected trip.

While he concentrated on digging a stick from under the snow several yards away I unzipped my jacket and closed my hand around the Luger jammed in my waistband. The Luger is a 9 millimeter automatic handgun with a parabellum action. Mine was manufactured in 1918 by the *Deutsche Waffen-und Munitionsfabriken* and is marked with their monogram, a flourished *DWM*. Its serial number is 4731 and all its parts are original, except for the clip which bears the number 6554. It is an excellent weapon—compact, powerful, accurate and extremely well balanced. Often you will hear that Lugers are unreliable, that they jam frequently. This is not true. When jamming does occur it is invariably due to poor quality ammunition. American shells are not to be depended upon. 9 millimeter is a sporting caliber in the United States, not military, and the powder charge is too weak to keep the weapon working at maximum efficiency. Foreign military loads are easily obtainable. Belgian, Canadian, British or Israeli cartridges are all quite acceptable.

I laid my finger alongside the trigger guard. The metal was only a little chilly. The clip, which holds eight rounds, was already in place. I snapped the first shell into the chamber and flicked the safety off. I curled my finger lightly around the trigger and took aim.

The first shot broke Ahab's right foreleg at the middle joint. He collapsed heavily. The second shot missed. The third passed high through the rear of his body, but did not break the spine. With difficulty and in obvious pain he struggled to his feet and limped toward me on three legs. "Don't," he called. "Oh please don't." I fired again. He fell, but continued squirming forward. "Please," he said, "I love you. Don't." His blood was trickling and spraying bright red onto the dirty gray snow. I kept firing. "Please, I love you. I love you, I love you." The seventh round split his skull. He spasmed and lay still, his broken leg bent beneath him.

I ejected the last round. It broke through the crust of rotten ice and disappeared, unspent. I went home.

It is summer now. Voraciously, I am eating life.

He intended this.

This is what he intended.

He did.

THE INTERCEPTOR

BY BARRY N. MALZBERG

Upper West Side

(Originally published in 1972)

Death wore five faces that grim night. Could I pierce those grinning, evil masks and spot the real murderer?

H e has been in the hotel room for a long time. No pleasure that but he thinks he has the crime figured out at last. It must have been his wife.

Everything, *everything* points to her. She must have killed Robinson in temper; then, when the placement of the securities next to the corpse would have tied the murder to her, turned the thing around and implicated him with that phone call which brought him to the scene just three minutes ahead of the police.

"Come over," she said. "Something really terrible has happened; I appeal to you" and linked to her in the end, unable to understand what was going on he had come and had nearly been apprehended.

If he had not run immediately—but no sense in thinking about that now. He had gotten away from the police, just barely, and now at last he had solved the mystery. No time for speculation. No need for it either.

The motives were clear. Robinson and his wife must have been having an affair, had carried it on under him for a long time, his business partner and wife, and Robinson, bored, had been looking for a way out. Wryly he thinks that he could have warned Robinson about entrapment if only the man had been frank with him. In fact, regardless of consequences, Robinson might well have broken off the relationship if only given a little more time. And she could not bear to see it end that way, being that kind of a woman.

Yes, that must be it. He has nailed it to the ground. He lights another cigarette, looks around the room, paces to the window and looks at 72nd Street three floors below him, addicts milling in front of the hotel. He had been smart to have selected a location like this to be hidden although the circumstances were not of the best. If nothing else, living in this hotel for some weeks has made him socially conscious.

Perhaps it was not merely a crime of passion, though. His wife must have known that sooner or later Robinson would let slip news of the affair and the divorce would have been shattering. At all costs the woman believed in appearances. She would not even have a bedroom fight unless she was made up for it.

He sighs, walks away from the window. Relief overtakes him. It is good to know that he has the matter straightened out for himself at last and not a moment too soon. The police are closing in; even with the help of the inspector he could not remain in flight from the authorities forever. And to be apprehended in a hotel like this—

He picks up the phone to call the inspector and give him the explanation that will, at last, set him free. As he inhales deeply to brace himself, a fragment of dust in the foul hotel room penetrates his lungs in the wrong way and he coughs. He coughs repeatedly, wheezing, feeling the first stab of an asthma attack. Enough. Enough of cigarettes. In his new life he will definitely give up the habit. He stubs out his forty-third cigarette of the day and dials the inspector's home number.

He thinks at last that he has got the thing clear in his mind. Not soon enough to have saved the agony of flight but not too late. Not by a damned sight too late. He lights a cigarette to celebrate this. When everything is over he will give up the habit but now he will indulge himself. The murderer was Robinson.

Robinson! It all ties together. His business partner and his wife must have been having an affair for many years until his wife had lost interest and had told the man that she had reached the end, that the worn-out affair was not worth the risk of a lost marriage.

In a fit of jealous rage Robinson must have killed her in the offices, then planted the incriminating securities next to her and fled.

The securities had led the police inevitably to him and with his wife dead and Robinson out of the country he did not have a chance. It had been clever of Robinson to arrange that illness of his father in Italy, diabolically so, and no details had ever been checked. Did Robinson even have a father?

And so he had no choice but to become a fugitive while he tried to piece the crime together himself. He had to find the explanation that would free him of the authorities and restore him to the life that for so long he had taken for granted. But it had been difficult. Now the police had infiltrated into the hotel itself. The dope traffic in the halls and outside might distract them for a while; still it could be only a matter of time until they traced down his room number, poured into his door holding guns, and arrested him.

Fortunately, he had at last worked out the true explanation

of the crime. He would be saved. If he could only reach the inspector quickly enough to start the process in motion—

He coughs. The air in this old and vicious hotel, once elegant, now destroyed, located in an undesirable area of the city he has always hated even in the good years when he and his young wife lived here, this air has become increasingly foul and in the bargain, due to the terrible impact of the murder and then the building pressures on him he has been smoking too much, even beyond his normal excess.

He has always had a morbid fear of getting lung cancer and dying slowly, although his own doctor had assured him just two months ago, shortly before the nightmare began, that for a man of forty-seven he had been in perfect health. Slight elevation of the blood pressure; suspicious fullness around the area of the spleen, yes, but these were not serious problems and could be controlled. Lung cancer was contradicted under all circumstances.

He thinks now of his doctor, a thin, nervous internist who had also treated his wife, been taciturn about her own condition, had insisted on the sanctity of that relationship and of his files.

Funny that the doctor had never known anything about the man's personal life, although he had been treating the two of them for seven years. No pictures on his desk that might be indicative, no wife or children squinting or smiling imbecilically at the degrees framed on the wall opposite.

Perhaps she was having an affair with the doctor then as well. This was not impossible. She was a passionate woman for whom he had had little time for many years. Pressures of business. Building the firm. Acquiring securities. There might have been quite a few.

Robinson's problem, in fact, might not have been the end

of the affair but the discovery that he was merely another in a procession. Robinson had vanity over his insecurity. This would have been unbearable to him. Looked at in that way the situation creates sympathy for Robinson as well. Tragic he thinks. All of it was tragic: missed circumstances, lapsed opportunities, an exercise in misdirection. No time to take the long view however or to want to go back. It is too late for this.

Procedures. Stick to the *modus operandi* as he has seen it established. First, the call to the inspector to clear himself. Then the meeting with the inspector to give the details, the abandonment of charges, the hunt for the true murderer, Robinson.

He thinks he knows how the man can be found. In Italy or New York Robinson's habits are still as naked to him as only those of a lifelong business partner can be. It is not for nothing that they have worked together, shared his wife.

At last, soon or late, in the presence of the police or alone he will come face to face with the man, possibly in some dismal hotel room just like this one. Staggering against the walls, sweating, coughing, mumbling, choking, Robinson may look very much as he has over these weeks. He will feel sympathy for the man as only one who has shared these circumstances could.

"I forgive you," he will say, reaching forward to touch Robinson. "I'm sorry, it was not merely your fault but mine too. I relieve you of your guilt. All right, it is all right," and will connect then, a springing clasp, wrist to wrist and Robinson will disintegrate before him, weeping.

"I didn't mean to do it," he will say, "I had no choice. It was just that I was so frightened," and will cast him a look so full of pleading and mercy that it will contain all the vengeance he ever needed. As for the rest of it, the arrest, arraignment, trial, incarceration, he will play no role. He will let the authorities do as they will for the urge for vengeance will be out of him. Will anyone understand this?

Passion and loss. That was what it was. He can surely make this clear to the inspector, who is himself an understanding man who in his business must have seen many interesting cases like this. He and the inspector someday will share those reminiscences in a cocktail lounge or at a good restaurant on the East Side. He and the inspector. His salvation and his friend.

He picks up the phone, knowing the number so well that he could, if a blind man, find it expertly. He dials the number.

Finally, as a suddenness, all of it falls into place for him. The doctor. *All of the time it would have had to have been the doctor.*

Yes, yes! The man must have known his wife well. It had been seven years after all. He had treated her, understood from the confidences she would have given that she was lonely and abandoned, resentful of the way his original interest in her had fragmented into a hundred other meaningless concerns.

The doctor, hearing all of this on late afternoons in the gray of the empty office, must have taken all of these for signals instead of desperate secrets and tried to interest her in having an affair with him—when suddenly, stunningly, she turned on him in revulsion and then laughed at his desires. How well he knew this; she was exactly that kind of a woman.

"Where did you ever get that idea?" his wife must have said. "Just because I told you a few things did you think it meant that I would go to bed with you? I wouldn't touch you,

you foul little man. Hire a good-looking nurse and try it on her."

"No," the doctor would have said, "you can't say this to me. You cannot. There must be some reason—"

"I'll say anything I want," his wife would have answered, "I'm paying the bills. You don't even exist in my life if I don't want you to. Where could you have gotten the idea I would touch you?" She had that streak; it would have been what she said. And the doctor, a simple man enthralled by his desires, would have been unable to deal with it.

So, he had killed her. After saying what she did, his wife must have turned to leave the office, but before she could even reach the door the doctor had, in a fit of passion, ended her life. With a scalpel or hypodermic injection or whatever else doctors kept in their examining rooms.

They weren't regulated, that was the trouble. An M.D. could get away with anything, once you had that degree on the wall. But it did not guarantee that you could have sex with your patients.

That was the point at which he had gone wrong. It would have been a clean wound—he knew his business, after all— with very little bleeding and after that with crazed skill the doctor would have disposed of the weapon and erased all signs of his own implication in the crime.

Had she died immediately? Or had she hung on, gasping on the floor for a few moments, her eyes slowly gazing as she stared at the fluorescence? Well, no need to be too graphic, he will think of that some other time. He wants to think that it was a clean, quick death; even for her cruelty she should not have suffered.

The securities then. With the woman lying at last dead before him the doctor's passion would have turned to panic and then at last to mad cunning as the thought came to him that without witnesses and with the fact of a sterile marriage there would be an available suspect.

If he could plant the securities near the body then the investigation would inevitably turn away from him, despite the fact that it was his office, and toward the husband with whose fate those securities were inextricably linked.

The doctor would not even have to worry about getting the corpse from the office; it would be credible that the husband would want to kill her in surroundings where someone else would be implicated.

Double reverse. Sitting in the hotel room he nods slowly, being able to appreciate, as he thinks the thing through, the doctor's cunning all the way down the line.

So the doctor had done it then. There was plenty of information from the wife over seven years and he knew exactly where to look. He had seized the securities, placed them on top of the corpse and then closed up his office, knowing that all of this would shortly be found by the authorities who would make the connections.

The trap had sprung well. If he had not finally had the alertness and good sense to consider the issue of the doctor, the man without whom, damningly, the crime could not have worked, he would never have gotten out. But finally, through his own thought and effort, the crime has been solved.

If he can get the facts to the right people in time.

Robinson first. He must call Robinson and give him the explanation slowly, carefully, just the way he has worked it out.

His business partner is a ponderous man; he must take time to explain and not confuse him by hurrying. Still, he knows that he can be counted on: if it were not for Robinson smuggling him away from home at the critical moment and into this dismal but safe hotel room he would at this moment be in a cell, awaiting trial and conviction.

Still, he thinks, Robinson could have shown better taste in hotels; even at this level there must be a better place and the drug traffic is incessant.

But his partner and friend of almost a quarter-century, the only man he could ever trust, had stood by him as none of the others would, not even the inspector. Robinson insisted steadfastly that he was innocent, that he never could have done it. And had bought just enough time from the inspector to put him, for the moment, out of their grasp.

But only for the moment. He must remember that. Like his poor wife, he had run out of time.

He will tell Robinson and his partner will go to the inspector on his behalf with the story. Once the police know which trail to investigate, the crime will open up before them just as for himself it has opened in this grim hotel room.

The doctor's hasty disappearance, his failure to contact the answering service, the peculiar aspect of the corpse, the way in which the office was left—all of these will assume a different cast in the inspector's mind. He is too tough and shrewd to deny the obvious once it is presented on him and will direct the police to close down on the evidence which must surely lurk in the doctor's file. And surely the doctor had had friends to whom he might have, before his flight, intimated the truth.

While he stays hidden, Robinson his one connection to the authorities, the crime will unravel about them and he will be able to come out of this with his life intact, his reputation restored.

The loss of his wife, the pitiful way in which his marriage

has ended are dreadful, of course, but he realizes that in some corridor of the heart he must have abandoned her long ago.

There had almost never been a marriage. For this and the murder itself he will have to make atonement in some intricate way, pay some measure of penance beyond what he has already by living these dreadful weeks.

But enough of that for now. The thing to do is to call Robinson and begin the springing of the levers which, as they are released one by one, will send him back to the world.

He returns from the window at which he has been pacing, casting idle looks downward at 72nd Street. Three teenage boys are assaulting someone's convertible and as scars appear on the old car's body he has been thinking about the less visible assassins who have been working on him all this time. He coughs at some rancid odor which whisks in and out of the window.

Then, swallowing determinedly he picks up the phone. He knows where Robinson will be. The number is engraved into him. He sighs and shakes his head. He dials.

At last he sees the answer and hopes that it is not too late. It must have been at the corner of his mind for a while. Again and again he had pushed it off because it had been too insane, too unreasonable, but now he can no longer turn back. The truth is agony but the truth will set him free.

It is the inspector.

The inspector from the beginning had been too casual about his involvement in the case, too insidious in wanting to know personal facts, not willing himself to yield hard facts or opinions which would establish his own thoughts on the case, the position which a legitimate police official would have to take.

And the matter of identity as well. Never once had the

inspector offered identification. And, accepting unthinkingly as he would have to the presence of an inspector on a major murder case, he had never asked for identification. If he had the whole case might have broken in front of him then, but it was a risk the man identifying himself as the "inspector" had been willing to take. He was clever, he was a brilliant actor, and it had turned out not to be a risk at all.

The inspector. The inspector! Oh, this man must have loved his wife for a long time, loved and hated her as well, watched her from a distance, then slowly infiltrated himself into her life.

Who knew what manner of man he might be? Who could even touch the mask? How could his wife, that gentle, diffuse woman distracted by her own sorrow, have doubted whatever nonsensical stories he gave her to explain his original appearance? The inspector had fooled him—a hard, sophisticated businessman with half a million dollars in hidden, accumulated, tax-free securities—for a long time; his wife would have never questioned any part of him.

So, it must have been with Robinson that the plan, in all its diabolicism, had been conceived. The "inspector" and Robinson bending their heads against one another, sharing dreadful confidences from the beginning. Murder his wife to begin and then plant the securities which Robinson somehow had remembered seeing that day when inadvertently he had left them on his desk and gone out for lunch near the corpse in order to tie the crime inextricably to the husband. He was already in trouble with the securities once discovered; what more logical, after tax evasion, than murder? Authorities, particularly police, thought in this way.

Robinson would have been the only possible means of divining the location of the securities in the office and the "inspector" must have worked with him carefully to set up the plan. How they must have laughed! and then their faces lapsing into purpose as they had gathered more tightly to roll up the net.

The "inspector's" motives would always be shrouded—he can accept this, there are things in life which he will never know—but Robinson's would not. He would have needed the securities for himself, control of the business, immunity from detection. An embezzlement of twenty-five long years' duration would have shortly been discovered anyway and everything would have collapsed. The annual audit, he thinks excitedly, was just about due under the new accounts for the first time.

Robinson would have known that he had very little time to act. This was part of the motive but will also make the solution easier. As it was, Robinson stood to benefit in two ways. He would hide the embezzlement forever and he would assume full control of the firm.

Until now, then, the plan in its malevolence and cunning had worked well. If it had not been for this last-minute deduction on which Robinson and the "inspector" could not have counted it would have succeeded. But now, given only a little more time he could clear himself and bring it down around them.

The police. He will call the police and tell them everything patiently, carefully. Already they have traced him to this miserable, dangerous hotel. Patrolmen have parked cars outside. They are prowling through the gray corridors pounding at doors, ignoring the drug traffic in their eagerness to get at him. It will not be long until they trace his room number through the little clerk downstairs and find him.

But the same drives, he hopes, that enabled them to trace

his whereabouts so skillfully will underline their willingness to listen.

Surely the authorities want this crime solved as much as he does.

And once the pieces begin to fall into place—the "inspector" who is not an inspector, the strange behavior of Robinson, the circumstances of the firm's accounting—the end will come quickly. The "inspector" at least must, as part of the plan, remain in sight, continuing his normal activities, being accessible. The police will find him quickly and quickly the confirming story will emerge.

For many years Robinson himself has been under great strain; these last few weeks must have been a nightmare for him as well—a dread tight-roping between necessity to continue and the urge to confess.

Robinson will be found. He will tell them everything quickly.

So. The police. He will call them now and set in motion that series of events which will free him. The authorities will not be able to bring back his wife and he realizes that to a certain extent that does make the crime his because he allowed their marriage to die. But this is something for which he will have to atone carefully, in a private way, in whatever years remain.

For an instant he thinks of phoning his doctor instead and having him make the call to the police to negotiate a meeting, but he realizes that it is too late for this kind of caution and so he picks up the phone with determination, choking slightly. Fetid air pours in from the walls. Decrepit. The hotel is impossible. You cannot blame tenants for the quality of lives they must lead living here.

But he, he at least will live in better circumstances soon.

In possession of himself for the first time in many weeks he leans forward intensely.

But it occurs to him in the midst of dialing that he has, so far, murdered his wife, his doctor, his business partner and the police inspector sent out for routine questioning on these murders and that he is very tired of hiding in a hotel room, becoming bored with the reduction he has made of his life. Figures. He needs more figures in his speculations, that is all. He cannot manipulate just the four of them forever.

"Pardon me," he says to the desk clerk who has come politely on the line after the long hold. "Pardon me, but would you bring me another cup of coffee and maybe a bottle of scotch up here?" He has a relationship with the desk clerk. It is a familiar errand.

"And I'll have something extra for you," he adds cunningly to speed the little clerk on his errand and puts down the phone.

"Yes, sir, here it is," the clerk says, entering a few moments later . . . and then falls dead with a .32 caliber bullet in his heart, falls dead on the sheets beside him and as he does so the doctor, the inspector, his wife and Robinson all turn to congratulate the clerk with relief on their faces and to welcome at last a new member into the club.

CROWDED LIVES

CLARK HOWARD

Sixth Avenue

(Originally published in 1989)

George Simms stood across the street on Sixth Avenue and looked at the old Algiers Hotel. It did not appear markedly different than he remembered it from years earlier. There were a couple of vagrants loitering outside and a few scruffy kids playing where previously a uniformed doorman would never have allowed, but the vagrants and the kids were there because the neighborhood had gone so far downhill. The hotel itself, twelve stories tall, standing formidably behind its marqueed entrance, was outwardly unchanged, as if its dignity, its style, might still be intact. George Simms knew, however, that inside would be a different story entirely.

When there was a lull in traffic, Simms crossed the street and tried five of the eight entry doors before he found one unlocked. Walking quietly across a marble floor, he stopped at the edge of the foyer and looked at the lobby. The Italian-marble columns were still there, and some leaded windows high up in the wall that faced an inner courtyard, but that was all that remained unscathed. Most of the mahogany wainscoting and pilasters was warped, scratched, scarred, or broken off. The velvet tapestries were dusty and torn. The carpeting was worn, ripped, curling up at the corners. A lot of the original lobby furniture was still there, overstuffed chairs and divans on which stylishly dressed women had once taken afternoon tea. The women sitting on them now, George Simms observed, wore sweatshirts and Levis, and drank their coffee out of cardboard cups. Their children, perhaps two dozen of them—like their mothers, of various colors—were playing on the worn carpet, hiding behind the torn tapestries, or scribbling on the mahogany with stubs of crayon. Off in the corners sat a few elderly persons who watched them silently.

Across the foyer, a stout, uniformed woman sat at an incongruous green-metal desk under a sign that read: ALL VISITORS MUST SIGN IN AND OUT. She had been watching Simms since he had walked in and finally said, "Can I help you?"

Simms went over to her. "I'm supposed to go to work for Charlie Hosey."

"You from the halfway house?"

"Yes."

"Okay, you got to see Max Wallace first. He's head of security on the premises. See the grand ballroom over there—those big doors that are chained shut? Go down the hall next to them—you'll see his office."

Simms threaded his way through the playing children, past the women whose conversation ceased as he went by, past the big ballroom doors which did have a length of chain connected to their brass handles by a padlock, and down a hall to a door that had ASSISTANT MANAGER lettered into its mahogany surface and a plastic sign reading *Security* thumbtacked above it.

A black man dressed in starched, creased khaki, Max Wallace was thick but not fat, built like a fire hydrant, with eyes that riveted wherever they focused. As soon as Simms entered, they riveted on him. "Let's see your assignment paper," he said without preliminary.

Simms hesitated. "The job counselor at the halfway house said I was supposed to give that to Charlie Hosey."

"I don't care what the job counselor at the halfway house told you, bud. *I'm* in charge of these premises, not him. I want to see your assignment paper—now." He held out a thick hand. Simms gave him the folded paper he wanted. Wallace's laser eyes flicked over it. "General maintenance man," he read, and grunted contemptuously. He tossed the paper back to Simms. "What'd you serve time for, Simms?" he asked, leaning forward, his words almost a challenge.

"You're not allowed to ask me that," Simms told him.

Wallace's eyes flashed anger, but just for an instant. He sat back. "They tell you that at the *halfway house?*" he asked.

"Yes." Simms wished he had a drink of water.

"Then I guess you also know that I can't ask where you did your time, or even how much time you did—that right?"

"Yes. Right."

"Well, since I'm not allowed to know anything about *you*, I'm going to tell you a few things about me. First of all, understand one thing: I'm in charge of every*thing* and every*body* inside these premises. The Algiers is a city welfare hotel. There are nearly three hundred indigent families living here, many of them just women with young children." Wallace tilted his head with a coyness surprising for his size. "I guess you been away from women for quite a spell, haven't you?"

Simms didn't say anything. Wallace's eyes narrowed. "Couldn't be that you were away for rape, could it, Simms? I mean, it would be just like those halfway-house fools to put a rapist in a building full of women to try to prove he's been re-ha-bil-i-tated. Is that it, Simms? You a rapo?"

"I told you, you're not allowed to—"

"I heard you the first time." Wallace pointed a threatening finger. "Every woman in this building is under my protection, Simms. I catch you out of line with any of them, you even look down one of their blouses when they bend over, and I'll have your ass back in the slammer so quick you'll think you never got out. Understand me?"

"I understand," Simms said quietly. He was relieved when Wallace looked away long enough to pick up the phone and dial two digits.

"Charlie, this is Max," he said. "Come to my office and get your new helper." When he hung up, he sat far back in his swivel chair, the springs squeaking with his weight, and carefully unwrapped a large black cigar that could have been designed with him in mind. Lighting it with an old-fashioned flip-top Zippo, he released several puffs of pungent smoke into the close little office. As he removed the cigar from his teeth, he actually smiled.

"Maybe I misjudged you, Simms," he said almost pleasantly. "Maybe you're not a rapo, after all." His smile, there for mere seconds, vanished and his voice turned harsh again. "Maybe you're a child molester. A pervert. Is that what you are, Simms?"

George Simms didn't have to worry about answering that one, because at that moment Charlie Hosey walked in.

"I can really use you," Hosey said as he showed Simms around the hotel. He was an older, short, balding man with a vague whiskey smell about him. "It ain't bad keeping up with the big stuff—the boiler, the hot-water heaters, the electrical system. It's the little stuff that runs me ragged. The minor plumbing repairs, jammed locks, hotplates shorted out, lighting fixtures that don't work. You can handle all that kinda stuff, can't you?"

"Sure," Simms said. "Those are the same problems I used to take care of in the cellhouse. Except for jammed locks, that is—I wasn't allowed to mess with locks."

"I guess not," Hosey said.

"Did you come here through the halfway house, too?" Simms asked.

"Me? No. I used to work here when the Algiers was a *real* hotel. I was maintenance superintendent when the place closed down. After that, I went to St. Luke's Hospital for a few years. Then when I seen in the paper where the city was gonna lease the Algiers as a welfare hotel, I went and seen about coming back. They was glad to get me. Keeping this place going is like working in a secondhand tire shop—it's patch, patch, patch all the time."

They paused at the chained doors. "That's the Moroccan Ballroom," Hosey said. "The Duke and Duchess of Windsor used to throw parties in there. I seen 'em. It's got picnic tables in it now—the Help for the Homeless people come in twice a day and serve free meals. Over here—" the little man led Simms across the lobby to a pair of locked leather-padded doors "—is the Casablanca Club. It used to be a real ritzy nightclub. All the big show people used to perform in there: Jolson, Helen Morgan, Blossom Seeley and Bennie Fields, Ruth Etting. I seen 'em." He sighed wistfully. "Yeah, this place used to be something."

They rode a service elevator, which Hosey had to unlock, down to the boiler room in the basement. On the way down, Simms asked, "What's with this guy Wallace, anyway? He comes on like a concentration-camp guard."

"Ex-cop," Hosey said. "Takes his job real serious." After a beat to think it over, he added, "I guess I ought to tell you—Max don't much like the halfway house sending guys to work here. You're the third one they sent. The other two didn't last long. Max, he don't give a guy much slack. He particularly don't like nobody messing around with one of the young women that lives here." Hosey shrugged. "I ain't telling you what to do, understand—but you asked and I thought you should know."

"Thanks," said Simms. "I appreciate it."

Off the big boiler room was the maintenance office: a badly scarred wooden desk littered with papers and miscellaneous junk in front of a padded chair that had a patch repaired with black electrical tape. A wooden straight chair stood in front of the desk, an old metal file-cabinet next to it. A pinup-girl calendar from a plumbing-supply company was thumbtacked to the wall. At the back of the office was a curtained doorway leading to a small storeroom. The curtain wasn't closed all the way and Simms caught a glimpse of a cot in the room.

"Here's where I list all the minor repairs to be done," Hosey said, showing Simms a clipboard hanging on a nail. "Every day you just go down the list and do as many of 'em as you can. I ain't gonna dog you as long as you do a reasonable amount of work. I know alls you're getting is minimum wage for now. But if you work out and want a permanent job when you're released from the halfway house, we can talk about it."

"I'll do a good job for you, Mr. Hosey," Simms told him.

"Just call me Charlie," said the little man.

A week later, Simms was sitting on the fire stairs at the end of the seventh-floor corridor having a smoke and drinking coffee from a small thermos he'd bought. His toolbelt and the clipboard of job orders lay on the step next to him. He had been sitting there for nearly an hour when the door to Room 704 opened and a little Puerto Rican girl, five or six years old,

198 // Manhattan Noir 2

came out into the corridor to play. Pretty, clay-colored, with raven hair, she had on jeans and a sweater and carried a doll that was missing a hand. Sitting on the worn carpet with her back to the wall, she propped up her knees, sat the doll on them, and began to braid the doll's hair.

Simms watched her for a couple of minutes, then leaned forward a little and spoke to her. "Hello." He said it very quietly so as not to frighten her.

She looked at him but didn't speak back.

"My name's George," he said. "I work here." He showed her the toolbelt. "See?" The little girl looked, then turned her attention back to the doll. "That sure is a pretty doll," Simms said. "But what happened to her hand?"

"She was in a accident," the child said, not looking at him.

"That's too bad," Simms said consolingly. "But she's a very lucky little doll to have you to take care of her." From the pocket of his denim workshirt, he took a pack of chewing gum. Slowly unwrapping a stick, he put it in his mouth. The little girl was watching him. "Would you like some gum?" he asked. She looked back at her doll without answering. "It's fruit-flavored," he said. "Here—" he held out a stick "—have some."

The girl rose and walked over to him. She stood before the stairs he was sitting on and Simms gave her the gum and watched as she unwrapped it and put it in her mouth. As she began to chew, she smiled.

"See, I told you it was good," Simms said. A lock of hair had fallen over her forehead and Simms reached out and brushed it back. "Now, I told you my name, but if we're going to be friends you've got to tell me yours."

Just then a woman came out of 704 and strode urgently

CLARK HOWARD // 199

over to them. "Debbie, what are you doing?" she said irritably.

Simms frowned. Debbie? *Debbie?* What the hell kind of name was that for a Puerto Rican kid?

The woman took the girl by one arm. "You know you're supposed to stay right by the door. And not talk to strangers."

"It's okay," Simms said, smiling. "I work here."

"I don't give a damn where you work!" the woman snapped. She was pretty—an older version of the child, except that her eyes had no innocence left in them. "What have you got in your mouth?" she demanded of Debbie. "Spit it out," she ordered, holding her hand under the child's mouth. "Now get back in the room!" As the little girl hurried away, the woman turned her anger on Simms. "What the hell do you think you're doing, giving gum to my kid? Who the hell are you, anyway?"

"My name's George," Simms said. "I work here." He held up the toolbelt. "I fix things—"

"Yeah. Well, if I ever catch you giving anything to my kid again I'm gonna fix *you*." The woman stuck the wad of gum on the handle of his screwdriver. "Stay away from my kid!"

She stalked away.

A few days later, Simms went down to the maintenance office for some new work orders and Hosey was not at his desk. Simms pulled the curtain aside and looked into the storeroom for him. He wasn't there, either. It was the first time Simms had seen the storeroom except for an occasional glimpse when the curtains were left open an inch or so. Now he looked around curiously. The cot he'd seen his first day was of the ordinary folding variety, with a blue-striped mattress and a couple of gray blankets that had ST. LUKE HOSPITAL printed on them. An upturned wooden crate served as a nightstand. On it was a cheap little lamp, an ashtray full of cigarette butts, and a glossy porno magazine with a nude woman in bondage on the cover. Standing on the floor next to the cot was an almost empty Jim Beam bottle. A few of Hosey's extra clothes hung from nails in the wall.

The phone on Hosey's desk rang. Simms closed the curtain and answered it. "Maintenance."

"Where's Charlie?"

Simms recognized Max Wallace's voice. "I don't know, I just walked in."

"Find him," Wallace ordered crisply. "Then the two of you get up to my office—*fast.*"

Simms found Hosey over in a section of the basement that had been converted into a laundry room for the welfare tenants. He had the drum out of a clothes dryer and was resetting its axle. Simms told him about Wallace's call and Hosey put aside his work. "Did he say what it was about?" he asked.

"No," said Simms. "He just sounded mad—as usual."

When they got to the security office, Max was with a little black girl of eight or nine and her mother. Wallace glanced at Hosey, glared at Simms, and knelt in front of the girl. "Sweetheart, I want you to look at these two men and tell me if it was either one of them that scared you." The child hesitated and Wallace gently patted her head. "It's all right. Come on now, take a look for me."

The little girl looked at Hosey and Simms, frowned, seemed to ponder, and finally said, "I'm not sure. It was so dark—" Her voice broke and she whimpered a little.

Wallace gestured to her mother. "I'll talk to her again later. Meantime, try to go on with her normal routine as much as you can. Don't avoid the subject, but don't talk about it like it was the end of the world, either. Understand?"

"Yes, all right," the mother replied in a strained voice. She took her daughter and left.

Wallace sat behind his desk and studied Hosey and Simms with cold eyes. "That little girl," he said evenly, "was on her way down the stairs to go to school this morning when a man accosted her on the landing between the lobby and two. She says the man tried to kiss her. The light on the landing was out, but she saw that he was a white man and she says he had a funny smell."

"Well, why pick on us?" Hosey said indignantly.

"You're white and you're in the building," Wallace said.

"For Christ's sake, there's probably two or three dozen white guys living in the place," Hosey argued. "And there's boyfriends that sneak in and spend the night, there's johns that some of these women go out and pick up for extra money. You got no right to single us out, Wallace."

"Nobody said I was singling you out. I always check the obvious first." The security man reached for his phone. "You can go," he told them.

His eyes lingered on Simms until he was out the door.

That afternoon, Simms was helping Hosey rehang one of the lobby doors that the kids had misaligned by swinging on it. "Maybe I shouldn't have got so hot at Max," the little man mused. "He's just trying to do his job. It ain't an easy one, either—there's lots going on in this place that shouldn't be going on. Prostitution, drug sales, stolen property being sold—"

"I guess you never expected to see those kind of things in the Algiers," Simms sympathized.

"Not stuff like that, never," Hosey declared. "'Course, in any big city hotel you're gonna get your share of illegal goings-on. Hell, I used to see Meyer Lansky and Lucky Luciano come in here regular to have a drink in the Oasis Bar—there's no telling what kind of crooked business they was talking about. And one time we found out there was a high-price call-girl ring operating out of what used to be the penthouse suite. It was supposed to be rented to this wealthy Texas dame and her four daughters—well, they wasn't her daughters at all, if you know what I mean."

Hosey grinned. "Funniest thing that ever happened was the time some teller over at Chase Manhattan got conned by a blonde who was a dead ringer for Lana Turner. She was supposed to run away with him, see, after he embezzled a bundle of dough, but what she really did was run away *from* him—*with* the dough. The cops arrested him right here in the hotel, sitting on the bed, suitcase all packed, waiting for her to come back." While Hosey was talking, Simms noticed Debbie's mother go into the coffee shop across the street from the hotel. Debbie wasn't with her. "She got caught later on," Hosey said.

"Who?"

"The blonde that looked like Lana Turner. She got caught down in Florida somewheres. Only had about ten thousand dollars left. Claimed the bank teller only gave her twenty. The bank said a hundred thousand was stole. If you ask me, the bankers probably took the difference." Hosey used an electric drill on a long extension cord to screw in the last door-hinge. "Well, that about does it. I wish there was some way to keep the kids from swinging on it, but I guess there ain't. We'll be fixing it again in a month."

"Okay if I take a few minutes off, Charlie?" Simms said.

He could see Debbie's mother sitting by the coffee-shop window with a cup in front of her.

"Sure, take a break," Hosey said, winding up his extension cord.

Simms trotted over to the coffee shop and went to the table where Debbie's mother sat. "Can I talk to you a minute?" he asked.

She looked up from a folded section of classified ads. "What about?"

Simms sat across from her. "I just wanted to tell you I was sorry for what happened about the gum. I guess I wasn't thinking. I mean, it was just a natural thing to offer the kid a stick of gum. It never occurred to me how it might look."

"Just stay away from her, okay?" the woman said firmly.

"Yeah, sure I will," Simms assured. "I just wanted you to know I didn't mean nothing by it. I was only trying to be friendly."

"Okay, but don't let it happen again." She sighed wearily. "That place over there—" she bobbed her chin at the hotel "—is a sewer. A mother with a kid can't be too careful."

"I know, I realize that now. I'm sorry, okay?" He took a pack of gum from his shirt pocket. "How about you?" he asked, raising his eyebrows. "*You* want a stick of gum?"

She half smiled in spite of herself. "Why not?" She took a stick and put it in her mouth.

"Looking for a job?" Simms asked, nodding at the classifieds.

"Yeah. Soon's I find one, I'm getting out of that dump over there."

"Listen," he told her, "I go to this place at night, it's kind of a community center, and sometimes I hear about job openings over there. If I hear of anything I think might interest you, I'll let you know."

Her eyes flashed suspicion. "What do you think that'll get you?"

"What do you mean?"

"I don't sleep around, man."

"Hey," Simms said righteously, "I'm just trying to be a nice guy. Lighten up a little."

She sighed again. "Well, you just never know. Seems like everybody's out to get something."

"I know. It's hard to tell who's being straight with you sometimes." Simms drummed his fingers on the tabletop. After a moment, he asked, "So where's Debbie?"

"She's in daycare until three."

"How'd you happen to give her a name like Debbie?" he asked. "I mean, that's kind of an all-American girl-next-door name."

"Maybe I'd like her to grow up to be an all-American girl-next-door. Anything wrong with that?"

"No, not at all. No offense intended," he said quickly. "Hey, speaking of names, what's yours?"

"Lupe Mercado," she told him.

"I'm George Simms," he said. He extended his hand and, after first hesitating, she shook it. "If you ever need anything fixed in your room," he said, "just let me know. You don't have to fill out a form and wait your turn, I'll do it for you right away."

Lupe shrugged. "Okay." There was a tiny pinch at the top of her nose.

"I better be getting back," Simms said, rising. "Thanks for not being mad at me anymore."

Outside, as he waited to cross the street, he looked back

and saw her watching him suspiciously. He smiled and waved. She still doesn't trust me all that much, he thought. But for his purposes, that was okay. All he needed was a little trust.

For a week, Simms watched Lupe Mercado come and go. Her routine never varied. First thing in the morning she took Debbie to daycare, then she spent the rest of the morning job-hunting. At noon she was usually back at the hotel for the free meal served by Help for the Homeless. After lunch she'd sit in the lobby or go across to the coffee shop and read the classifieds again to see if there was anything she missed that morning. Sometimes Simms would see her using one of the pay phones in the lobby to call about jobs. Then, just before three, she'd leave to get her daughter from daycare.

Now and then Simms would speak to her in passing or wave to her across the lobby, but he didn't intrude on what she was doing or in any way act as if he was presuming a friendship. All he wanted to do was keep her aware of him until he was ready.

He picked Thursday as the day. Thursday: late in the week when people were tired, not as alert, laboring toward the weekend. Simms had already selected the boiler-room door that led to the alley as the way by which he'd leave the hotel. He knew he'd have to move fast—Max Wallace would be after him very quickly.

At three-thirty, Simms was on the seventh floor when Lupe Mercado got off the elevator with Debbie and came down the corridor to 704. Simms pretended to be in a hurry.

"I was hoping I'd run into you," he said in a rush of words. "I only got a second—there's a bad leaky pipe in the basement I got to tend to." Fumbling in his pocket, he pulled out a slip of paper. "This lady's got a dress shop down in the Village.

She wants somebody to work in her stockroom—says she'll train somebody with no experience, says it's good pay plus a discount on clothes. Give her a call as soon as you can, the job might still be open." Pressing the slip of paper into her hand, he hurried down the corridor to the fire stairs. He made sure his footsteps sounded loudly as he ran down to six, and half-way down to five. Then he abruptly turned and crept quietly back up to seven. Standing just around the corner from the corridor, he heard Lupe speaking to her daughter.

"I'll be at the phone in the lobby—just for a few minutes. You stay inside until I get back. Don't play in the hall."

Hearing a door close, Simms peered around the corner. Lupe Mercado was hurrying toward the elevator. He waited until she got on the elevator, then walked quickly to Room 704. When he knocked, Debbie opened the door on a chain.

"Debbie," he said easily, "call your mother to the door—I gave her the wrong phone number."

"She went downstairs."

"Oh. Well, let me in and I'll wait for her. I have to give her the right number."

He took a pack of gum from his pocket and put a stick in his mouth. "It's okay," he assured her. "Your mother and I are friends. You know I'm helping her find a job." Unwrapping another stick of gum, he held it through the opening.

Debbie hesitated. Then she took it. Simms unfolded several work orders he had stuck under his toolbelt. "While I'm waiting, I want to check something in your bathroom that needs fixing." He added just a hint of firmness to his voice. "Open the door now, Debbie, so I can get to work."

Debbie took the chain off and opened the door. When Simms got inside, he closed and locked the door behind him.

* * *

In the lobby, Lupe hung up the telephone and stared at the slip of paper in confusion. It was the number of a dress shop in the Village, all right, but the sales clerk Lupe had talked to knew nothing of any stockroom job that was open. The clerk had called the manager to the phone, but the manager knew nothing about it, either. And the owner of the store was out of town on a buying trip.

Puzzled, Lupe started back toward the elevators. Charlie Hosey was near the elevator bank, repairing a drinking fountain. Max Wallace had just walked up to him. "Where's Simms?" she heard Wallace ask the maintenance man.

"He went up to seven to do something," Hosey said. "He ain't come down yet."

Lupe stopped and stared at them. "Oh, my God!" she said.

"What's the matter?" Wallace asked.

Without answering, Lupe ran toward the elevators.

"Simms," Wallace said tightly. "I knew it!" He ran after Lupe.

Hosey ran after both of them.

In the bathroom of 704, Debbie was sitting on the edge of the tub, watching Simms in fascination. He had emptied the medicine cabinet of all its contents, piling them in the sink. Then, with a power screw-remover, he had unscrewed four three-inch wood screws that held the metal medicine cabinet into the wall studs on each side of it. With a small chisel, he'd pried loose the top, bottom, and both sides of the cabinet and taken it out of the wall. Then he had stuck his arm far down into the opening between the walls and pulled up a pillow-case with *Algiers Hotel* embroidered across the hem. "Thanks, kid," he said, tucking the pillowcase under one arm. "Tell your mother to call Maintenance to have this put back in."

He started for the door and Debbie followed him. At the door, he paused and gave her the rest of the pack of gum. "Your mother's right, you know," he told her. "You really shouldn't talk to strangers or take gum or anything. Promise me you won't do it again."

Smiling shyly, Debbie said, "I promise, George."

Simms opened the door and stepped into the corridor. Max Wallace, just hurrying up, put a gun in his face. "Move a muscle and you're gone," he said coldly.

Simms froze. Lupe Mercado rushed past him to gather Debbie into her arms. "My baby! What did he do to you?" she cried.

"I didn't do anything to her—" Simms started to protest.

"Shut up!" Wallace ordered.

Peering past Wallace's shoulder, Charlie Hosey's face brightened. "Now I remember you! You're the bank teller! I always thought you looked familiar—"

Wallace frowned. "That Chase Manhattan embezzler you told me about?"

"That's the one," said Hosey. "The one who hooked up with the Lana Turner lookalike."

Wallace snatched the pillowcase from Simms and looked inside it. "Well, I'll be damned," he whispered.

"It must have been hidden in that room all these years," Hosey said. "Eighty thousand dollars."

Lupe stared at the bundles of currency in the pillowcase, then turned her eyes incredulously to Simms, her lips parted in stunned disbelief. Wallace put handcuffs on Simms and started leading him away.

"Why didn't you tell me?" Lupe asked, following them down the hall, indignation rising. "We could have shared it!

We could have both got out of this sewer! Why didn't you trust me enough to tell me?"

"Me trust *you?*" Simms said. "You didn't even trust me enough to give your kid a stick of gum!"

In the middle of the corridor, Wallace pushed Simms onto the elevator. "You could have *tried!*" Lupe said. Then more softly she added, "*I* could have tried—"

"Well, it's too late now," Simms said flatly as the elevator door closed them off from each other for the last time.

YOUNG ISAAC

JEROME CHARYN

Lower East Side

(Originally published in 1990)

I t was West Broadway, a land of small factories that could
have produced every button and zipper in the world.
Isaac loved to spy on all these button and zipper men,
who would leave their lofts in the middle of the afternoon
and congregate in a candy store, where they drank a curious
concoction of malt and cream soda. They'd arrived in the '20s
from London's East End. The language they spoke was almost
indecipherable, even though Isaac's dad had come out of the
same streets. But Joel Sidel didn't struggle over zippers. He was
the fur-collar prince, and he was gathering a nice little nest.
He had an exclusive contract with the Navy to manufacture
fur collars for foul-weather coats. It kept him out of the war.
He was already a millionaire in 1943, but he wouldn't give
up the tiny house that was ensconced between two button
factories. "I'm one of the downtown Sidels," he liked to say.
"Never was an uptown man." He wore suspenders lined with
jewels. He had mistresses of every persuasion. He neglected
his wife and children and ran to the Salmagundi Club, where
he mingled with artists, because Joel would rather have been
a painter than a fur-collar prince. He wanted the Germans to
get the hell out of Paris, so he could move in. "How can I go
to Montmartre and meet Picasso when there's storm troopers
on every block?"

If Isaac tried to reason with him—"Dad, Dad, you have your business in Manhattan"—the West Broadway Picasso would cuff him on the ear.

"What would you know? You're a truant. You lie. You steal."

Isaac could have returned the cuff. At thirteen he was a head taller than Joel. But he wouldn't have hit his own dad. He loved the old man, as much as he could love a father who played the Bedouin with his own family. If Isaac had become a thief, wasn't it out of some dread that Joel would abandon him? Joel had his new Jerusalem: the hills of Montmartre. And Isaac had his wealth of ration stamps.

The stamps came in buff-colored booklets issued by the OPA, Office of Price Administration. It was a federal offense to traffic in stolen stamps. "Persons who violate rationing regulations are subject to $10,000 fine or imprisonment, or both." That's what it said on the front of each book. But Isaac prized the blue and red stamps, with their pictures of cannons and tanks, aircraft carriers and fighter planes . . .

He never sold a book to individual clients. That would have been dumb. Because the OPA had their own detectives. Isaac always used a middleman, Stoney Whitehall, the air raid warden. Stoney could work up a deal during air raid drills, while he wore his white helmet and poked around with a whistle and a flashlight, snarling, "Close the blinds, will ya? It has to be midnight."

He took whatever merchandise Isaac had, paying him in old, crumpled bills that could never be traced back to Stoney himself. When Isaac's supply was low, the warden would mutter, "I need product, kid. I can't go out empty-handed. I might get killed."

Isaac wasn't a wholesaler. He could clip only one book at a time, from absentminded mothers who left their purses open or forgot to lock their doors, from housewives at the Essex Street indoor market who were much too busy counting their change to notice Isaac Sidel. He was very agile for a boy who resembled a bear. He had none of the obvious signs of a thief. He wasn't nervous. His eyes didn't wander. He didn't drool at the mouth, or play with himself in front of the housewives. He could linger at a merchant's stall. He was the son of Joel Sidel. He would buy fruit for his woeful family. There was always an alibi for Isaac.

But the warden wouldn't leave him alone. He waylaid Isaac outside the Essex Street market.

"Stoney," Isaac said, "you shouldn't come here. People will talk."

"Never mind. Gimme what you got."

He ripped at Isaac, removed the single booklet Isaac had pocketed in his pants. The booklet cost Isaac an hour's work. The boy had waited like a spider, hovered between two stalls, to catch the right victim. And now Stoney was ruining Isaac.

He slapped the boy. Isaac swallowed blood. Merchants wandered in and out of the market. Stoney walked away.

It was one more piece of bitterness Isaac had to bear. He was losing his dad to the Salmagundi Club and some phantom idea of art. His mom had opened a junk shop to show the fur-collar prince she could survive without him, while his baby brother Leo still pissed in his pants.

Isaac couldn't forget that slap. He met Florsheim, the assistant principal, near the Loew's Delancey. Florsheim was a failed scholar of Greek. He'd abandoned Euripides to become a glorified custodian in the public schools of New York. It was from Florsheim that Isaac had learned about the terrible fate of men and women in a wounded world. Isaac had been his best pupil before he eloped from P.S. 88 to begin his career as a criminal.

"I know," Florsheim said, sadness on his scholar's face. He looked like a consumptive child. He was much more delicate than the girls and boys he had to guard. Isaac had disappointed him.

"Fourteen days."

"I don't feel good," Isaac said. "I need the fresh air."

"Is that why you live inside a market, breathing chicken feathers?"

"I have to shop," Isaac said. "We're alone. My father's new address is the Salmagundi Club."

Florsheim touched him with a hand that felt like a broken wing. Isaac couldn't even consider it a slap.

"You're stealing ration stamps."

"Prove it," Isaac said.

"Fourteen days. I can't cover for you, Sidel. Soldiers are dying and you steal stamps."

It's a living, Isaac wanted to say, but he wouldn't provoke the scholar into another pathetic slap. He liked Florsheim the way he liked the button men, with their crazy talk.

He left Florsheim and marched to the air raid wardens' barracks, a storefront on Attorney Street. Isaac had no fear of the wardens, who were idlers and opportunists, peddlers of other people's merchandise. They wore white armbands, sleeping with helmets over their eyes, like some slothful army. He would have enjoyed shaking them out of their bunks, copping their helmets, and tossing those hard white hats over the Williamsburg Bridge.

"Where's Stoney?"

He had to ask again, going from bunk to bunk, before one

of the wardens sang from under his hat, "Mendel's. He's at Mendel's if anyone wants to know."

Isaac was disheartened. He could never walk into Mendel's bar. He wouldn't have dared. Mendel's had been the Manhattan headquarters of Murder, Inc., until Governor Dewey kicked all those gunmen in the pants. The bar was on Clinton Street, near the Williamsburg Bridge. It had beer mugs in the window, rotting flowers from one of the brethren's funerals, a peeling photograph of FDR, whom the gangsters considered *their* President, old hunting scenes of New Amsterdam, with bare-chested Indians and peg-legged Peter Stuyvesant, who was as unkind to criminals as Dewey himself. Isaac dreamt that he would be welcomed into the brotherhood of Mendel's some day. Nothing seemed more important. Not ration stamps. Not the war. Not the New York Giants, who sat in the cellar in 1943, orphans of their own little war. Nothing mattered as much as an open ticket to Mendel's. Isaac arrived on Clinton Street, his nose against the glass, watching and waiting for a miracle to happen.

The door opened. Stoney stood with a beer mug, his little eyes like rodents. He talked that crazy talk of the button men.

"Come in, will ya, love? Don't stand there like a silly cow."

And Isaac, with a blush on his face, entered the heartland of Mendel's. It stank of beer and sawdust and foul breath. Isaac didn't mind. He'd never seen women in a bar, but the women of Mendel's had broad shoulders and a thick, raucous laugh. They inspected Isaac as if he were some prize cattle. They felt his arm and reached down to stroke his thigh. Isaac was ashamed, because he had on his winter underwear.

"A cute one, Stoney, will you lend him out?"

"Not a chance," the warden said, basking over Isaac. "The twit is my property." He winked at the barman, who brought Isaac a glass of seltzer water with a cherry at the bottom. The warden whispered in Isaac's ear. "Make a toast, will ya, you ungrateful little sod."

Isaac clutched the glass of seltzer, but he didn't know what to say.

"To hell with Tom Dewey!" shouted one of the women.

"May he rot with Kid Twist!"

Twist was a Murder, Inc. gunman until he became a stoolie for the Brooklyn D.A. He fell out the window of a Coney Island hotel while he was in the company of six cops. He was the shame of Mendel's bar, because in the old days Twist would come over from Brooklyn to sit at Mendel's and buy drinks for the whole population.

The gassy water must have woken Isaac. "To the Bomber," he said, "the greatest center-fielder in the world."

"To the Bomber."

"To the Bomber."

Harry "Bomber" Lieberman was a utility man the Giants had brought up in the second winter of the war, while their best men were overseas. But he didn't play like a utility man. He was an antelope, crashing into fences and catching fly balls on a team that had already died.

"To the Bomber," Stoney said, smiling at Isaac. "Now kid, what the hell is it you want?"

"You owe me money, Mr. Whitehall. I came to collect."

The warden turned to Mendel's clientele, his nostrils flaring with pretended rage.

"I made this boy. God is my witness. I gave him his start. I bring him through the door, and this is the thanks I get."

"I came to collect."

Mendel's women were beginning to admire the brevity of Isaac's style. They liked his bearish looks and the scratchy feel of his long johns. They shut their eyes and imagined Isaac riding them in one of Mendel's back rooms.

"Leave the boy alone," said Diana Moon, the huskiest of these sisters. "Leave him alone."

"None ya business," said Stoney, and he went to slap Isaac. But Diana Moon hooked her fingers into his belt. And the boy began to pound Stoney Whitehall in the middle of a long afternoon. Stoney fell under the bar, and Mendel's forgot about him. He was only an air raid warden who'd delivered contraband ration booklets to Eric Fish, a renegade police captain and survivor of Murder, Inc. Fish had escaped the prosecutors because he wasn't flamboyant or greedy. It was Fish who'd complained about Stoney's fallen quota of stamps, Fish who'd promised to set the warden's little house on fire if the quota didn't rise. He was a Clinton Street boy who'd become a cop, made captain, and then resigned to run with Dasher Abbandando and Kid Twist. Dasher died in the electric chair. And Captain Fish? He had a dark, unsmiling face. He could walk into headquarters on Centre Street and drink coffee with his old chiefs.

He didn't sell any of the contraband books. He had the names on the covers removed with eradicating ink. His own forgers wrote in the names of particular police commanders, and the captain offered these dun-colored books as gifts. That's how he'd built his own immunity during the war. He loansharked a little, always careful to waltz around his former comrades at 240 Centre Street. He got rich, but he never smiled. He must have been a student of Euripides, like Florsheim, the assistant principal.

Fish had his own table at the far side of the bar. He was always there. He sat in his old captain's tunic, the sleeves gone gray, the ribbons on his chest leaking a strange liquid. He called to Isaac across the smoke and gloom of Mendel's, beer mugs hanging upside down from the wall. "I want the child that beat up my air raid warden."

Isaac approached the captain's table, shivering with a curious joy. He imagined himself among the retinue of Eric Fish, the captain's own little specialist in ration stamps. He looked upon the darkest face he'd ever seen. All Isaac could catch were eyes and the wings of a nose.

"Who are you, then?"

"Isaac Sidel."

"Son of Joel, the fur-collar prince?"

"The same," Isaac said, refusing to falter in front of that black mask.

"Did you know that your father hires scabs?"

"I'm not surprised," Isaac said.

"I threatened to kill him a couple years ago." Isaac said nothing. "Tom Dewey got between me and your dad . . . Did you know I can never leave Manhattan? The D.A.'s men got together with the Treasury boys. They decided it might not look good on their scorecard to prosecute an ex-captain who had enough medals and ribbons to paper a district attorney's ass. So I made a deal. I promised never to leave this fucking island. Otherwise you think I'd be sitting here, smelling piss? I'm a prisoner, Mr. Isaac."

Like the Man in the Iron Mask, Isaac thought, because the captain himself had become a mask in the darkness of Mendel's.

"Twist," Isaac said.

"What? Are you talking about Abe Reles? Go on. Ask me anything."

"What happened to the Kid?"

"Loved him like a brother. But I couldn't protect no songbird. They hid him on Coney at the Neptune Hotel. But I got to the cops that were minding Reles. It was simple business. Because Abe would have ratted on everybody."

"I figured you were the Coney Island connection," Isaac said.

"You figured right. But I'm still short one air raid warden. Stoney's my butcher. He supplies me with stamps."

"But I did all the work."

"You? Your father's a fucking millionaire."

"But he's forgotten about the Sidels."

"I could break his head . . . as long as I don't have to leave Manhattan island. How old are you, Mr. Isaac?"

"Fourteen," Isaac muttered, adding a year to his personal calendar.

"One of Florsheim's brats?"

"Yes. But I've decided to leave school, Captain. I have a talent for stealing stamps."

"What do you think of Florsheim?"

"He has egg on his tie. He'll always be what he is. A small-time philosopher."

"Ah, you're not particularly fond of him."

"I am. He taught me Euripides. But Euripides can't put food on the table."

"And I suppose you'd like to become my new air raid warden."

"You won't regret it, Captain," Isaac said, looking into that bloodless mask. "I could diversify. I don't have to stick to stamps."

"And you'd break heads for me, keep whoever I wanted in line."

"Anything," Isaac said.

The captain leaped from his chair and pummeled Isaac into the ground. Ribbons fell off his chest. Medals flew everywhere. And Isaac felt the captain's fists. Knobs of stone. Mendel's women began to shriek. Diana Moon begged Eric Fish to stop this terrible vocation of slaughtering Isaac Sidel.

The captain breathed on Isaac. "Go to school. If I catch you in Mendel's, I'll kill you to death."

Diana Moon washed his swollen face with a wet rag, and Isaac crawled out of Mendel's. He returned to school, convinced that Florsheim was the captain's favorite cousin. The world belonged to Euripides. And Isaac was left with the grief of having to become a student again. He envied the clarity of other people's lives. The button men had their malt and cream soda. Sophie Sidel had her rags. Joel had the Salmagundi Club. Leo Sidel had the piss in his pants. Isaac looked in the mirror. There were lines of bitterness. The boy was beginning to grow some kind of mask.

He went to Euripides. The assistant principal had been avoiding Isaac in the halls of P.S. 88. But Isaac sneaked into Euripides's office. "How did you do it?"

Euripides wouldn't look at Isaac's wounds. "I'm sorry," he said.

"How did you do it?"

"I went to school with Eric Fish. I coached him in geometry. He wouldn't have graduated. He does me favors from time to time. We talk on the phone. I told him about the stamps. But I never dreamed he would hurt you, Isaac. I thought . . ."

"I could have had a brilliant career. Now I'm Euripides . . . like you."

Isaac walked out of P.S. 88. He passed the copper dome of police headquarters, with its four clocks, its stone figures representing the five boroughs, its porches, its balustrades, its two lions out front with their big teeth, and he wondered about his fall from grace. The policemen had their own palace. But it wasn't Mendel's.

He took the subway up to the Polo Grounds, crawled under a gate, sat in the bleachers while the wind howled in that empty shell. He wasn't lying to conjure up Harry Lieberman. It felt safe among the empty seats, the green railing, the dead grass. He wasn't a soldier or a center-fielder. He was a retired thief.

A groundsman saw him in the bleachers. "Hey, you, you son of a bitch."

Isaac didn't run. He sat in his green chair. The groundsman arrived with a hoe. "What the hell are you doing here?"

"Waiting for the Bomber."

"Jesus, you from out of town? Harry don't play in winter. The Giants are asleep . . . You figuring to sit until April or May?"

"If I have to," Isaac said.

The groundsman laughed. He tried not to stare at Isaac's face.

"Sit, but don't pee on the benches."

He abandoned Isaac, shoved across the stadium, and started to dig along some imaginary line between second base and the Bomber's own big country of center field.

LOVE IN THE LEAN YEARS

BY DONALD E. WESTLAKE

Wall Street

(Originally published in 1992)

C harles Dickens knew his stuff, you know. Listen to this: "Annual income twenty pounds, annual expenditure nineteen nineteen six, result happiness. Annual income twenty pounds, annual expenditure twenty pounds ought and six, result misery."

Right on. You adjust the numbers for inflation and what you've got right there is the history of Wall Street. At least, so much of the history of Wall Street as includes me: seven years. We had the good times and we lived high on that extra jolly sixpence, and now we live day by day the long decline of shortfall. Result misery.

Where did they all go, the sixpences of yesteryear? Oh, pshaw, we know where they went. You in Gstaad, him in Aruba, her in Paris and me in the men's room with a sanitary straw in my nose. We know where it went, all right.

My name's Kimball, by the way, here's my card. Bruce Kimball, with Rendall/LeBeau. Account exec. May I say I'm still making money for my clients? There's a lot of good stuff undervalued out there, my friend. You can still make money on the Street. Of course you can. I admit it's harder now, it's much harder when I have only thruppence and it's sixpence I need to keep my nose filled, build up that confidence, face the world with that winner's smile. Man, I'm only hitting on one nostril, you know? I'm *hurtin'*.

Nearly three years a widow; time to remarry. I need a true heart to share my penthouse apartment (unfurnished terrace, unfortunately) with its grand view of the city, my cottage (fourteen rooms) in Amagansett, the income of my portfolio of stocks.

An income—ah, me—which is less than it once was. One or two iffy margin calls, a few dividends undistributed, bad news can mount up, somehow. Or dismount and move right in. Income could become a worry.

But first, romance. Where is there a husband for my middle years? I am Stephanie Morwell, forty-two, the end product of good breeding, good nutrition, a fine workout program and amazingly skilled cosmetic surgeons. Since my parents died as my graduation present from Bryn Mawr, I've more or less taken care of myself, though of course, at times, one does need a man around the house. To insert lightbulbs and such-like. The point is, except for a slight flabbiness in my stock portfolio, I am a fine catch for just the right fellow.

I don't blame my broker, please let me make that clear. Bruce Kimball is his name and he's unfailingly optimistic and cheerful. A bit of a blade, I suspect. (One can't say *gay* blade anymore, not without the risk of being misunderstood.) In any event, Bruce did very well for me when everybody's stock was going up, and now that there's a—oh, what are the pornographic euphemisms of finance? A shakeout, a mid-term correction, a market adjustment, all of that—now that times are tougher, Bruce has lost me less than most and has even found a victory or two amid the wreckage. No, I can't fault Bruce for a general worsening of the climate of money.

In fact, Bruce . . . hmmm. He flirts with me at times, but

only in a professional way, as his employers would expect him to flirt with a moneyed woman. He's handsome enough, if a bit thin. (Thinner this year than last, in fact.) Still, those wiry fellows. . . .

Three or four years younger than I? Would Bruce Kimball be the answer to my prayers? I do already know him and I'd rather not spend *too* much time on the project.

Stephanie Kimball. Like a schoolgirl, I write the name on the note pad beside the telephone on the Louis XIV writing table next to my view of the East River. The rest of that page is filled with hastily jotted numbers: income, outgo, estimated expenses, overdue bills. *Stephanie Kimball.* I gaze upon my view and whisper the name. It's a blustery, changeable, threatening day. *Stephanie Kimball.* I like the sound.

"There is a tide in the affairs of men, which, taken at the flood, leads on to fortune." Agatha Christie said that. Oh, but she was quoting, wasn't she? Shakespeare! Got it.

There was certainly a flood tide in my affair with Stephanie Morwell. Five years ago, she was merely one more rich wife among my clients, if one who took more of an interest than most in the day-to-day handling of the portfolio. In fact, I never did meet her husband before his death. Three years ago, that was; some ash blondes really come into their own in black, have you noticed?

I respected Mrs. Morwell's widowhood for a month or two, then began a little harmless flirtation. I mean, why not? She was a widow, after all. With a few of my other female clients, an occasional expression of male interest had eventually led to extremely pleasant afternoon financial seminars in midtown hotels. And now, Mrs. Morwell; to peel the layers of black from that lithe and supple body. . . .

Well. For three years, all that was merely a pale fantasy. Not even a consummation devoutly to be wished—now, who said that? No matter—it was more of a daydream while the computer's down.

From black to autumnal colors to a more normal range. A good-looking woman, friendly, rich, but never at the forefront of my mind unless she was actually in my presence, across the desk. And now it has all changed.

Mrs. Morwell was in my office once more, hearing mostly bad news, I'm afraid, and in an effort to distract her from the grimness of the occasion, I made some light remark, "There are better things we could do than sit here with all these depressing numbers." Something like that; and she said, in a kind of swollen voice I'd never heard before, "There certainly are."

I looked at her, surprised, and she was arching her back, stretching like a cat. I said, "Mrs. Morwell, you're giving me ideas."

She smiled. "Which ideas are those?" she asked, and forty minutes later we were in her bed in her apartment on Sutton Place.

Aaah. Extended widowhood had certainly sharpened *her* palate. What an afternoon. Between times, she put together a cold snack of salmon and champagne while I roved naked through the sunny golden rooms, delicately furnished with antiques. What a view she had, out over the East River. To live such a life. . . .

Well. Not until this little glitch in the economy corrects itself.

"Champagne?"

I turned and her body was as beautiful as the bubbly. Smiling, she handed me a glass and said, "I've never had such a wonderful afternoon in my entire life."

We drank to that.

We were married, my golden stockbroker and I, seven weeks after I first took him to bed. Not quite a whirlwind romance, but close. Of course, I had to meet his parents, just the once, a chore we all handled reasonably well.

We honeymooned in Caneel Bay and had such a lovely time we stayed an extra week. Bruce was so attentive, so charming, so—how shall I put it?—ever ready. And he got along amazingly well with the natives; they were eating out of his hand. In no time at all, he was joking on a first-name basis with half a dozen fellows I would have thought of as nothing more than dangerous layabouts, but Bruce could find a way to put almost anyone at ease. (Once or twice, one of these fellows even came to chat with Bruce at the cottage. I know he lent one of them money—it was changing hands as I glanced out the louvered window—and I'm sure he never even anticipated repayment.)

I found myself, in those first weeks, growing actually fond of Bruce. What an unexpected bonus! And my warm feeling toward this new husband only increased when, on our return to New York, he insisted on continuing with his job at Rendall/LeBeau. "I won't sponge on you," he said, so firm and manly that I dropped to my knees that instant. *Such* a contrast with my previous marital experience!

Still, romance isn't everything. One must live as well; or, that is, some must live. And so, in the second week after our return, I taxied downtown for a discussion with Oliver Swerdluff, my new insurance agent. (New since Robert's demise, I mean.) "Congratulations on your new marriage, Mrs. Kimball," he said, this red-faced, portly man who was so transparently delighted with himself for having remembered my new name.

"Thank you, Mr. Swerdluff." I took my seat across the desk from him. "The new situation, of course," I pointed out, "will require some changes in my insurance package."

"Certainly, certainly."

"Bruce is now co-owner of the apartment in the city and the house on Long Island."

He looked impressed. "Very generous of you, Mrs., uh, Kimball."

"Yes, isn't it? Bruce is so important to me now, I can't imagine how I got along all those years without him. Oh, but this brings up a depressing subject. I suppose I must really insure Bruce's life, mustn't I?"

"The more important your husband is to you," he said, with his salesman's instant comprehension, "the more you must consider every eventuality."

"But he's priceless to me," I said. "How could I choose any amount of insurance? How could I put a dollar value on *Bruce?*"

"Let me help you with that decision," Mr. Swerdluff said, leaning that moist red face toward me over the desk.

We settled on an even million. Double indemnity.

"Strike while the widow is hot." Unattributed, I guess.

It did all seem to go very smoothly. At first, I was merely enjoying Stephanie for her own sake, expecting no more than our frequent encounters, and them somehow the idea arose that we might get married. I couldn't see a thing wrong with the proposition. Stephanie was terrific in bed, she was rich, she was beautiful and she obviously loved me. Surely, I could find some fondness in myself for a package like that.

And what she could also do, though I had to be very careful she never found out about it, was take up that shortfall, those pennies between me and the white medicine that makes me such a winning fellow. A generous woman, certainly generous enough for that modest need. And I understood from the beginning that if I were to keep her love and respect and my access to her piggy bank, I must never be too greedy. Independent, self-sufficient, self-respecting, only dipping into her funds for those odd sixpences which would bring me, in Mr. Dickens's phrase, "result happiness."

The appearance of independence was one reason why I kept on at Rendall/LeBeau, but I had other reasons as well. In the first place, I didn't want one of those second-rate account churners to take over the Morwell—now Kimball—account and bleed it to death with percentages of unnecessary sales. In the second place, I needed time away from Stephanie, private time that was reasonably accounted for and during which I could go on medicating myself. I would never be able to maintain my proper dosages at home without my bride sooner or later stumbling across the truth. And beyond all that, I've always enjoyed the work, playing with other people's money as if it were merely counters in a game, because that's all it is when it's other people's money.

Four lovely months we had of that life, with Stephanie never suspecting a thing. With neither of us, in fact, ever suspecting a thing. And if I weren't such a workaholic, particularly when topped with my little white friend, I wonder what eventually might have happened. No, I don't wonder; I know what would have happened.

But here's what happened instead. I couldn't keep my hands off Stephanie's financial records. It wasn't prying, it wasn't suspicion, it wasn't for my own advantage, it was merely a continuation of the work ethic on another front. And I wanted to do something nice for Stephanie because my fondness had grown—no, truly, it had. Did I love her? I believe I did. Surely, she was lovable. Surely, I had reason. Every day, I was made happy by her existence; if that isn't love, what is?

And Stephanie's tax records and household accounts were a mess. I first became aware of this when I came home one evening to find Stephanie, furrow-browed, huddled at the dining-room table with Serge Ostogoth, her—our—accountant. It was tax time and the table was a snowdrift of papers in no discernible order. Serge, a harmless drudge with leather elbow patches and a pathetic small mustache, was patiently taking Stephanie through the year just past, trying to match the paperwork to the history, a task that was clearly going to take several days. Serge had been Stephanie's accountant for three years, I later learned, and every year they had to go through this.

So I rolled up my sleeves to pitch in. Serge was grateful for my help. Stephanie, with shining eyes, kept telling me I was her savior, and eventually we managed to make sense of it all.

It was then I decided to put Stephanie's house in order. There was no point mentioning my plan; Stephanie was truly ashamed of her record-keeping inabilities, so why rub her nose in it? Evenings and weekends, if we weren't doing anything else, not flying out to the cottage or off to visit friends or out to theater and dinner, I'd spend half an hour or so working through her fiscal accounts.

Yes, and her previous husband, Robert, had been no help. When I got back that far, there was no improvement at all. In fact, Robert had been at least as bad as Stephanie about keeping records, and much worse when it came to throwing money around. A real wastrel. Outgo exceeded income all through that marriage. His life insurance, at the end, had been a real help.

And so had Frank's.

It was a week or two after I'd finished rationalizing the Robert years—two of them, though in three tax years—that my work brought me to my first encounter with Frank. Another husband, last name Bullock. Frank Bullock died three and a half years before Stephanie's marriage to Robert Morwell. Oh, yes, and he, too, had been well-insured. And with him, too, insurance paid double indemnity for accidental death.

Robert had been drowned at sea while on a cruise with Stephanie. Frank had fallen from the terrace of this very apartment while leaning out too far with his binoculars to observe the passage of an unusual breed of sea gull; Frank had been an amateur ornithologist.

And Leslie Hanford had fallen off a mountain in the Laurentians while on a Canadian ski holiday. Hanford was the husband before Bullock. Apparently, the first husband. Leslie's insurance, in fact, had been the basis for the fortune Stephanie now enjoyed, supplemented when necessary or convenient by the insurance of her later husbands. After each accidental death, Stephanie changed insurance agents and accountants. And each husband had died just over a year after the policy had been taken out.

Just over a year. So that's how long my bride expected to share my company, was it? Well, she was right about that, though not in the way she expected. I, too, could be decisive when called upon.

Whenever the weather was good, Stephanie took the sun on our terrace. Although it would be plagiarizing a bit from my bride, I could one day, having established an alibi at the office. . . .

The current insurance agent was named Oliver Swerdluff. I went to see him. "I just wanted to be sure," I said, "that the new policy on my life went through without a hitch. In case anything happened to me, I'd want to be certain Stephanie was cared for."

"An admirable sentiment," Swerdluff said. He was a puffy, sweaty man with tiny eyes, a man who would never let suspicion get between himself and a commission. Stephanie had chosen well.

I said, "Let me see, that was—half a million?"

"Oh, we felt a million would be better," Swerdluff said with a well-fed smile. "Double indemnity."

"Of course!" I exclaimed. "Excuse me, I get confused about these numbers. A million, of course. Double indemnity. And that's exactly the amount we want for the new policy, to insure Stephanie's life. If that's what I'm worth to her, she's certainly that valuable to me."

Call me a fool, but I fell in love. Bruce was so different from the others, so confident, so self-reliant. And it was so clear he loved me, loved *me*, not my money, not the advantages I brought him. I tried to be practical, but my heart ruled my head. This was a husband I was going to have to keep.

Many's the afternoon I spent sunbathing and brooding on the terrace while Bruce was downtown at the firm. On one hand, I would have financial security for at least a little while. On the other hand, I would have Bruce.

Ah, what this terrace could be! Duckboarded, with wrought-iron furniture, a few potted hemlocks, a gaily striped awning. . . .

Well, what of it? What was a row of hemlocks in the face of true love? Bruce and I could discuss our future together, our finances. A plan, shared with another person.

We would have to economize, of course, and the first

place to do so was with that million-dollar policy. I wouldn't be needing it now, so that was the first expense that could go. I went back to see Mr. Swerdluff. "I want to cancel that policy," I said.

"If you wish," he said. "Will you be canceling both of them?"

A MANHATTAN ROMANCE

BY JOYCE CAROL OATES

Central Park South

(Originally published in 1997)

Your Daddy loves you, that's the one true thing.
Never forget, Princess: that's the one true thing in your life
of mostly lies.

That wild day! I'd woken before it was even dawn; I
seemed to know that a terrible happiness was in store.

I was five years old; I was feverish with excitement; when
Daddy came to pick me up for our *Saturday adventure* as he
called it, it had just begun to snow; Momma and I were standing at the tall windows of our eighteenth-floor apartment
looking out across Central Park when the doorman rang;
Momma whispered in my ear, "If you said you were sick, you
wouldn't have to go with—him." For she could not utter the
word *Daddy*, and even the words *your father* made her mouth
twist. I said, "Momma, I'm not sick! I'm not." So the doorman sent Daddy up. Momma kept me with her at the window,
her hands that sometimes trembled firm on my shoulders and
her chin resting on the top of my head so I wanted to squirm
away but did not dare, not wanting to hurt Momma's feelings
or make her angry. So we stood watching the snowflakes—a
thousand million snowflakes drifting downward out of the sky
glinting like mica in the thin sunshine of early December. I
was pointing and laughing; I was excited by the snow, and by
Daddy coming for me. Momma said, "Just look! Isn't it beauti-

ful! The first snow of the season." Most of the tall trees had
lost their leaves, the wind had blown away their leaves that
only a few days before had been such bright, beautiful colors,
and you could see clearly now the roads curving and dipping
through the park; you could see the streams of traffic—yellow
taxis, cars, delivery vans, horse-drawn carriages, bicyclists;
you could see the skaters at Wollman Rink, and you could
see the outdoor cages of the Children's Zoo, which was closed
now; you could see the outcroppings of rock like miniature
mountains; you could see the ponds glittering like mirrors laid
flat; the park was still green, and seemed to go on forever; you
could see to the very end at 110th Street (Momma told me
the name of this distant street, which I had never seen close
up); you could see the gleaming cross on the dome of the Cathedral of St. John the Divine (Momma told me the name of
this great cathedral, which I had never seen close up); our
new apartment building was at 31 Central Park South and so
we could see the Hudson River to the left, and the East River
to the right; the sun appeared from the right, above the East
River; the sun vanished to the left, below the Hudson River;
we were floating above the street seventeen floors below; we
were floating in the sky, Momma said; we were floating above
Manhattan, Momma said; we were safe here, Momma said,
and could not come to harm. But Momma was saying now
in her sad angry voice, "I wish you didn't have to go with—
him. You won't cry, will you? You won't miss your momma
too much, will you?" I was staring at the thousand million
snowflakes; I was excited waiting for Daddy to ring the bell at
our front door; I was confused by Momma's questions because
wasn't Momma me? so didn't Momma know? the answer to
any question of Momma's, didn't Momma already know? "I
wish you didn't have to leave me, darling, but it's the terms of

the agreement—it's the law." These bitter words *It's the law* fell from Momma's lips each Saturday morning like something dropped in the apartment overhead! I waited to hear them, and I always did hear them. And then Momma leaned over me and kissed me; I loved Momma's sweet perfume and her soft-shining hair but I wanted to push away from her; I wanted to run to the door, to open it just as Daddy rang the bell; I wanted to surprise Daddy, who took such happiness in being surprised; I wanted to say to Momma, *I love Daddy better than I love you, let me go!* Because Momma was me, but Daddy was someone so different.

The doorball rang. I ran to answer it. Momma remained in the front room at the window. Daddy hoisted me into his arms, "How's my Princess? How's my Baby-Love?" and Daddy called out politely to Momma, whom he could not see, in the other room, "We're going to the Bronx Zoo, and we'll be back promptly at 5:30 p.m. as agreed." And Momma, who was very dignified, made no reply. Daddy called out, "Goodbye! Remember us!" which was like Daddy, to say mysterious things, things to make you smile, and to make you wonder; things to make you confused, as if maybe you hadn't heard correctly but didn't want to ask. And Momma never asked. And in the elevator going down Daddy hugged me again saying how happy we were, just the two of us. He was the King, I was the Little Princess. Sometimes I was the Fairy Princess. Momma was the Ice Queen who never laughed. Daddy was saying this could be the happiest day of our lives if we had courage. A light shone in Daddy's eyes; there would never be a man so handsome and radiant as Daddy.

"Not the Bronx, after all. Not today, I don't think."

Our driver that day was an Asian man in a smart visored

cap, a neat dark uniform, and gloves. The limousine was shiny black and larger than last week's and the windows were dark-tinted so you could see *out* (but it was strange, a scary twilight even in the sun) but no one could see *in*. "No plebeians knowing our business!" Daddy said, winking at me. "No spies." When we passed traffic policemen Daddy made faces at them, waggled his fingers at his ears and stuck out his tongue though they were only a few yards away; I giggled frightened Daddy would be seen and arrested, but he couldn't be seen, of course—"We're invisible, Princess! Don't worry."

Daddy liked me to smile and laugh, not to worry; not ever, ever to cry. He'd had enough of crying, he said. He'd had it up to here (drawing a forefinger across his throat, like a knife blade) with crying, he said. He had older children, grown-up children I'd never met; I was his Little Princess, his Baby-Love, the only one of his children he did love, he said. Snatching my hand and kissing it, kiss-tickling so I'd squeal with laughter.

Now Daddy no longer drove his own car, it was a time of rented cars. His enemies had taken *his driver's license* from him to humiliate him, he said. For they could not defeat him in any way that mattered. For he was too strong for them, and too smart.

It was a time of sudden reversals, changes of mind. I had been looking forward to the zoo; now we weren't going to the zoo but doing something else—"You'll like it just as much." Other Saturdays, we'd driven through the park; the park had many surprises; the park went on forever; we would stop, and walk, run, play in the park; we'd fed the ducks and geese swimming on the ponds; we'd had lunch outdoors at Tavern on the Green; we'd had lunch outdoors at the boathouse; on a windy March day, Daddy had helped me fly a kite (which we'd lost—it broke, and blew away in shreds); there was the promise of skating at Wollman Rink sometime soon. Other Saturdays we'd driven north on Riverside Drive to the George Washington Bridge, and across the bridge, and back; we'd driven north to the Cloisters; we'd driven south to the very end of the island as Daddy called it—"The great doomed island, Manhattan." We'd crossed Manhattan Bridge into Brooklyn, we'd crossed the Brooklyn Bridge. We'd gazed up at the Statue of Liberty. We'd gone on a ferry ride in bouncy, choppy water. We'd had lunch at the top of the World Trade Center, which was Daddy's favorite restaurant—"Dining in the clouds! In heaven." We'd gone to Radio City Music Hall, we'd seen *Beauty and the Beast* on Broadway; we'd seen the Big Apple Circus at Lincoln Center; we'd seen, the year before, the Christmas Spectacular at Radio City Music Hall. Our *Saturday adventures* left me dazed, giddy; one day I would realize that's what *intoxicated, high, drunk* means—I'd been drunk with happiness, with Daddy.

But no other *drunk*, ever afterward, could come near.

"Today, Princess, we'll buy presents. That's what we'll do—'store up riches.'"

Christmas presents? I asked.

"Sure. Christmas presents, any kind of presents. For you, and for me. Because we're special, you know." Daddy smiled at me, and I waited for him to wink because sometimes (when he was on the car phone, for instance) he'd wink at me to indicate he was joking; for Daddy often joked; Daddy was a man who loved to laugh, as he described himself, and there wasn't enough to laugh at, unless he invented it. "You know we are special, Princess, don't you? And all your life you'll remember your Daddy loves you?—that's the one true thing."

Yes, Daddy, I said. For of course it was so.

* * *

I should record how Daddy spoke on the phone, in the back-seats of our hired cars.

How precise his words, how he enunciated his words, polite and cold and harsh; how, though he spoke calmly, his handsome face creased like a vase that has been cracked; his eyes squinted almost shut, and had no focus; a raw flush like sunburn rose from his throat. Then he would remember where he was, and remember *me*. And smile at me, winking and nodding, whispering to *me*; even as he continued his conversation with whoever was at the other end of the line. And after a time Daddy would say abruptly, "That's enough!" or simply, "Goodbye!" and break the connection; Daddy would replace the phone receiver, and the conversation would have ended, with no warning. So that I basked in the knowledge that any one of Daddy's conversations, entered into with such urgency, would nonetheless come to an abrupt ending with the magic words "That's enough!" or "Goodbye!" and these words I awaited in the knowledge that, then, Daddy would turn smiling to *me*.

That wild day! Breakfast at the Plaza, and shopping at the Trump Tower, and a visit to the Museum of Modern Art where Daddy took me to see a painting precious to him, he said . . . We had been in the café at the Plaza before but this time Daddy couldn't get the table he requested, and something else was wrong—it wasn't clear to me what; I was nervous, and giggly; Daddy gave our orders to the waiter, but disappeared (to make another phone call? to use the men's room?—if you asked Daddy where he went he'd say with a wink, That's for me to know, darlin', and you to find out); a big plate of scrambled eggs and bacon was brought for me; eggs Benedict was brought for Daddy; a stack of blueberry pancakes with warm syrup was brought for us to share; the silver pastry cart

238 // MANHATTAN NOIR 2

was pushed to our table; there were tiny jars of jams, jellies, marmalade for us to open; there were people at nearby tables observing us; I was accustomed, in Daddy's company, to being observed by strangers; I took such attention as my due, as Daddy's daughter; Daddy whispered, "Let them get an eyeful, Princess." Daddy ate quickly, hungrily; Daddy ate with a napkin tucked beneath his chin; Daddy saw that I wasn't eating much and asked was there something wrong with my breakfast; I told Daddy I wasn't hungry; Daddy asked if "she" had made me eat, before he'd arrived; I told him no; I said I felt a little sickish; Daddy said, "That's one of the Ice Queen's tactics—'sickish.'" So I tried to eat, tiny pieces of pancakes that weren't soaked in syrup, and Daddy leaned his elbows on the table and watched me, saying, "And what if this is the last breakfast you'll ever have with your father, what then? Shame on you!" Waiters hovered near in their dazzling white uniforms. The maitre d' was attentive, smiling. A call came for Daddy and he was gone for some time and when he returned flush-faced and distracted, his necktie loosened at his throat, it seemed that breakfast was over; hurriedly Daddy scattered $20 bills across the table, and hurriedly we left the café as everyone smiled and stared after us; we left the Plaza by the side entrance, on 58th Street, where the limousine awaited us; the silent Asian driver standing at the curb with the rear door open for Daddy to bundle me inside, and climb inside himself. We had hardly a block to go, to the elegant Trump Tower on Fifth Avenue; there we took escalators to the highest floor, where Daddy's eyes glistened with tears, everywhere he looked was so beautiful. Have I said my Daddy was smooth-shaven this morning, and smelled of a wintergreen cologne; he was wearing amber-tinted sunglasses, new to me; he was wearing a dark pinstriped double-breasted Armani suit and over it an Armani camel's-hair coat with shoulders that made him appear more muscular than he was; he was wearing shiny black Italian shoes with a heel that made him appear taller than he was; Daddy's hair had been styled and blown dry so that it lifted from his head like something whipped, not lying flat, and not a dull flattish white as it had been but tinted now a pale russet color; how handsome Daddy was! In the boutiques of Trump Tower Daddy bought me a dark blue velvet coat, and a pale blue angora cloche hat; Daddy bought me pale blue angora gloves; my old coat, my old gloves were discarded—"Toss 'em, please!" Daddy commanded the saleswomen. Daddy bought me a beautiful silk Hermès scarf to wrap around my neck, and Daddy bought me a beautiful white-gold wristwatch studded with tiny emeralds, that had to be made smaller, much smaller, to fit my wrist; Daddy bought me a "keepsake" gold heart on a thin gold chain, a necklace; Daddy bought for himself a half-dozen beautiful silk neckties imported from Italy, and a kidskin wallet; Daddy bought a cashmere vest sweater for himself, imported from Scotland; Daddy bought an umbrella, an attaché case, a handsome suitcase, imported from England, all of which he ordered to be delivered to an address in New Jersey; and other items Daddy bought for himself, and for me. For all these wonderful presents Daddy paid in cash; in bills of large denominations; Daddy no longer used credit cards, he said; he refused to be a cog in the network of government surveillance, he said; they would not catch him in their net; he would not play their ridiculous games. In the Trump Tower there was a café beside a waterfall and Daddy had a glass of wine there, though he chose not to sit down at a table; he was too restless, he said, to sit down at a table; he was in too much of a hurry. Descending then the escalators to the ground floor, where a cool breeze lifted to touch our heated faces; I was terribly excited in my lovely new clothes, and wearing my lovely jewelry; except for Daddy gripping my hand—"Care-ful, Princess!"—I would have stumbled at the foot of the escalator. And outside on Fifth Avenue there were so many people, tall rushing rude people who took no notice of me even in my new velvet coat and angora hat, I would have been knocked down on the sidewalk except for Daddy gripping my hand, protecting me. Next we went—we walked, and the limousine followed—to the Museum of Modern Art, where again there was a crowd, again I was breathless riding escalators, I was trapped behind tall people seeing legs, the backs of coats, swinging arms; Daddy lifted me to his shoulder and carried me, and brought me into a large, airy room; a room of unusual proportions; a room not so crowded as the others; there were tears in Daddy's eyes as he held me in his arms—his arms that trembled just slightly—to gaze at an enormous painting—several paintings—broad beautiful dreamy-blue paintings of a pond, and water lilies; Daddy told me that these paintings were by a very great French artist named "Mon-ay" and that there was magic in them; he told me that these paintings made him comprehend his own soul, or what his soul had been meant to be; for as soon as you left the presence of such beauty, you were lost in the crowd; you were devoured by the crowd; it would be charged against you that it was your own fault but in fact—"They don't let you be good, Princess. The more you have, the more they want from you. They eat you alive. Cannibals."

When we left the museum, the snowflakes had ceased to fall. In the busy Manhattan streets there was no memory of them now. A bright harsh sun shone down almost vertically between the tall buildings but everywhere else was shadow, without color, and cold.

* * *

By late afternoon Daddy and I had shopped at Tiffany &
Co., and Bergdorf Goodman, and Saks, and Bloomingdale's;
we had purchased beautiful expensive items to be delivered
to us at an address in New Jersey—"On the far side of the
River Styx." One purchase, at Steuben on Fifth Avenue, was
a foot-high glass sculpture that might have been a woman, or
an angel, or a wide-winged bird; it shone with light, so that
you could almost not see it; Daddy laughed, saying, "The Ice
Queen!—exactly"; and so this present was sent to Momma at
31 Central Park South. As we walked through the great glittering stores Daddy held my hand so that I would not be lost
from him; these great stores, Daddy said, were the cathedrals
of America; they were the shrines and reliquaries and cata-
combs of America; if you could not be happy in such stores,
you could not be happy anywhere; you could not be a true
American. And Daddy recited stories to me, some of these
were fairy tales he'd read to me when I'd been a little little
girl, a baby; when Daddy had lived with Momma and me, the
three of us in a brownstone house with our own front door,
and no doorman and no elevators; on our ground-floor windows there were curving iron bars, so that no one could break
in; there were electronic devices of all kinds, so that no one
could break in; our house had two trees at the curb, and these,
too, were protected by curving iron bars; we lived in a narrow,
quiet street a half-block from a huge, important building—
the Metropolitan Museum of Art; when Daddy had been on
television sometimes, and his photograph in the papers; they
would say I knew nothing about this, I was too young to know,
but I did; I knew. Just as I knew it was strange for Daddy to
be paying for our presents with cash from his wallet, and out
of thick-stuffed envelopes in his inside coat pockets; it was

strange, for no one else paid in such a way; and others stared at him; stared at him as if memorizing him—the vigor of his voice and his shining face and his knowledge that he, and I, who was his daughter, were set off from the dull, dreary ordinariness of the rest of the world; they stared, they were envious of us, though smiling, always smiling, if Daddy glanced at them, or spoke with them. For such was Daddy's power.

I was dazed with exhaustion; I was feverish; I could not have said how long Daddy and I had been shopping, on our *Saturday adventure*; yet I loved it, that strangers observed us, and remarked how pretty I was; and to Daddy sometimes they would say, *Your face is familiar, are you on TV?* But Daddy just laughed and kept moving, for there was no time to spare that day.

Out on the street, one of the wide, windy avenues, Daddy hailed a cab like any other pedestrian. When had he dismissed the limousine?—I couldn't remember.

It was a bumpy, jolting ride. The rear seat was torn. There was no heat. In the rearview mirror a pair of liquidy black eyes regarded Daddy with silent contempt. Daddy fumbled paying the fare, a $50 bill slipped from his fingers—"Keep the change, driver, and thanks!" Yet even then the eyes did not smile at us; these were not eyes to be purchased.

We were in a dark, tiny wine cellar on 47th Street near Seventh Avenue where Daddy ordered a carafe of red wine for himself and a soft drink for me and where he could make telephone calls in a private room at the rear; I fell asleep, and when I woke up there was Daddy standing by our table, too restless to sit; his face was rubbery and looked stretched; his hair had fallen and lay in damp strands against his forehead; globules of sweat like oily pearls ran down his cheeks.

He smiled with his mouth, saying, "There you are, Princess! Up and at 'em." For already it was time to leave, and more than time. Daddy had learned from an aide the bad news, the news he'd been expecting. But shielding me from it of course. For only much later—years later—would I learn that, that afternoon, a warrant for Daddy's arrest had been issued by the Manhattan district attorney's office; by some of the very people for whom, until a few months ago, Daddy had worked. It would be charged against him that as a prosecuting attorney Daddy had misused the powers of his office, he had solicited and accepted bribes, he had committed perjury upon numerous occasions, he had falsely informed upon certain persons under investigation by the district attorney's office, he had blackmailed others, he had embezzled funds . . . such charges were made against Daddy, such lies concocted by his enemies who had been jealous of him for many years and wanted him defeated, destroyed. One day I would learn that New York City police detectives had come to Daddy's apartment (on East 92nd Street and First Avenue) to arrest him and of course hadn't found him; they'd gone to 31 Central Park South and of course hadn't found him; Momma told them Daddy had taken me to the Bronx Zoo, or in any case that had been his plan; Momma told them that Daddy would be bringing me back home at 5:30 p.m., or in any case he'd promised to do so; if they waited for him in the lobby downstairs would they please please not arrest him in front of his daughter, Momma begged. Yet policemen were sent to the Bronx Zoo to search for Daddy there; a manhunt for Daddy at the Bronx Zoo!— how Daddy would have laughed. And now an alert was out in Manhattan for Daddy, he was a "wanted" man, but already Daddy had shrewdly purchased a new coat in Saks, a London Fog trench coat the shade of damp stone, and made arrangements for the store to deliver his camel's-hair coat to the New Jersey address; already Daddy had purchased a gray fedora hat, and he'd exchanged his amber-tinted sunglasses for darker glasses, with heavy black plastic frames; he'd purchased a knotty gnarled cane, imported from Australia, and walked now with a limp—I stared at him, almost I didn't recognize him, and Daddy laughed at me. In the Shamrock Pub on Ninth Avenue and 39th Street he'd engaged a youngish blond woman with hair braided in cornrows to accompany us while he made several other stops; the blond woman had a glaring-bright face like a billboard; her eyes were ringed in black and lingered on me—"What a sweet, pretty little girl! And what a pretty coat and hat!"—but she knew not to ask questions. She walked with me gripping my hand in the angora glove pretending she was my momma and I was her little girl, and Daddy behind hobbling on his cane; shrewdly a few yards behind so it would not have seemed (if anyone was watching) that Daddy was with us; this was a game we were playing, Daddy said; it was a game that made me excited, and nervous; I was laughing and couldn't stop; the blond woman scolded me—"Shhh! Your Daddy will be angry." And a little later the blond woman was gone.

Always in Manhattan, on the street I wonder if I'll see her again. *Excuse me* I will cry out *do you remember? That day, that hour?* But it's been years.

So exhausted! Daddy scolded me carrying me out of the taxi, into the lobby of the Hotel Pierre; a beautiful old hotel on Fifth Avenue and 61st Street, across from Central Park; Daddy booked a suite for us on the sixteenth floor; you could look from a window to see the apartment building on Central Park South where Momma and I lived; but none of that was very real to me now; it wasn't real to me that I had a momma, but only real that I had a daddy. And once we were inside the suite Daddy bolted the door and slid the chain lock in place. There were two TVs and Daddy turned them both on. He turned on the ventilator fans in all the rooms. He took the telephone receivers off their hooks. With a tiny key he unlocked the minibar and broke open a little bottle of whiskey and poured it into a glass and quickly drank. He was breathing hard, his eyes moving swiftly in their sockets yet without focus. "Princess! Get up *please*. Don't disappoint your Daddy *please*." I was lying on the floor, rolling my head from side to side. But I wasn't crying. Daddy found a can of sweetened apple juice in the minibar and poured it into a glass and added something from another little bottle and gave it to me saying, "Princess, this is a magic potion. Drink!" I touched my lips to the glass but there was a bitter taste. Daddy said, "Princess, you must obey your daddy." And so I did. A hot hurting sensation spread in my mouth and throat and I started to choke and Daddy pressed the palm of his hand over my mouth to quiet me; it was then I remembered how long ago when I'd been a silly little baby Daddy had pressed the palm of his hand over my mouth to quiet me. I was sickish now, and I was frightened; but I was happy, too; I was drunk with happiness from all we'd done that day, Daddy and me; for I had never had so many presents before; I had never understood how special I was, before; and afterward when they asked if I'd been afraid of my daddy I would say no! no I hadn't been! not for a minute! I love my daddy I would say, and my daddy loves me. Daddy was sitting on the edge of the big bed, drinking; his head lowered almost to his knees. He was muttering to himself as if he were alone—"Fuckers! Wouldn't let me be good. Now you want to eat my heart. But not *me*." Later I was wakened to something loud on the TV. Except it was a pounding at the door. And men's voices calling "Police! Open up, Mr.—"—saying Daddy's name as I'd never heard it before. And Daddy was on his feet, Daddy had his arm around me. Daddy was excited and angry and he had a gun in his hand—I knew it was a gun, I'd seen pictures of guns—this was bluish-black and shiny, with a short barrel—and he was waving the gun as if the men on the other side of the door could see him; there was a film of sweat on his face catching the light, like facets of diamonds; I had never seen my Daddy so furious calling to the policemen—"I've got my little girl here, my daughter—and I've got a gun." But they were pounding at the door; they were breaking down the door; Daddy fired the gun into the air and pulled me into another room where the TV was loud but there were no lights; Daddy pushed me down, panting; the two of us on the carpet, panting. I was too scared to cry, and I started to wet my pants; in the other room the policemen were calling to Daddy to surrender his weapon, not to hurt anyone but to surrender his weapon and come with them now; and Daddy was sobbing shouting—"I'll use it, I'm not afraid—I'm not going to prison—I can't!—I can't do it!—I've got my little girl here, you understand?"—and the policemen were on the other side of the doorway but wouldn't show themselves saying to Daddy he didn't want to hurt his daughter, of course he didn't want to hurt his daughter; he didn't want to hurt himself, or anyone; he should surrender his weapon now, and come along quietly with the officers; he would speak with his lawyer; he would be all right; and Daddy was cursing, and Daddy was crying, and Daddy was crawling on his hands and knees on the carpet trying to hold me, and the gun; we were crouched in the farthest darkest corner of the room by the heating unit; the ventilator fan was throbbing; Daddy was hugging me and crying, his breath was hot on my face; I tried to push out of Daddy's arms but Daddy was too strong calling me Princess! Little Princess! saying I knew he loved me didn't I. The magic potion had made me sleepy and sickish, it was hard for me to stay awake. By now I had wet my panties, my legs were damp and chafed. A man was talking to Daddy in a loud clear voice like a TV voice and Daddy was listening or seemed to be listening and sometimes Daddy would reply and sometimes not; how much time passed like this, how many hours—I didn't know; not until years later would I learn it had been an hour and twelve minutes but at the time I hadn't any idea, I wasn't always awake. The voices kept on and on; men's voices; one of them saying repeatedly, "Mr.—, surrender your weapon, will you? Toss it where we can see it, will you?" and Daddy wiped his face on his shirt sleeve, Daddy's face was streaked with tears like something melting set too near a fire, and still the voice said, calmly, so loud it seemed to come from everywhere at once, "Mr.—, you're not a man to harm a little girl, we know you, you're a good man, you're not a man to harm anyone," and suddenly Daddy said, "Yes! Yes that's right." And Daddy kissed me on the side of the face and said, "Good-bye, Princess!" in a high, happy voice; and pushed me away from him; and Daddy placed the barrel of the gun deep inside his mouth. And Daddy pulled the trigger.

So it ended. It always ends. But don't tell me there isn't happiness. It exists, it's there. You just have to find it, and you have to keep it, if you can. It won't last, but it's there.

IN FOR A PENNY

BY LAWRENCE BLOCK

Eighth Avenue

(Originally published in 1999)

P aul kept it very simple. That seemed to be the secret. You kept it simple, you drew firm lines and didn't cross them. You put one foot in front of the other, took it day by day, and let the days mount up.

The state didn't take an interest. They put you back on the street with a cheap suit and figured you'd be back inside before the pants got shiny. But other people cared. This one outfit, about two parts ex-cons to one part holy joes, had wised him up and helped him out. They'd found him a job and a place to live, and what more did he need?

The job wasn't much, frying eggs and flipping burgers in a diner at 23rd and Eighth. The room wasn't much, either, seven blocks south of the diner, four flights up from the street. It was small, and all you could see from its window was the back of another building. The furnishings were minimal—an iron bedstead, a beat-up dresser, a rickety chair—and the walls needed paint and the floor needed carpet. There was a sink in the room, a bathroom down the hall. No cooking, no pets, no overnight guests, the landlady told him. No kidding, he thought.

His shift was four to midnight, Monday through Friday. The first weekend he did nothing but go to the movies, and by Sunday night he was ready to climb the wall. Too much time to kill, too few ways to kill it that wouldn't get him in trouble. How many movies could you sit through? And a movie cost him two hours' pay, and if you spent the whole weekend dragging yourself from one movie house to another . . .

Weekends were dangerous, one of the ex-cons had told him. Weekends could put you back in the joint. There ought to be a law against weekends.

But he figured out a way around it. Walking home Tuesday night, after that first weekend of movie-going, he'd stopped at three diners on Seventh Avenue, nursing a cup of coffee and chatting with the guy behind the counter. The third time was the charm; he walked out of there with a weekend job. Saturday and Sunday, same hours, same wages, same work. And they'd pay him off the books, which made his weekend work tax-free.

Between what he was saving in taxes and what he wasn't spending on movies, he'd be a millionaire.

Well, maybe he'd never be a millionaire. Probably be dangerous to be a millionaire, a guy like him, with his ways, his habits. But he was earning an honest dollar, and he ate all he wanted on the job, seven days a week now, so it wasn't hard to put a few bucks aside. The weeks added up and so did the dollars, and the time came when he had enough cash socked away to buy himself a little television set. The cashier at his weekend job set it up and her boyfriend brought it over, so he figured it fell off a truck or walked out of somebody's apartment, but it got good reception and the price was right.

It was a lot easier to pass the time once he had the TV. He'd get up at ten or eleven in the morning, grab a shower in the bathroom down the hall, then pick up doughnuts and coffee at the corner deli. Then he'd watch a little TV until it was time to go to work.

After work he'd stop at the same deli for two bottles of cold beer and some cigarettes. He'd settle in with the TV, a beer bottle in one hand and a cigarette in the other and his eyes on the screen.

He didn't get cable, but he figured that was all for the good. He was better off staying away from some of the stuff they were allowed to show on cable TV. Just because you had cable didn't mean you had to watch it, but he knew himself, and if he had it right there in the house how could he keep himself from looking at it?

And that could get you started. Something as simple as late-night adult programming could put him on a train to the big house upstate. He'd been there. He didn't want to go back.

He would get through most of a pack of cigarettes by the time he turned off the light and went to bed. It was funny, during the day he hardly smoked at all, but back in his room at night he had a butt going just about all the time. If the smoking was heavy, well, the drinking was ultralight. He could make a bottle of Bud last an hour. More, even. The second bottle was always warm by the time he got to it, but he didn't mind, nor did he drink it any faster than he'd drunk the first one. What was the rush?

Two beers was enough. All it did was give him a little buzz, and when the second beer was gone he'd turn off the TV and sit at the window, smoking one cigarette after another, looking out at the city.

Then he'd go to bed. Then he'd get up and do it all over again.

The only problem was walking home.

And even that was no problem at first. He'd leave his

rooming house around three in the afternoon. The diner was ten minutes away, and that left him time to eat before his shift started. Then he'd leave sometime between midnight and twelve-thirty—the guy who relieved him, a manic Albanian, had a habit of showing up ten to fifteen minutes late. Paul would retrace his earlier route, walking the seven blocks down Eighth Avenue to 16th Street with a stop at the deli for cigarettes and beer.

The Rose of Singapore was the problem.

The first time he walked past the place, he didn't even notice it. By day it was just another seedy bar, but at night the neon glowed and the jukebox music poured out the door, along with the smell of spilled drinks and stale beer and something more, something unnameable, something elusive.

"If you don't want to slip," they'd told him, "stay out of slippery places."

He quickened his pace and walked on by.

The next afternoon the Rose of Singapore didn't carry the same feeling of danger. Not that he'd risk crossing the threshold, not at any hour of the day or night. He wasn't stupid. But it didn't lure him, and consequently it didn't make him uncomfortable.

Coming home was a different story.

He was thinking about it during his last hour on the job, and by the time he reached it he was walking all the way over at the edge of the sidewalk, as far from the building's entrance as he could get without stepping down into the street. He was like an acrophobe edging along a precipitous path, scared to look down, afraid of losing his balance and falling accidentally, afraid too of the impulse that might lead him to plunge purposefully into the void.

He kept walking, eyes forward, heart racing. Once he was past it he felt himself calming down, and he bought his two bottles of beer and his pack of cigarettes and went on home.

He'd get used to it, he told himself. It would get easier with time.

But, surprisingly enough, it didn't. Instead it got worse, but gradually, imperceptibly, and he learned to accommodate it. For one thing, he steered clear of the west side of Eighth Avenue, where the Rose of Singapore stood. Going to work and coming home, he kept to the opposite side of the street.

Even so, he found himself hugging the inner edge of the sidewalk, as if every inch closer to the street would put him that much closer to crossing it and being drawn mothlike into the tavern's neon flame. And, approaching the Rose of Singapore's block, he'd slow down or speed up his pace so that the traffic signal would allow him to cross the street as soon as he reached the corner. As if otherwise, stranded there, he might cross in the other direction instead, across Eighth Avenue and on into the Rose.

He knew it was ridiculous but he couldn't change the way it felt. When it didn't get better he found a way around it.

He took Seventh Avenue instead.

He did that on the weekends anyway because it was the shortest route. But during the week it added two long cross-town blocks to his pedestrian commute, four blocks a day, twenty blocks a week. That came to about three miles a week, maybe a hundred and fifty extra miles a year.

On good days he told himself he was lucky to be getting the exercise, that the extra blocks would help him stay in shape. On bad days he felt like an idiot, crippled by fear.

Then the Albanian got fired.

* * *

He was never clear on what happened. One waitress said the Albanian had popped off at the manager one time too many, and maybe that was what happened. All he knew was that one night his relief man was not the usual wild-eyed fellow with the droopy mustache but a stocky dude with a calculating air about him. His name was Dooley, and Paul made him at a glance as a man who'd done time. You could tell, but of course he didn't say anything, didn't drop any hints. And neither did Dooley.

But the night came when Dooley showed up, tied his apron, rolled up his sleeves, and said, "Give her my love, huh?" And, when Paul looked at him in puzzlement, he added, "Your girlfriend."

"Haven't got one," he said.

"You live on Eighth Avenue, right? That's what you told me. Eighth and 16th, right? Yet every time you leave here you head over toward Seventh. Every single time."

"I like the exercise," he said.

"Exercise," Dooley said, and grinned. "Good word for it."

He let it go, but the next night Dooley made a similar comment. "I need to unwind when I come off work," Paul told him. "Sometimes I'll walk clear over to Sixth Avenue before I head downtown. Or even Fifth."

"That's nice," Dooley said. "Just do me a favor, will you? Ask her if she's got a sister."

"It's cold and it looks like rain," Paul said. "I'll be walking home on Eighth Avenue tonight, in case you're keeping track."

And when he left he did walk down Eighth Avenue—for one block. Then he cut over to Seventh and took what had become his usual route.

He began doing that all the time, and whenever he headed

east on 22nd Street he found himself wondering why he'd let Dooley have such power over him. For that matter, how could he have let a seedy gin joint make him walk out of his way to the tune of a hundred and fifty miles a year?

He was supposed to be keeping it simple. Was this keeping it simple? Making up elaborate lies to explain the way he walked home? And walking extra blocks every night for fear that the Devil would reach out and drag him into a neon-lit Hell?

Then came a night when it rained, and he walked all the way home on Eighth Avenue.

It was always a problem when it rained. Going to work he could catch a bus, although it wasn't terribly convenient. But coming home he didn't have the option, because traffic was one-way the wrong way.

So he walked home on Eighth Avenue, and he didn't turn left at 22nd Street, and didn't fall apart when he drew even with the Rose of Singapore. He breezed on by, bought his beer and cigarettes at the deli, and went home to watch television. But he turned the set off again after a few minutes and spent the hours until bedtime at the window, looking out at the rain, nursing the beers, smoking the cigarettes, and thinking long thoughts.

The next two nights were clear and mild, but he chose Eighth Avenue anyway. He wasn't uneasy, not going to work, not coming home, either. Then came the weekend, and then on Monday he took Eighth again, and this time on the way home he found himself on the west side of the street, the same side as the bar.

The door was open. Music, strident and bluesy, poured through it, along with all the sounds and smells you'd expect.

He walked right on by.

You're over it, he thought. He went home and didn't even turn on the TV, just sat and smoked and sipped his two long-neck bottles of Bud.

Same story Tuesday, same story Wednesday.

Thursday night, steps from the tavern's open door, he thought, Why drag this out?

He walked in, found a stool at the bar. "Double scotch," he told the barmaid. "Straight up, beer chaser."

He'd tossed off the shot and was working on the beer when a woman slid onto the stool beside him. She put a cigarette between bright red lips, and he scratched a match and lit it for her.

Their eyes met, and he felt something click.

She lived over on Ninth and 17th, on the third floor of a brownstone across the street from the projects. She said her name was Tiffany, and maybe it was. Her apartment was three little rooms. They sat on the couch in the front room and he kissed her a few times and got a little dizzy from it. He excused himself and went to the bathroom and looked at himself in the mirror over the sink.

You could go home now, he told the mirror image. Tell her anything, like you got a headache, you got malaria, you're really a Catholic priest or gay or both. Anything. Doesn't matter what you say or if she believes you. You could go home.

He looked into his own eyes in the mirror and knew it wasn't true.

Because he was stuck, he was committed, he was down for it. Had been from the moment he walked into the bar. No, longer than that. From the first rainy night when he walked home on Eighth Avenue. Or maybe before, maybe ever since

Dooley's insinuation had led him to change his route.

And maybe it went back further than that. Maybe he was locked in from the jump, from the day they opened the gates and put him on the street. Hell, from the day he was born, even.

"Paul?"

"Just a minute," he said.

And he slipped into the kitchen. In for a penny, in for a pound, he thought, and he started opening drawers, looking for the one where she kept the knives.

TWO OVER EASY

BY SUSAN ISAACS

Murray Hill

(Originally published in 2008)

On the morning of his forty-ninth birthday, Bob Geissendorfer sat in the recently remodeled Tuscan farmhouse kitchen in his apartment in the Murray Hill section of Manhattan and explained to himself that it was his own fault. *If you hadn't been such a decent guy, you'd have been a genuine media star, the most quoted reporter in the* New York Times' *Business section. You could have owned Enron, talked tough with Chris Matthews, joked with Imus. You know you've got the stuff: an analytical mind, a clear writing style, and—let's face it, this is a visual culture—the tight-cheeked, blue-eyed, square-jawed, graying-hair good looks of an actor who'd be cast as a CEO in a Super Bowl commercial.* In real life (Bob had to laugh to himself) CEOs were mostly Dennis Kozlowski/Ken Lay types, men who looked made of mashed potatoes rather than muscle and bone.

But irony of irony, in this era of diversity, his name had held him back. "Geissendorfer" reeked of lederhosen. At best. And at worst, a Nuremberg defendant—a name that should have "Oberstgruppenführer" in front of it. Yet at the last minute he hadn't been able to hurt his father's feelings by Anglicizing it.

All during J school at Northwestern, though, he'd been picturing his byline as Robert Giles. There he'd be, at his first job at some small yet first-rate paper, muttering *Bob Giles here* into the phone with Woodwardian sang froid as he read over his copy. Bob Giles: two crisp syllables he wouldn't have to spend half of every single goddamn day spelling. The cosmic joke of his decision? Honor your father and you get fucked.

He sipped his orange juice. Whole Foods. Good. Well, like so much in life, everybody knows it's the best. Except it wasn't. Too pulpy. You're interviewing the chairman of Delta and suddenly there's a giant strand of orange fiber attached to a mini-blob of pulp that's flossed its way between your teeth and feels Velcroed to your gums and you forget your follow-up question.

When Bob got to the *Times*, lesser reporters, Williams and Wu and even Shapiro, developed ten sources to his one just because nobody could remember his last name. Who wanted to call the paper and say, *Oh, operator, give me the guy in the Business section with, uh, the German name—Gibbelhoffer or Sauerkraut or some damn thing?*

"Almost ready!" Chrissie Geissendorfer chirped. Or maybe trilled. Some adjective to describe a cute voice. Cute, even though once any woman who happened to have a brain turned twenty-five, she'd know enough to turn her back on cute. She'd march, shoulders back, boobs front, directly into life.

But not his wife. Here she was, back toward him, busy at the six-burner stove she'd had to have. *Almost ready*, he mimicked to himself. With that voice like one of the "Christmas Don't Be Late" chipmunks. That was the problem with short women: They embraced Cute, or, to be fair, maybe had it foisted on them, and then, when other women were becoming interesting or sensual or elegant, they couldn't let go of Cute. About ten years ago, when he asked her casually,

"Hey, would you like me to call you Christina now?" she doubled over and pretended to throw up. Then she tweeted, or possibly twittered, "Christina? Couldn't you just kill my parents? Way back when, like when I was nine or ten years old, I remember thinking my name sounded like I had grandma denture breath."

Steak and eggs, his ritual birthday breakfast. Early in their marriage, he must have made a positive reference to steak and eggs, although why he couldn't imagine. But that's what he got on his next birthday, along with her Alvin the Chipmunk rendition of the Happy Birthday song. Same thing the following year. Right then and there, he said to himself, *Oh fuck, this is what I'm going to be facing 365 mornings from now and for the rest of my life. Unless I can get rid of her. Divorce. Or maybe she'll die young: nothing painful, something quick.*

And here it was, before him, the egg whites thicker than liquid, yet runnier than mucous. The yolks—three of them, for God's sake—were more orange than yellow and shadowed by ripples, as if they were lying above some egg-world fault line about to give way. Two over easy did not mean three under-fried eggs that probably came from some organic farm where chickens ran amok and pecked particles in cow shit. Another thing: Chrissie had cut the steak into an inch-high rectangle before broiling it, so it looked like a bad joke birthday gift—a greasy brown box rather than a piece of meat.

She was singing, "Happy birthday to yoooou . . ." although with her accent, it was more like, "Hyappy beerthday . . ." He suppressed a groan—*I'm getting too damn good at groan suppression,* he mused—and offered her his I-dazzle-women smile. Naturally, Chrissie flashed one in return, her show-every-tooth-while-you're-at-it smile emphasized how the Crest Whitestrips hadn't worked on her molars.

Well, he couldn't *not* act appreciative. She was trying so hard, and she loved him so much. Truth be told, Bob ached for her. Christina Johnston Geissendorfer was a genuinely decent human being. Yet he'd stopped loving her six months into their marriage.

No reason: Maybe his feelings changed when he realized that what he'd first viewed as a warm personality and lively mind turned out to be no more than extravagant perkiness. He asked the question he posed himself frequently: How did I talk myself into believing she had a mind when she'd been in the marketing department of a costume jewelry company. Her Great Moment was renaming the six hundred "Big Apple" bracelets from an order cancelled by Macy's "Original Sin" bracelets and selling them to Victoria's Secret.

He should have turned his attention back to his plate right then, but he caught sight of the crumbs embedded among the fibers of her terry cloth bathrobe, crumbs the unmistakable dark amber of Pepperidge Farm cookies. Over the years of their marriage, what had once been Chrissie's hourglass figure had spread into the boxy solidity of a grandfather clock. Sex was largely a defensive act now, because if he gave in to feelings for her—namely, utter indifference—she'd start demanding to know if she was doing something to turn him off, and, *Please, Bob, be straight with me; don't worry about my feelings.* Or she'd be suggesting to him—in what she thought was her gentle voice—*Maybe you should go to see Dr. Gratz and ask for a testosterone count. You don't have to feel self-conscious, it's more common than you know with guys your age.*

She sat across from him, resting her elbows on the rough wood table that the decorator said came from an olive-grower's house near Sienna. Another idiot extravagance, but then his Aunt Beryl had left him enough that they could live in a CFO-of-a-NASDAQ-listed-company manner rather than managing on his *Times* salary. Chrissie's chin perched on the heels of her upturned hands. What the hell was she sitting there for? To watch him eat? He cut a large slice of the egg, figuring he had to do it now. If he waited, he'd probably gag on cold egg-white slime, and she'd spend his entire birthday leaving apologies on his voice mail about how truly sorry she was that breakfast had been a fiasco, then call back to say she hoped her messages hadn't sounded passive-aggressive.

"I have that cabinetmaker coming over today for an estimate," Chrissie said. "On the wood paneling for your library." Bob nodded, and noted that she'd said "your library," which was appropriate because her idea of reading was "25 Treasures in Your Garbage" in *Real Simple*. "You want to know something? You're the only man I know who'd want a library." Was this a compliment? A criticism? Compliment, he decided, because her eyes had that I-love-you Hallmark greeting card haze.

A library. Their daughter Jordana was graduating from NYU Law School, and as there was no way she'd ever live at home again, they were turning her bedroom into his own private space. Wall-to-wall bookshelves and a sound system designed to resonate off wood. "Everybody else's husband would want a media room. Do you know what a library says? *This man has class.*" He nodded and swallowed quickly, so egg ooze wouldn't coat his throat. "Bobby," she went on, "since the cabinetmaker is coming anyway—"

"No."

"Could you please just hear me out?" she squealed. Whenever her voice rose this high, stretched by tension, he wanted to cover his ears to protect himself, the way people did in news footage when bombs plunged to earth, from her screeching.

"No, because whatever it is, we can't do it now. You your-self said let's go with custom shelves because in the long run it's the same price as buying and installing, but it's costing—"

"It's not! And if we give him cash, he won't charge us tax." She smoothed back her hair, preening, as if she'd just come up with a financial coup worthy of Jay Gould. "It's sim-ple economics. Tell me if I'm wrong: You know better than anyone. He'll be here, so isn't this the time to put a new front on the medicine cabinet, so it'll look like an old mirror in a fabulous antique frame—not a real antique, but distressed wood—instead of just an ugly piece of crap from Tacky Bath-room Expo 1967 or something?"

Bob realized then that his thinking of Chrissie as a gen-uinely decent human being had been a momentary lapse brought on by birthday sentimentality. *The truth, the real truth? She does love me, as far she is able. Except she has the emotional range of a pigeon, and ultimately she's never been able to think beyond feathering her own nest. Now, with Jordana finishing law school and James at Hampshire at $45,000 a year, happy though still unsure whether he wants to continue making clay pots (cit-ing Picasso's success in ceramics) or switch to Asian Studies, it's within my power to be free. Not to have to hear that voice—* "Good merrning!"—*as the first human contact every single day of my life.*

"You probably think I'm terrible," she said, "asking for something on *your* birthday. But number one, this is for both of us, our medicine cabinet, and number two . . ."

Babble, babble. If the Apocalypse came in their lifetime, she'd jabber right through it, then look around and ask: *Did something happen?* Bob lowered his head and eyed the rect-angular box, the steak, that sat on his plate. A small, broiled curlicue of fat hanging from the left corner. When he glanced back at her, he saw an almost-fifty-year-old woman who not only didn't get the meaning of life, but didn't care whether or not there was one.

A genuinely decent person? Forget it. He was being too decent, talk about decency. Chrissie was now and always had been completely self-absorbed. And superficial? She should have her very own superlative adjective: *superficialest*. If she could have, she would have demoed the kids along with the kitchen and redesigned them to fit her banal vision of what was desirable. Turn Jordana into an editor at *Vogue* instead of an aspiring intellectual property lawyer. As Chrissie saw it, "property" was good, but "intellectual" demoted it to a topic impossible to introduce as dinner party conversation. (Jordana's unduly hairy boyfriend Clark was a lawyer, Harvard, which made him okay in Chrissie's view, along with the fact that the *Times*'s Style section had called his father *the* go-to radiation oncologist at Sloan-Kettering.)

As for their son James, Chrissie would grow him five inches taller, give him some career she could drop at cocktail parties: astrophysicist, Deputy Assistant Secretary of the Treasury for Terrorist Financing and Financial Crimes. Actually, Bob had been taken aback when his son reached five-foot-eight and nothing more happened height-wise. He himself was five-eleven, but you don't think about having your son only come up to your ear in family pictures when you marry a short woman.

She was resting her chin on her hands to hide the froggy sac that was developing. Ribbit. Ribbit. Distaste barely surfaced before it turned into disgust, and an instant later a wave of hatred rose within him and pressed against the inside of his skull until he had to stifle a moan of pain. God, did he hate her! Honestly, he wasn't at all a violent man, but he'd like to

264 // Manhattan Noir 2

put his thumbs right under her froggy chin and press on her . . . What the hell do they call an Adam's apple in a woman?

He didn't even try banishing these sorts of thoughts anymore, and had long stopped feeling guilty about having them. Like a sex fantasy, it gave him pleasure and it didn't hurt anybody.

". . . it would give the whole room a look of . . . I don't know. Solidity. Elegance."

"What?"

Chrissie gave him her weary, stoic reaction. Flared nostrils, followed by a sigh blown through her nose. He hated her nostrils; they were isosceles triangles. "The mirror. Framing the medicine-cabinet mirror."

No, not throttle her. Truth be told, on and off over the years he played a kind of whodunit game about getting rid of her. Not seriously, because obviously that would be immoral. His ideas were more like putting poison into those giant antioxidant capsules she took every morning with a hideous *glug*. Oh, and the old defective electrical appliance business, tossing it into the bathtub. If he really wanted to be nasty, he'd buy a plug-in vibrator, so the cops and people from the medical examiner's office would snicker. No, then they might think she died because he couldn't satisfy her. Anyway, ninety-nine percent of the time, the husband was the top suspect and he was never able to think of a way he wouldn't be.

"Look, it's my birthday and I don't want to get into a whole discussion, but we did what you wanted to do. The kids' bathrooms." He waved his arm in a grand gesture, like a conductor introducing a hundred-piece orchestra. "The kitchen. We agreed to hold off on the master bath and do the library first. One project at a time."

Her nostrils flared again, but she managed a smile, and

that seemed to bring back her perkiness. "You're not enjoying your cholesterol festival?" she asked.

"No, no, it's fine," he said, smiling back. "I appreciate the fuss." He cut through the steak and wondered how he was ever going to get down enough of it—it must be close to a pound of meat—to stop her from asking a million times, *Didn't you like it?* It looked good, as if she'd gone to one of the chic, boutique butchers on the Upper East Side. But it was good for a big-deal dinner, not for breakfast. She knew he could never eat this much, but she probably didn't want the butcher thinking she could only afford four ounces of sirloin or tenderloin, whatever the hell it was. It was a little too well-done for him, but at least not her usual revolting, underdone beef-as-wounded-flesh. He'd thought about telling her he wasn't going to eat red meat anymore, but of course that would mean he couldn't order it in restaurants where people actually understood the meaning of medium-rare.

"Oh, speaking of fuss, when we go out with the McDevitts and the Schottlands Saturday night for your birthday, would you mind if I asked Jordana and Clark to join us?" Bob knew exactly where this came from: the *Times.* They had run something about how people with younger friends live longer and they'd run shots of a couple of gatherings where kids in their twenties were mingling with what appeared to be forty- and sixty- and eighty-somethings.

"No. It would be inappropriate. I mean, we've been doing birthdays with these people for years, so how, all of a sudden, can we suddenly say, 'We want to bring our daughter along'? Anyway, they're just dating."

"Living together and, in my humble opinion, very, very serious. Don't the names Jordana and Clark sound great together? Very modern but not too hip. I only wish he wasn't so hairy. I hear his father is too. When he's sitting down and I walk around in back of him, I can see the hair on his back kind of merging with the hair on his head, except it's curlier . . ." Endless babble. But the steak wasn't bad, and at least she had stopped salting it before putting it under the broiler, which would have turned it into striated muscle with rigor mortis. ". . . but he's really very impressive, on the partner track at one of the top firms, and don't forget he's thirty, so he can hold his own in conversation. I was a little surprised, frankly, that someone like him would look at a summer associate, but she does keep herself in fabulous shape and . . ."

Bob swallowed. Good, actually good. He gave her a nod. In the old days he would have said something like, *Here's looking at you, kid,* except then she'd be repeating it back to him, ad nauseum, for weeks, raising a Diet Coke to him in a toast, or as a salute when he was putting on a tie in front of the mirror, or as an overworked conversational comma to punctuate her babble. Another bite. Maybe if he ate enough of the steak she'd cut him a little slack on the eggs.

". . . right before she began dating him," Chrissie was saying, "I started noticing packages from Sephora.com. I mean, it never ceases to amaze me that there's a generation that buys makeup online, but there you go."

He swallowed again. A little too big of a bite, not quite enough chewing. The steak was right there, at the top of his throat, but it wasn't going down. He tried to cough it up quietly, but that didn't work, so he coughed harder. Except then he realized he couldn't cough. She was looking at him quizzically: head cocked to the side so that half her chin lifted up from her hands. Maybe she had a puzzled look in her eyes, but, as her brow had been Botoxed out of commission, he couldn't be sure.

The steak is caught in my throat, he started to say, but then realized he couldn't speak. Couldn't breathe. *My airway is blocked!* he thought, amazed because he always thought of that happening in restaurants, seeing all those Heimlich maneuver notices on his way to the men's room. *No, one good, really hard cough.* Bob brought his fist up to his mouth and almost stabbed himself with his fork, so he let it fall from his hand to clank on the plate. The hardest cough he could manage, but the cough wouldn't come. *Look! Don't you see I'm trying to cough up that fucking glob of steak, you stupid bitch?*

Chrissie's hands clutched the edge of the table and she said something brilliant like, "Huh?" Didn't understand what was happening, because all she did was sit there, her jaw dropping as though she couldn't believe her eyes. No, more like she was waiting for some terrible, shocking thing to happen as she watched the horror movie.

Bob banged his fist on the table, knocking over his juice glass. She started to look around for a napkin, so he banged it twice more to get her attention, then pointed to his throat. *Yes, yes, that's right, I'm choking, you idiot, and I can't breathe and obviously I can't talk.*

"Is something wrong?" she squeaked.

Oh my God, this is a goddamn nightmare. No air, no air could get through. He'd always been one of those if-at-first-you-don't-succeed-try-try-again types, but nothing he could do—

His chest felt like it was about to expand, but then it wouldn't. Trying harder didn't work. *Be calm. Don't panic. Maybe try to inhale through my nose.* No. Nothing happened.

He could die. He could. He could actually die. He could choke to death and that moron was just sitting on her tub of a butt asking if something was wrong.

The Heimlich maneuver. He put his hands mid-torso and pushed to demonstrate. No reaction. Okay, maybe her jaw dropped a little more so she looked like the idiot she was. Desperately, he made a grand arc with his finger to tell her, *Come around here. Get off your ass and . . .* Pushing against the table, he managed to stand, although he was bent over, as if taking a bow. Then he mimed the Heimlich business again. *What do you need, you stupid twit? Written directions? Voice-over narration? How stupid are you that you can't see that this is an emergency?* He'd show her. He swept his forearm across the table, knocking off plates and silverware, coffee cups and the steak and eggs. The stupid piece of parsley she put on practically everything that came to the table seemed to be in a universe with different gravity. It floated . . .

I'll do it myself! Stay calm. He'd read about it. If you're alone and you find yourself choking, you do the Heimlich on yourself. But he couldn't remember illustrations. The same: probably the same way. He pressed his hands against his diaphragm and pushed and pushed. Powerful arms, the guy in the gym told him once, seeming not to hold it against him that even after the free demonstration lesson Bob had decided against one-on-one training.

No. It wouldn't come out. Nothing he could do . . . He was starting to feel . . . lack of oxygen. Woozy. Not faint, he wasn't going to faint. And it was like getting punched over and over again, fear! fear! fear! as if his panic was a sadist attacking him.

Finally, she was getting up out of her chair, but like a movie in slo-mo. Maybe time was stretching, the way people say it does during a car accident. So Chrissie was finally getting it, and was actually moving, but it was like she was just a fucking fat turtle on two legs.

"I'll call 911," she said, as if she were saying something routine, like, *I'll call my mother*. Now she was strolling—fucking ambling, goddamn it, as if browsing a sale at Bloomingdale's—to the phone. What was she thinking? Didn't she get that this was the biggest emergency ever? What did she want him to do, die?

Die? No. She loved him, which showed how dumb she was, because he'd fallen out of love . . . What did she have to gain by his death? Nothing. Freedom. What would she do with freedom? Who the hell would want her? No, ridiculous. But she was taking her time. He couldn't see her face because the phone was on her stupid little bill-paying desk that she called *command central,* as if she were a person who could command anything.

Bob shook the table to get her attention but it barely moved. Not much sound. Swept everything off except her water bottle and the salt and pepper. Getting worse than woozy now. Hurry, bitch. She had nothing to gain by—

Aunt Beryl's money. The last statement, bottom line. Three mil something. Can't remember. He managed to grab the salt and pepper shakers, bang them together, and they made a dull, ceramic clonk. Clonk, clonk, clonk. Chrissie stank in a crisis, froze, but she did love him. Some things you just know.

She turned toward him with the last clonk. "You should see yourself," she said. "Your face is a weird dark color." She squinted. "Your lips are actually turning blue."

What? What is this, some kind of deranged power play in which she shows she has the power of life and death? And then she'll come running over and squeeze and then when I cough it out she'll say something like, This is to show you what it feels like when someone acts like they don't give a shit about you. *Doesn't she get it? I am dying.* Dying.

"Don't worry," Chrissie said, "I'm going to call 911 . . . the second you stop breathing." She ran her hands over the lapels of her bathrobe as if they were the collar of a sable coat. "If this surprises you, it shouldn't. Do you know you treat me like I'm nothing? How long I've hated you?" She asked it so casually, like, *Do you know how long it's been since you got the car washed?* "Your contempt, your absolute contempt for me." Strange, her voice wasn't a screech, but lower, much lower than he'd ever heard it. "When we go out with *Times* people, you're embarrassed by me."

Then she gave him the finger. Standing there, three feet from the phone, sticking it up high.

"Did you think you were dealing with such an idiot that I didn't see it? Or someone without feelings? I can't tell you how many nights I prayed you'd get run over by the 34th Street bus." He tried coughing again, but he couldn't. "This is a gift from God, you bastard. Your birthday, my gift. Half the time you say something and I'm thinking, *Drop dead, you cheap fuck.*" She smiled, her face luminous. "And now you are!"

Last ounce of life. Bob lurched toward his wife knowing she was probably thinking, *He's walking like Frankenstein,* but he was dizzy and his legs . . . his pants had turned to lead and every step . . . Lift the leg up, put it down, now the other leg.

"I tried so hard! And the harder I tried, doing new sex things, reading every single boring section of the *Times* and trying to make meaningful conversation, the more disgust I saw in you. But you never had the balls to leave me, did you? You know why, Mr. Hyena Breath? Because you knew nobody else would have you."

He wasn't going to make it over to her. So dizzy, and falling . . .

Bob fell over one of her Shaker chairs that she said went

absolutely perfect with the Tuscan farmhouse look. The chair crashed to the travertine floor and he collapsed on top of it. A microsecond before his forehead banged onto the cold tile, his stomach and chest hit the back post. The force of his al-most-dead weight against the wood was so violent that even as two ribs cracked, his torso was rammed in such a way that all the air in him was pushed up and out, along with Chrissie's overdone steak.

She must have thought he was dead, or so close to it, because she turned her back to him and went to the phone. She was press-ing the 9 and didn't see Bob Geissendorfer take three breaths and put his hand over the big new lump on his forehead. Only when he began to rise, lifting himself off the floor with surprising ease, and emitted only a soft "ug" of effort—not a word precisely, but also not a sound made by a dead body—did Chrissie turn.

He was moving toward her, not lurching at all. In seconds he was beside her, grabbing the phone from her hand, slam-ming it back into its cradle. She took a step, a prelude to run-ning from him, but his hands were already around her throat. "I'm going to kill you!" he blared, perhaps unnecessarily, as his thumbs began compressing her larynx. "Choke to death? You want to see choke to death? I'll give you choke to death!" He thought of her vicious "Mr. Hyena Breath" and he bellowed, "Choke to death, fatso!"

The doorbell rang, but naturally in the heat of the mo-ment neither Bob nor Chrissie heard it. He was too intent on strangling her and she was engaged, unsuccessfully, in trying to knee him in the testicles. Then she attempted something she must have seen on a self-defense segment of *Oprah*, put-ting her thumbs into his eyeballs, but he simply stretched out his arms further and continued to snuff out his wife's life.

"Happy birthday to you, Happy birthday to you . . ."

Chrissie and Bob stared, huge-eyed, at each other. Two voices moved from the front door toward the kitchen. His thumbs lost their strength and his hands fell to his sides. Chrissie took a step back and massaged her throat. Bob comforted the lump on his head with gentle pats. "Happy birthday, dear Dad . . ." Only one voice on the *Dad*, Jordana's, and a moment later, she and her boyfriend Clark entered the kitchen, holding hands.

"Oh my God," Jordana said, shaking her head so her long, dark blond hair fanned out prettily. Clark, his shirt open at the collar to afford a view of a triangle of hair of the sort found on black poodles, put his arm around her. She was gazing at the table and chairs and not at her parents. "What happened?"

"There was something slippery on the floor," said Chrissie, "and Daddy got up for a second and—" Somehow she got out a giggle and in her squealiest voice went on: "—he started to slip and I ran over to catch him and—"

"We kind of knocked over the chair and then Mom landed on the table and most of the stuff went flying off."

"Well," Jordana said, "I'm glad everybody's okay. Because here—" She rooted inside her pocketbook which, to Bob, looked like a tan leather laundry bag. He swallowed. His throat hurt. "—is your birthday gift. From both of us."

Together, they handed him a wrapped gift . . . a book. People always got him books. He tore off the paper and, sure enough, it was that new book about the lives of ordinary Afghans in Kandahar province. He'd read half the review and decided that was more than enough, but now he'd have to read it and enthuse. His head hurt and he wanted to vomit. "Do you know, I've been dying to read this. The review was terrific. Thank you. Great gift."

"And we have one other gift for you." He glanced at Chrissie for a second. She was rubbing her fingers gently over her throat. She looked him straight in the eye and he turned back to his daughter. "Actually, this is a gift for both of you. I guess you can call it a gift."

"I hope you'll call it a gift," Clark added. As always, Bob had to strain to hear what he was saying. Nobody else seemed to have that problem, but Clark spoke in some decibel range that was beyond Bob's ability to decipher clearly. "It's a gift to me."

"We're engaged!" Jordana announced.

Chrissie squealed with joy and ran over to embrace them. Now he had to go and kiss Jordana and offer Clark a manly handshake. Maybe grasp his shoulder too as they shook. That would show warmth, but kept Bob from actually having to give him a hug.

"This is the happiest news ever!" Chrissie declared.

As he took the three steps to them, he noticed the rest of the steak had bled all over the tile. Well, if you like gorillas, Clark was all right, and he was certifiably smart. Harvard undergrad and law school, yet egalitarian enough to get engaged to a girl from Swarthmore and NYU Law School.

The happiest news ever. Except now Bob could not kill his wife in cold blood, or indeed in any other fashion. They had a wedding to plan. Then James would be graduating. Then—who knew?—grandchildren. There was so much the Geissendorfers had to look forward to.

ABOUT THE CONTRIBUTORS

GEOFFREY BARTHOLOMEW has tended bar at McSorley's Old Ale House in Manhattan since 1972, when East 7th Street still resembled the setting of a noir novel. Upon publication, his 2001 volume *The McSorley Poems* became the best-selling poetry title at St. Mark's Bookshop in Manhattan, and it still enjoys robust sales from behind the bar at McSorley's. He is currently working on a memoir and a second volume of McSorley's poems.

LAWRENCE BLOCK was born in Buffalo, New York, and first came to Manhattan with his father. In a whirlwind weekend they stayed at the Commodore Hotel, saw *Where's Charlie?* on Broadway, went up to the top of the Empire State Building, and rode the Third Avenue El down to the Bowery. The year was 1948, and the future author, ten years old at the time, never got over it. He returned eight years later, and has lived in the borough ever since, but for brief sojourns in Ohio, Florida, and Brooklyn. The editor of *Manhattan Noir* and winner of many writing awards, he is nevertheless thrilled to share space in an anthology with Edith Wharton, Irwin Shaw, Stephen Crane, and Damon Runyon. His mother would be so proud . . .

JEROME CHARYN'S novel *The Green Lantern* was nominated for a PEN/Faulkner Award. His most recent novel, *Johnny One-Eye*, is about a double agent during the American Revolution. He lives in New York and Paris, where he teaches film theory at the American University. He has written ten novels about Isaac Sidel, the first four of which are being turned into graphic novels.

STEPHEN CRANE, born on November 1, 1871 in Newark, New Jersey, was a journalist, poet, and author. His first novel, *Maggie, A Girl of the Streets: A Story of New York* (1893) was self-published and unsuccessful. Crane attended the College of Liberal Arts at Syracuse University, after which he moved to the Bowery district in New York where he wrote sketches and short stories for newspapers. Crane became ill and died at the age of twenty-eight on June 5, 1900. His other works include *The Black Riders and Other Lines* (1895), "The Little Regiment" (1896), "The Bride Comes to Yellow Sky" (1897), *The Third Violet* (1897), "The

Blue Hotel" (1898), "War Is Kind" (1899), *The Monster and Other Stories* (1899), and *Active Service* (1899).

HORACE GREGORY was a poet and critic, born on April 10, 1898 in Milwaukee, and died on March 11, 1982. He graduated from the University of Wisconsin in 1923 and was a professor of English at Sarah Lawrence College in New York. In 1965 he won the Bollingen Prize for Poetry for lifetime achievement. His works include *Chelsea Rooming House* (1930), *Pilgrim of the Apocalypse* (1933), *Poems, 1930-1940* (1941), and *Dorothy Richardson: An Adventure in Self-Discovery* (1967).

O. HENRY was a reporter, columnist, and great American short story writer whose works explored the daily lives of the people of New York City. Born William Sydney Porter in Greensboro, North Carolina, O. Henry moved to New York City after serving three years in a penitentiary in Columbus, Ohio for embezzlement. He was released in 1901 and changed his name to O. Henry. He wrote for the *New York World* as well as other magazines. His works include *Cabbages and Kings* (1904), "The Last Leaf" (1907), *The Heart of the West* (1907), and "The Ransom of Red Chief" (1910).

CLARK HOWARD is an Edgar Award winner (and eight-time finalist) and has also won the Derringer and five *Ellery Queen* Readers Awards. Although he has written novels and true crime books, the short story has always been his favorite form. He has two short story collections and has been included in dozens of anthologies since 1975.

LANGSTON HUGHES was one of the most significant and prolific figures of the Harlem Renaissance. Through his fiction, poetry, plays, and essays, Hughes helped define black America's literary consciousness by celebrating cultural nationalism while tackling social injustice and racial inequality with equal dexterity. Though a subversive humor pervades much of his work, it is the vibrant spirit of Harlem that resonates most deeply and informs his unique sensibility as the voice of New York City's black working class.

EVAN HUNTER, also known as Ed McBain, was a screenwriter and best-selling novelist, born on October 15, 1926 in New York City. In

1998 he became the first American to receive the Diamond Dagger, the highest award from the British Crime Writers Association; he also won the Grand Master Award from the Mystery Writers of America for lifetime achievement in 1986. He published hundreds of books under his own name and various pen names, including the screenplay *The Birds* (1962), the play *Curtain* (1969), the novels *The Moment She Was Gone* (2002), *Money, Money, Money* (2001), a series of 87th Precinct novels, and the short story collections *Happy New Year, Herbie* (1963) and *Barking at Butterflies* (2000).

SUSAN ISAACS has been called "Jane Austen with a schmear" (*Washington Post*) and a "witty, wry observer of the contemporary scene" (*New York Times*). She is chairman of the board of the literary organization *Poets & Writers*, a past president of Mystery Writers of America, and is a member of PEN, the National Book Critics Circle, the Authors Guild, and the International Association of Crime Writers. Although her work includes film (*Compromising Positions, Hello Again*) and nonfiction (*Brave Dames and Wimpettes: What Women Are Really Doing on Page and Screen*), she's happiest working alone, writing novels. For more information, visit www.susanisaacs.com.

BARRY N. MALZBERG, one of science fiction's most prolific writers, has written over seventy-five novels in the field, as well as novels of suspense, crime fiction, and dark humor, both under his own name and under a number of pseudonyms. He has also written over four hundred short stories, in similarly varied fields. As an editor, he was in charge of *Amazing Stories*, *Fantastic*, and other magazines, and has produced a number of anthologies. A winner of the John W. Campbell Award and the *Locus* Award, he has been nominated several times for the Hugo and Nebula Awards, and was the Shubert Foundation Playwriting Fellow at Syracuse University.

JERROLD MUNDIS is a novelist and nonfiction writer who came out of the Midwest to Manhattan as a young man and has lived there on-and-off (mostly on) for more than forty-five years. His best-known novels are *Gerhardt's Children* and *The Dogs*. He enjoys Central Park and dogs and other elements that appear in his story in this volume. He has two grown sons, currently lives in Manhattan, and is generally in good spirits.

JOYCE CAROL OATES is a recipient of the National Book Award and the PEN/Malamud Award for Excellence in Short Fiction. Author of numerous works including the national best sellers *We Were the Mulvaneys, Blonde,* and *The Falls,* which won the 2005 Prix Femina, Oates is the Roger S. Berlind Distinguished Professor of the Humanities at Princeton University and has been a member of the American Academy of Arts and Letters since 1978.

EDGAR ALLAN POE, arguably one of the greatest American poets, was born on January 15, 1809 in Boston. Poe was orphaned at the age of two after both of his parents died and was adopted by John Allan. Poe's first book, *Tamerlane and Other Poems* was published in 1827. Nine years later, he and his family moved to New York. "The Raven" was published in 1845 in the *New York Evening Mirror,* and became his most famous poem. Poe died on October 7, 1849 and was inducted into the United States Hall of Fame in New York in 1910. His other works include *The Raven and Other Poems* (1845), *The Works of the Late Edgar Allan Poe* (1850), *The Narrative of Arthur Gordon Pym* (1838), and *Tales by Edgar A. Poe* (1845).

DAMON RUNYON was born in 1884 in Manhattan, Kansas to Elizabeth Damon Runyan and Alfred Lee Runyan, a storyteller and newspaper publisher. Runyan followed in his father's footsteps at an early age and began working for the *Pueblo Evening Press*. His surname was misspelled as *Runyon* and he kept the change. He was a sportswriter for the *Denver Post* and also wrote short stories for *McClure's* and *Harper's Weekly*. He moved to New York City in 1910 to work for the *Hearst Daily* and the *New York American* and published his first book, *The Tents of Trouble*, a collection of poems, in 1911. Several of his short stories from the collection *Guys and Dolls* were made into films, including *The Lady for a Day* (1933) and *The Lemon Drop Kid* (1951). Runyon developed throat cancer and died in 1946, two years after having an operation which left him unable to speak.

IRWIN SHAW, born in the Bronx, New York in 1913 to Jewish immigrants from Russia, was a playwright, screenwriter, and author. His parents moved the family to Sheepshead Bay in Brooklyn and changed their name from *Shamforoff* to *Shaw*. Irwin Shaw attended Brooklyn

College and wrote for the school newspaper. He graduated with a B.A. in 1934, and by age twenty-one was producing scripts for radio shows. He also wrote for magazines such as the *New Yorker* and *Esquire*. His works include the play *Bury the Dead* (1936), the short stories "The Sailor off the Bremen" (1939) and "Welcome to the City" (1942), and the film *I Want You* (1951).

JEROME WEIDMAN was born on April 4, 1913 in the Lower East Side section of New York City to immigrant parents. Along the way, he became a novelist, playwright, and short story writer. His novel *I Can Get It for You Wholesale* (1937) was published when he was twenty-four and later became a film in 1951 and a Broadway musical in 1962. He also frequently wrote short stories for the *New Yorker*, *Story*, and *American Mercury*. His other works include the plays *Fiorello!* (1959) and *Asteriski* (1969), and the novels *Fourth Street East: A Novel of How It Was* (1970) and *A Family Fortune* (1978).

DONALD E. WESTLAKE has written over eighty novels under his own name and pseudonyms, including Richard Stark. He is a Grand Master of the Mystery Writers of America, a three-time Edgar Award winner, and an Academy Award nominee for his screenplay of *The Grifters*. Westlake was born in Brooklyn in 1933, grew up in Albany, attended the State University of New York from which he received an Honorary Doctorate in 1996, and served in the U.S. Air Force.

EDITH WHARTON was born in New York during the "Old New York" era, when women were socially prepared for only marriage. She became one of America's greatest writers and published over forty books in her lifetime. She was the first woman to receive the Pulitzer Prize for Fiction (in 1920 for her novel *The Age of Innocence*), an Honorary Doctorate of Letters from Yale Academy, and full membership in the American Academy of Arts and Letters. Her works include *Greater Inclination* (1899), *The Valley of Decision* (1902), *The House of Mirth* (1905), and *The Custom of the Country* (1913).

CORNELL WOOLRICH, born on December 4, 1903 in New York City, is known by many as the father of noir fiction. His first novel, *Cover Charge* (1926), was written while he attended Columbia University. He wrote suspense stories for the magazines *Argosy*, *Black Mask*, and *Thrilling Mystery,* and his story "Rear Window" (1954) was the basis for Alfred Hitchcock's film by the same name. His novels include *Children of the Ritz* (1927), *The Time of Her Life* (1931), *The Bride Wore Black* (1940), *I Married a Dead Man* (1948), *Hotel Room* (1958), and *The Doom Stone* (1960).